Dancer
from
the Dance

DANCER

FROM

THE DANCE

A Novel by

ANDREW HOLLERAN

William Morrow and Company, Inc.

New York / 1978

Library of Congress Cataloging in Publication Data

Holleran, Andrew.
    Dancer from the dance.

    I. Title.
PZ4.H73778Dan   [PS3558.03496]   813'.5'4   78-6600
ISBN 0-688-03357-1

Printed in the United States of America.

2   3   4   5   6   7   8   9   10

Labor is blossoming or dancing where
The body is not bruised to pleasure soul,
Nor beauty born out of its own despair,
Nor blear-eyed wisdom out of midnight oil.
O chestnut tree, great rooted blossomer,
Are you the leaf, the blossom or the bole?
O body swayed to music, O brightening glance,
How can we know the dancer from the dance?

—WILLIAM BUTLER YEATS,
"Among School Children"

Dancer
from
the Dance

Ecstasy,

*It's finally spring down here on the Chattahoochee—
the azaleas are in bloom, and everyone is dying of cancer.
I am writing you very late at night. We have just one kero-
sine lamp, and the bugs outside are positively battering the
screen at my elbow, trying to get at the light—like so many
people we knew in New York trying to get Love,* n'est-ce
pas?—*pushy, pushy, pushy.*

*I cannot tell you where I am, because I want to make a
clean break with my former life. At this moment I know my
apartment is rotting beneath a swarm of rats and roaches;
the woman downstairs is coughing her tubercular cough;
the man next door is beating up his wife; the sound of
canned laughter from an* I Love Lucy *rerun reverberates up
the stairwell; the phone is ringing, and I do not care. I cannot go back. I would rather die like a beast in the fields,
amigo, with my face to the moon and the empty sky and
the stars, than go back; expire with the dew on my cheeks.*

*For example: At this instant a rust-red moon is hanging
low above the water lilies on the lake, and the leaves of the*

9

live oaks gleam in its light. There is not a sound in the world except the ducks in the weeds that take up when the frogs die down. The egrets are nesting there, too, white egrets that, every afternoon at dusk, fly in great flocks to roost in the golden weeds, and after a long, hot day, we sit out under the trees to watch them and feel the breeze that comes up across the water. Everything is in bloom, azaleas and dogwood, the air is soft as talcum powder, so soft you can't imagine people dying here; you imagine them crumbling to death, like biscuits left out in the rain, biscuits and talcum powder and azaleas rotting beneath the bushes in drifts of petals—and at noon, dear, the odor of pine needles rises up from the earth when I walk through the woods, rises up and envelops me in a cloud, and one feels like swooning.

There are convicts along the roads down here, cutting the grass while a man with a rifle watches them; there are convicts and egrets and azaleas and rust-red moons, and water moccasins and pecan farms, and outside my window at this moment a brown thrasher sleeps by the nest he is building. He brings one twig at a time and then stands on the branch outside it, looking all around, guarding his work; it is fascinating, and so much nicer than those sooty pigeons. (How do they live in that filth up there? How did I?)

And the boys downtown who walk around in blue jeans and no shirts, lanky, long-limbed southern boys—and our Irish priest who just returned from the missions in Guinea! We go to mass every week and are quite active in church affairs. I am in love with him, and the mockingbirds and hot blue skies and intense white clouds under the noonday sun, and the pine trees that bristle in the heat, as if they were plugged into electric sockets, and the flies droning over the gardenias, and the red skies at dusk crossed by

egrets flying low over the lake. At noon I lie in the ham-
mock in our garden and listen to the mockingbirds carrying
on high up in the live oaks and watch the cardinals dart
through the Spanish moss.

I will tell you this much: We live on a farm near a small
town filled with retired postmasters, most of whom are
dying of cancer. Tomorrow Ramon and I are gong over to
the neighbors to help them install a septic tank. I cannot
tell you how happy I am to be helping people install a sep-
tic tank, instead of listening to friends who call at three
A.M. to tell me they're committing suicide. Americans are
a practical people! We need practical problems. I would
MUCH rather help someone install a septic tank than pro-
vide him with a reason for living—it is very easy to install
a septic tank, but the latter is of course impossible. There
are no Suicide Hotlines down here. If they want to end it
all, they row out onto the lake, very early in the A.M. when
the family is asleep, and blow their brains out where only
the ducks can hear! Saves so many message units, don't you
think?

Do write. We pick up our mail in Atlanta once a week,
when Ramon goes up to buy fertilizer, pumps, and things
like that—big girl stuff.

Agathe-Hélène de Rothschild

The Lower East Side
New York, N.Y.

Vision,

It was spring here, too, last week—Sunday afternoon I
walked down the steps off Columbus Circle into Central
Park, and the odor of piss rose up from the rest rooms, and

I knew a year had passed. And down in your old neighbor-hood, darling, the bag ladies were sleeping outside again on the steps of the St. Marks Dispensary, and the whores were in hot pants, and the Polish men standing in front of your building in those dark suits & hats, as if they were waiting for a cortege to begin. EVeryone thought spring had come! And then it dropped thirty degrees in one afternoon, snowed the next morning, Bob was mugged on Ninth Street, and we are right back to a New York winter.

Flamingo had a White Party last night—two muscle numbers came in DIAPERS, Bob wore a sequined Halston top, the Baron Ambert was there, and two Egyptian women who were running around with Sutherland and who asked me if I thought they should paint their cunts! I told them that one should not draw attention to unpleasant things. Sutherland said the only reason he came was that he dared not defy the evening papers; Hobbs told him that a well-bred woman appears in print on only three occasions: her birth, marriage, and death. "Yes, darling," said Sutherland, "but I'm not that well-bred." The music was atrocious: that roller-skating music they're turning out now that discos are big business. It wasn't till six, when most everyone had gone, that he started to play the good stuff. Gene Harris sat on a banquette all night with a celestial Puerto Rican boy who was licking his arm every time I looked—I was ready to be taken to Bellevue.

So much for the life of the mind—I am in fact so de-pressed that last night while Bob Cjaneovic was sitting on my face, I began to think how futile life is, no matter what you do—it all ends in Death, we are given such a short time, and everything truly is, as Ecclesiastes says, Vanity, Vanity, Vanity. (Of course that only made me burrow deeper, but still—to have the thought.)

Perhaps that's why I walked out of Cadwalader, Wicker-sham & Taft last month. It's true. I could not write another will, or letter of credit, or memorandum, so I've started to hook for a living. I'm very good. I can do it with anyone: old men, harelips. I give enemas, and one fellow who lives on Sutton Place just asks to smell my wet hair. THAT'S an easy hundred! I have one marvelous old guy who used to be a screenwriter, and knew EVeryone in Hollywood in the thirties, and during sex the phone rings and it's always Joan Fontaine!!

I'm also doing lots of jockstrap things, at fifty bucks a throw (less the price of the jockstrap, which they get to keep). I have a man on Sixty-fourth Street who pours Bosco and whipped cream into my jock while I stand there, and he jerks off!!

(There's a big market in stained underwear, and smelly jockstraps, I'm told, darling—could we make a killing?)

As for Sutherland, he spent yesterday in Bergdorf's IN FULL DRAG—in a Halston George smuggled out of the shop for him. He had the saleswomen bill his purchases to a house in East Hampton! Whom the gods would destroy, they first make mad.

Your first lover is very depressed; he thinks the West is being destroyed by the labor unions, that people no longer believe in anything, and the blacks have ruined the city, et cetera. Then he was mugged last night—by a white teen-ager—and spent the evening in Bellevue.

I myself was roughed up by three Serbo-Croatian security guards at the Plaza Hotel last night, where I went on a call. (And I thought these things only happened in East Ger-many!) I will not bore you with the rest of the story, except to say my left leg is now in a cast, and we're suing everyone.

So you see, you're missing nothing up here. Although

everyone misses you. *I have one more thing to tell you,
more shocking than my new career, no doubt, and it's this:
While recuperating from last night's "interrogation" I've
started writing a novel that I want you to read. A gay novel,
darling. About all of us. Would you, could you, give it a
read?*

Yours in Christ,
Madeleine de Rothschild

P.S.   *I'm sorry everyone is dying of cancer, but be careful; I'm beginning to think cancer is contagious. I
wouldn't want to lose you just yet.*

Three o'clock
The Deep South

Madness,

   *I just finished scrubbing the church altar for the World
Day of Prayer.*

   *Please do send your novel on. This is the perfect place
to read, and that is all I want to do with that life—read
about it. One thing Ramon says is: Keep the chapters short.
Ramon says no one has a very long attention span anymore,
and that's why the world is so unhappy. (God knows it was
true of us.)*

   *However, I must caution you, love: Those things may be
amusing to us, but who, after all, wants to read about sis-
sies? Gay life fascinates you only because it is the life you
were condemned to live. But if you were a family man
going home on the 5:43 to Chappaqua, I don't think you'd
want to read about men who suck each other's wee-wees!
Even if people accept fags out of kindness, even if they
tolerate the poor dears, they don't want to know WHAT*

THEY DO. Canons of taste must be observed, darling. People are tired of hearing about sex, anyway. And the story of a boy's love for a boy will never capture the world's heart as the story of a boy's love for a girl. (Or a boy's love for his DOG—if you could tell that story again, this country would make you rich as Croesus!) Also you would have to make your novel very sad—the world demands that gay life, like the life of the Very Rich, be ultimately sad, for everyone in this country believes, down deep in their heart, that to be happy you must have a two-story house in the suburbs and a FAMILY—a wife and 2.6 kids and a station wagon and a big dog and an elm tree with a tire hanging from it on a rope. Please, darling, there is not much variation of opinion in this country, or any country, for that matter; the whole world wants to be like My Three Sons. *So (a) people would puke over a novel about men who suck dick (not to mention the Other Things!), and (b) they would demand it be ultimately violent and/or tragic, and why give in to them?*

Anyway—contrary to the activists who want the world to believe not only that Gay Is Good, but Gay Is Better— gay life does have its sadness.

Your novel might serve a historical purpose—if only because the young queens nowadays are utterly indistinguishable from straight boys. The twenty-year-olds are completely calm about being gay, they do not consider themselves doomed. Someone should record the madness, the despair, of the old-time queens, the Great Queens whose stories, unlike Elizabeth of Austria(!), have never been told: Sutherland, She Who Must Be Obeyed, and Epstein—the true loonies of this society, refusing to camouflage themselves for society's sake.

However, I don't think a novel is a historical record; all

15

a piece of literature should do, I think, is tell you what it was like touching Frank Romero's lips for the first time on a hot afternoon in August in the bathroom of Les' Café on the way to Fire Island. If you can do that, divine!

So I think your task is nearly impossible, but send it on. I'd love to sit under the Spanish moss with a glass of lemonade and some pecan pralines, and read a novel written by a dear friend! How very southern! And I grow more fond of the South every day. The only part of this country with any manners whatsoever, and it's merely because people have no manners anymore that they are going to blow themselves up. I enclose one azalea, a faded shrimp color; I don't know what it will be when you get it.

Hélène de Sévigné

Midnight
The Lower East Side

Delirium,

Just returned from an Episcopalian priest, who is apparently very popular with his congregation in a little town in Connecticut—très chic, *of course. The man is so handsome, and so witty, and so charming—he recited psalms for me, and then had me beat him up with the butt of a machete and spit all over his face (the strain of being popular, I guess). And* then *I went to the Pierre, where lives Duncan Uhr, a boy with one of the biggest trust funds in New York, and one of the biggest dicks (a double legacy). He is quite intelligent, but he sits in the Pierre all day eating spaghetti and watching reruns of* I Love Lucy *and having callboys come over; or he goes to the Baths at night. It was rather embarrassing, however, because WE KNEW EACH*

16

OTHER AT CHOATE! However, he had forgotten this till I reminded him, after *our transaction was complete.*

I do not know whether to use as a quote to open my novel a line of Nietzsche or the Shirelles:

> The world can never be
> Exactly what you want it to be.

(from "Will You Still Love Me Tomorrow?")

In fact, I don't know whether the novel should be done along the lines of Auntie Mame, *or* Decline and Fall of the Roman Empire; *it has elements of both.*

About your objections—which I appreciated—agree with Ramon, everyone's attention span is too short, and that is what's wrong with the world; however, as to nobody wants to read about fags!

I can't help its being gay. I have been a full-time fag for the past five years, I realized the other day. Everyone I know is gay, everything I do is gay, all my fantasies are gay, I am what Gus called those people we used to see in the discos, bars, baths, all the time—remember? Those people we used to see EVERYWHERE, every time we went out, so that you wanted to call the police and have them arrested?—I am a doomed queen.

I would LIKE to be a happily married attorney with a house in the suburbs, 2.6 kids, and a station wagon, in which we would drive every summer to see the Grand Canyon, but I'm not! I am completely, hopelessly gay!

In fact when Stanford sent me a questionnaire asking what was the peak experience of the past ten years of my life, a voice inside answered without hesitation: sucking Alfredo Montavaldi's cock. (It certainly meant more than Professor Leon's Chaucer seminar.)

But let me reassure you, my novel is not about fags. It is

about a few characters who just happen to be gay (I know
that's a cliché, but it's true). After all, most fags are as boring as straight people—they start businesses with lovers and
end up in Hollywood, Florida, with dogs and double-knit
slacks and I have no desire to write about them. What can
you say about a success? Nothing! But the failures—that
tiny subspecies of homosexual, the doomed queen, who puts
the car in gear and drives right off the cliff! That fascinates
me. The fags who consider themselves worthless because
they are queer, and who fall into degradation and sordidness! It was those whom Christ befriended, not the assholes
in the ad agencies uptown who go to St. Kitts in February!
Those people bore me to DEATH! (One of my clients has
an account with a potato chip firm—I sit on his face.)

So you see I've written about a small subspecies only,
I've written about doomed queens. Capisce?

It's very cold again; I passed the woman who lives next
door coming up the stairs—she was drunk, as usual, and
had to grab the railing to keep from falling over. She has
such a sad face, the faded face of a woman who was once
pretty, and now her face is just resigned, and it gives me a
chill in my bones. THAT is what I want to write about—
why life is SAD. And what people do for Love (everything)
—whether they're gay or not.

                                                    Victor Hugo

                                        High Noon
                                        Chiggers & Spanish Moss

Life Itself,
    Just came in from picking strawberries—big, beautiful
ones—it is so good to work in the earth, dearest, to have

Dirt under your fingernails—and not coming through the telephone, for a change! (Oh, that greasy receiver!) I cannot tell you how peaceful it is outside in the yard. It is high noon, love; everything is stunned by the heat; perfect silence, even the birds are napping; a faint wind blows through the screen, a wind far more caressing than any human lover's lips; and I feel at perfect peace with the universe. And how much there is in it! Yesterday I cleared some grass around a palm tree to fertilize it (the farmers down here use banana skins, it gives the soil potassium) and I uncovered the glistening, almost liquid body of a baby snake—a striped, gray, wet body, which until then had been growing in a little cavern of grass and earth beside the palm tree trunk; I found, too, a turtle egg, very white and veined, like marble, or hard sugar; and a beautiful boy in a rowboat, fishing in the weeds offshore, with a hunting knife in his belt, in all the stillness and the heat.

Forgive me for boring you with all of this. However, there is no news down here, as you can well imagine—other than my turtle egg, and that the organist at church is sick, and Ramon's grandmother, too, who is visiting us. It occurred to me last night as I was bathing Señora Echevarria that the real sadness of gay life is that it cuts us off from experience like this: to be in a shadowed room at dusk on a spring evening, wiping the forehead of an old Cuban lady (who at least does not claim to have come from a Wealthy, Aristocratic Family of Havana, like all those queens in New York) while Ramon spoke to her in Spanish (alas, I know only French; and why? Because when I first came to New York, Sutherland told me there were only two requirements for social success with those queens in the Hamptons: a perfect knowledge of French and a big dick) and there was so much LIFE in that room, not the hothouse, artificial, desperate life we led up there in Gotham, but LIFE as it is in all its complexity and richness. For what is the real sadness of doomed queens? That they run in packs with one another waiting for the next crow's foot to appear, and wondering how many more seasons they can spend on Fire Island before they have to take a house in upstate New York. Homosexuality is like a boarding school in which there are no vacations. My God!

Duncan Uhr is a perfect example, and he was driven mad by it years ago. You know he is crazy. He loses control if anyone rejects him, he used to break into houses at Fire Island, and climb over the cubicles in the Baths to get at people. I was once in a room at the Everard having sex with a Korean cellist, and I looked up in the throes of passion to see Duncan climbing down the wall above me like a Human Fly. He said, "Don't mind me, just go on as you were," and proceeded to mount the Korean boy, who was already mounted on me *(the Korean said nothing; Orientals are so polite). I asked Duncan if sex like that wasn't difficult, and he said, "No, it's all a matter of rhythm, one-two-three, one-two-three, kind of like doing the Beguine!" (It was remarks like that, darling, that made me realize I had to get out of New York, divine as the city is!)*

Where is the novel?

le Duc de Saint-Simon

Seven A.M.
The Lower East Side

Existence,

There is no heat, no hot water, and the wind is rattling the windows as I type this letter to you after staying up all night to finish the novel. I can see right into the kitchen of the apartment behind this one, over the fire escape. The kitchen is very neat—a Japanese girl lives there—and on her shelf are lined up the following products: Tide, Comet, Dove Dishwashing, Woolite, and Clorox—exactly the things on my shelf!!!!

Adored your story about Duncan Uhr, and believe me, it is only one of many. He was a very bright boy at school but always desperately in love, of course. Somewhat embarrassing to see him in that context, but when you're hooking, you never know who will open the door.

Flamingo had a Black Party last night—quite a crush; live models being fist-fucked on platforms, pornographic movies on all the walls, and every leather queen in New York pissing on each other in the back room. Too decadent, n'est-ce pas? Also too boring—I left before two, but as I was going out the door, a voice in my ear said: "We're having a small Crucifixion, just a few friends, at Park and Seventy-fifth after the party, can you make it?" I turned and it was Sutherland, with his two Egyptian heiresses, completely covered in leather with zippers up the back and tiny holes for their ears and nose/mouth! They are indefatigable! And so chic!

So, vision, the novel is ready at last; it is, in the end, about Sutherland—and Malone. Did you expect that? People are celebrated for all the wrong reasons, I think—people should be famous for being good—and Malone was—and his story is the saddest of all, somehow. I've called it Wild Swans; *do you think people will think it's about* birds?

So I'm off, darling, to mail this at the post office, and then to go on a call: a pilot for Lufthansa Airlines. It sounds like something I'd do for free! But then sex has no meaning for me anymore; it's too pointless.

Oh—I discovered venereal warts on my ass last week. Had them burned off by Dr. Jones, in that VD Mill he runs on Lexington Avenue; if you went to him with a broken leg, he'd tell you it was syphilis—too too depressing/cheers.

Oh—the azaleas arrived a dark purple. Thanks. I decided on Santayana & Yeats.

Enclosed: one first novel (I did not change the names; there are no innocents to protect!)

Yours in Christ,
Marie de Maintenon

1

HE was just a face I saw in a discotheque one winter, but it was I who ended up going back to Fire Island to pick up his things. Now my father used to say, and I agree: There is nothing so unhappy as going through the clothes of a friend who has died, to see what may be used and what should be given to charity.

But Malone was hardly even a friend—something much more, and much less, perhaps—and so it felt odd to be traveling out there yesterday afternoon. It was a fine autumn day, the last week of October, and as the taxi drove from the train station in Sayville to the docks, that village had never looked more attractive. There was an unspoken celebration in the very silence, of the end of that long summer season, when a hundred taxis a day like ours crisscrossed the streets between the train station and the docks, taking the inhabitants of Manhattan across that shallow bay to their revelries on the beach of Fire Island. It was a journey between islands, after all: from Manhattan, to Long Island, to Fire Island, and the last island of the three was nothing but a sandbar, as slim as a parenthesis, enclosing the Atlantic, the very last fringe of soil on which a man might put up his house, and leave behind him all—absolutely all—of that huge continent to the west. There are New Yorkers who boast they've never been west of the Hudson, but the exhausted souls who went each weekend of summer to their houses on that long sandbar known among certain crowds as the Dangerous Island (dangerous because you could lose your heart, your reputation, your contact lenses), they put an even more disdainful distance between themselves and America: free, free at last.

Well, now the village of Sayville had been left in perfect peace. The strenuous season was behind, and as the taxi drove, more slowly, through the puddles of sunlight and crimson leaves, we passed one tableau after another of small-town life. Kids were playing football in the town park, and another football game swept across the high school field, and boys on bicycles were drawing lazy circles in the supermarket parking lot, and families were out in their backyards raking leaves. It was the sort of scene Malone turned sentimental over. He always passed through Sayville with a lingering regret for its big white houses and friendly front yards with picket fences and climbing roses. He always looked back as he went through, saying this might be that perfect town he was always searching for, where elms and lawns would be combined with the people he loved. But those summer taxis drove inevitably through it, like vans bearing prisoners who are being transferred from one prison to another—from Manhattan to Fire Island—when all we dreamed of, really, in our deepest dreams, was just such a town as this, quiet, green, untroubled by the snobberies and ambition of the larger world; the world we could not quit.

"Isn't this beautiful?" Malone would exclaim as we drove past the girl doing handstands on the lawn, a young woman walking a flock of children down a dappled sidewalk. "Why don't we take a house here next summer instead?" But he knew we wouldn't, and he knew he wouldn't, for even now the drums were in our blood, we sat forward almost hearing them across the bay, and the van raced on through the streets so that the driver could hustle back for another load of pleasure-seekers, so bent on pleasure they were driving right through Happiness, it seemed, a quieter brand of existence that flourished under these green elms. We kept driving right through all the dappled domesticity, like prisoners, indeed, being moved from jail to jail imprisoned in our own sophistication. The truth was the town reminded Malone of his days at boarding school in Vermont; the sight of a football arcing across a green wall of woods made him sigh with a passionate regret. He always looked like a student who has just come in off the playing fields, eyes glowing from an afternoon of soccer. He always looked like that, even in the depths of a subway station, on the dingiest street in Manhattan.

"People are fools to go back after Labor Day," Malone murmured that sunny afternoon. "We should come *out* after Labor Day," he said; but then he was always trying to refine his pleasures. He loved the shore in autumn when the crowds had vanished, and in the winter he used to go out dancing at five in the morning, and why? Because then the crowd had gone, the discaire was no longer playing for them, but for his friends, and that was the best dancing. And that was why he wanted all his friends to be with him in the country and watch the seasons change in a rustic valley he never found.

The nasal voice that crackled on the taxi's radio in summer was silent now, as silent as the still air, except for a single burst of static requesting the driver to pick up Mrs.

Truscott, who wanted to go shopping, at 353 Elm Street. The driver said he would pick the lady up in five minutes— news that must have gladdened her heart, for in the summer Mrs. Truscott had to wait for the minions of advertising agencies, the doctors, designers, models, and producers to get to their houses on the beach.

As we waited at that streetcorner in the vivid, fiery air of late October, we stared dumbly through the windows at the autumn we'd forgotten, living in the city, the autumn blazing out here in the villages along the bay. The van went down one last dappled street and then rounded a bend to present us with a sight that never failed to make our hearts beat faster: the marshy inlets where the trees stopped and the masts of ships rose instead into the air.

The ferries had stopped running a month ago, however, and as we waited for the motorboat we'd hired to take us across, the only sound in all that crisp, clean air was the sound of hammers clattering around us as men in woolen caps repaired their boats in dry dock. Malone had said one day: "I am not spending next summer here. I'll go out west, I'll live in a tent in Africa, I'll do anything but waste another summer on the Island."

"Waste?" said Sutherland, turning his head slightly as if he had heard a bird chirp behind him in the bushes. "Who can waste a summer on the Island? Why, it's the only antidote to death we have. Besides," he said, blowing out a stream of smoke, "you know very well that if you did go to Africa, you would be lying in your tent among the gazelles and lions, and you would not even pull back the flap to look at them, because you will be wondering only who is dancing with Frank Post and whether Luis is playing 'Law of the Land.' Don't be a fool," he said. "Don't think for a moment of escaping. You can't!"

There was nothing very sinister about the place that Malone had protested hopelessly against that day when our motorboat puttered into the harbor across the bay. The Island lay bathed in the same autumn light falling on Sayville. Only one big white boat was still moored there, sharing the inlet with a family of migratory geese, and as we floated past, a big woman in a cerise caftan sat playing cards on the afterdeck with a young man in a hooded sweat shirt. They waved to us, improbable couple, and we waved back. The awnings had been taken down from the Botel, the sliding glass doors were boarded up with sheets of plywood, pasted with the dead leaves an earlier rainstorm had blown against them. It had never looked so bare. There wasn't a soul in sight when we got off.

It was easy to see how thieves from the villages of Long Island crossed over in the winter and looted houses. We passed one big, forlorn place after another, houses with turrets and skylights, houses with pennants drooping in the windless air, houses like castles, houses like cottages, houses hiding in the woods, and houses on display. The sagging electrical lines glistened in the clear October light. Leaves had accumulated under the holly trees, and portions of the shrubbery had turned a dull maroon. Above, the thinnest skein of clouds served only to emphasize the aching blue. We walked to a high point and saw, stretching down the beach, in the nooks of houses, a string of bright turquoise swimming pools, absurdly full. When we got to Malone's we stopped at the pool and stared at it—the pool that all the Puerto Rican boys used to dive into from the balcony, the roof, in the exhilaration of drugs—and then we walked around the deck and looked for a moment at the listless sea. It was the green of an empty Coke bottle. It was very still. But it had been very stormy, for the beach bore no resemblance at all to the one we had sprawled on all summer long—it had been completely washed away, and with it the summer itself: the music, clothes, dances, lovers. The sea had gouged out a new beach, with new coves and hillocks. I turned back to the house—famous for its electricity bills (three thousand a month), for the parties, for the people who had come here and their amusements. In an airy bedroom on the second floor, overlooking the pool and the ocean, we opened the closets and the drawers and began sorting Malone's clothes.

The clothes! The Ralph Lauren polo shirts, the Halston suits, the Ultrasuede jackets, T-shirts of every hue, bleached fatigues and painter's jeans, plaid shirts, transparent plastic belts, denim jackets and bomber jackets, combat fatigues and old corduroys, hooded sweat shirts, baseball caps, and shoes lined up under a forest of shoe trees on the floor; someone had once left the house and all he could tell his friends was that Malone had forty-four shoe trees in his closet. There were drawers and drawers of jump suits, shirts by Ronald Kolodzie, Estee Lauder lotions and astringents, and drawers and drawers of bathing suits, of which he had twenty-eight, in racing and boxer styles. And then there were the drawers of the clothes Malone really wore: the old clothes he had kept since his days at boarding school in Vermont—old khaki pants, button-down shirts with small collars (for someone who ran around with the trendiest designers, he loathed changes in style), a pair of rotten tennis sneakers, an old tweed jacket. There was one drawer filled with nothing but thirty-seven T-shirts in different colors, colors he had bleached them or dyed them, soft plum and faded shrimp and celery green and all shades of yellow, his best color. He had scoured the army-navy surplus stores in lower Manhattan looking for T-shirts, for underwear, plaid shirts, and old, faded jeans. There was a closet hung with thirty-two plaid shirts, and a bureau filled entirely with jeans faded to various shades of blue.

I finally stood up, depressed at all these things—for what were they but emblems of Malone's innocent heart, his inexhaustible desire to be liked?

There are boys in New York whose lovers die of drugs, and who give the dead lover's clothes to their new lover without a second thought; but a dead man's clothes have always seemed ghoulish to me, and so I gave up sorting the clothes, and left it all to my friend and began wandering through the rest of the house.

The house, with all its redundant pavilions, had been taken by an Italian princess, who had remained in Manhattan all summer in her air-conditioned rooms above Central Park eating hot dogs—and who wanted the place there in case she should want, some summer day, to go to the beach. She had taken it and Sutherland—with his peculiar talent for producing these bizarre benefactors—had used it the latter half of the summer for himself and Malone.

But the house was silent now, and as I turned and walked back through the empty rooms, they were devoid of the spirits who had once wasted all that electricity, both human and inhuman, humming through the rooms. A succession of houseboys had passed through the place and they had been replaced as casually as fuses. One of them, a dancer from Iowa, had been discovered renting rooms to strangers for fifty dollars a day during the week. He later had his head blown off on St. Marks Place by a Mafia hit man when he started a new career as a drug dealer; his funeral had been more glittering than any party of the winter. Well, these personalities had vanished and now the house was empty. And as I wandered through I felt a guilty pleasure I have always known in places the crowd has departed—a dormitory room on graduation day, a church after mass, bungalows by the sea when the season is past. There was something mute yet eloquent about such places, as if they were speaking a very old tale of loss, futility, and peace. Post offices in small towns, late at night . . .

October on Fire Island was lovely partly because it had been abandoned by the crowd. And wasn't that the whole allure of love, and why Malone had been such a genius at it: our struggle, always, to isolate from the mob the single individual, having whom society meant nothing? There were lovers whose affair was purely public, whose union consisted of other people's considering them lovers, but the reason I loved the beach in autumn (besides the elegance of the weather, the enameled light that layered everything from carpenters to butterflies to the tips of the dune grass) was that now the false social organism had vanished and left it what Malone had always wished it to be: a fishing village, in which, presumably, no one lied to one another.

A sudden wish to feast on the past made me sit down on the steps leading to the beach for a moment, the steps where in the hot August sunlight we had rested our feet from the burning sand and shaded our eyes to look out at the figures in the dazzling light. There had been a dwarf that summer, a squat hydrocephalic woman who wandered up and down the beach among those handsome young men like a figure in an allegory. And there had been the Viet Nam veteran who had lost a leg, and walked along the water's edge in a leather jacket in the hottest weather, hobbling with a cane. He had drowned that Sunday so many swimmers had drowned. Not twenty feet from the steps on which I sat now, a corpse had lain all afternoon beneath a sheet because the police were too busy to remove it, and five feet away from the corpse, people lay taking the sun and admiring a man who had just given the kiss of life to a young boy. Death and desire, death and desire.

The whole long, mad summer came back in the warmth of that pale, distant sun burning high above the deserted sea. The summer gym shorts had become fashionable as bathing suits, the summer Frank Post (who each spring contemplated suicide because he could not rise to the occasion again—of being the most voluptuous, beautiful man on the Island, the homosexual myth everyone adored—but managed to go to the gym, take his pills, and master yet another season) shaved his body and wore jockstraps to Tea Dance, and his lover died of an overdose of Angel Dust and Quaaludes. The summer "I'll Always Love My Mama" lasted all season and we never grew tired of it. The summer that began with the Leo Party and ended with the Pink and Green Party (which Sutherland had given, and from which Malone had vanished). The summer nude sunbathing began, the summer Todd Keller, from Laguna Beach, was the "hot number" and Angel Dust the favorite drug. The summer Kenny Lamar was arrested in the bar for sniffing a popper, the summer certain people got into piss, the summer his guests threw a birthday cake into Edwin Giglio's face, they all loathed him so, the summer Lyman Quinn's deck collapsed at the Heat Wave Party, with two thousand people on it; the summer a whale beached itself near Water Island in July, and a reindeer appeared swimming offshore in August. The summer Louis Deron dressed in gas masks, the summer Vuitton became pretentious, along with Cartier tank watches, and Lacostes were out. The summer the backpacking look began, the summer the grocery store changed hands, and people began to worry about the garbage floating three miles out in the Atlantic Ocean, the summer George

31

Renfrew took the Kane House and built a new pool for the Esther Williams Party, the summer the new policeman drove everyone crazy, and Horst Jellaby began flying the flag of the country of his lover for one week: One only had to see the flag of Argentina to know he had snared the gorgeous physician visiting from Buenos Aires, or the flag of Colombia to know the coach of the national soccer team was in his bed at that moment. The summer the models moved to Water Island to get away from the mobs who had started to come to this place in greater numbers each summer. The summer two Cessnas collided in midair and the sky rained bodies into a grove of trees where everyone was in the middle of having afternoon sex. The summer some nameless ribbon clerk died trying to sniff a popper at the bottom of a pool . . . it was a blur, all of it, of faces, and parties, and weekends and storms; it vanished, as did all weeks, months, years in New York in one indistinguishable blur, life speeded up, life so crowded that nothing stood out in relief, and people waited, as they had one autumn weekend here, for a hurricane to provide some kind of sublime climax that never came . . .

A single figure was walking along the ravaged beach frowning at the sand and then looking out to sea: alone with the late October sky, the coming storm. As we had watched so many figures approach, and pass, and disappear those furious summers given over to nothing more than watching figures like this one come near, and then finding them flawed or flawless, this late-autumn visitor assumed a face and body—and I recognized one of Malone's first lovers: a Hungarian nuclear physicist we had all adored one summer. This place, the city, was full of Malone's former lovers. He compared them once to the garbage of New York accumulating in a giant floating island off the coast of this very beach, floating nearer each year, as if accumulated loves, like waste, could choke us. The physicist passed by brooding over private sorrows. We had all of us wanted him with scant success. Which recalled a rule of Malone's, with which he used to comfort those who despaired of ever wedding their dreams, spoken with a rueful regret that it was true (for, if true lovers are either chaste or promiscuous, Malone belonged, in the end, to the first school): "Over a long enough period of time, everyone goes to bed with everyone else." And cheap as it was, that was the truth.

They had taken no notice of his disappearance, these people: no funeral pennants on the turrets of their houses, no black sash across the swimming pool. The Island waited now in bleak desuetude for next season; the very beach of that particular summer had been mercifully obliterated by autumn storms so that next summer's strand might assume its shape; and it was right. One came here for very selfish reasons; after all, it was a purely pagan place. Malone would be memorialized in gossip. He would be remembered at a dozen dinner parties next summer, or in those casual conversations after sex in which two strangers discover they know exactly the same people and live exactly the same lives. One would expect as much sentiment for the departure of an Island beauty as one would for the patron of a gambling casino who walks away from the roulette wheel. For such a private place, it was very public: Anyone could come here, and anyone did. If not this gypsy throng, who would mourn Malone? He lived perhaps in my memory: I would always think of this place, this sea, this sky, his face together, and wonder if he had wasted his life.

Can one waste a life? Especially now? "Well," Malone would say when some conceited beauty refused to even meet his eyes, "we're all part of the nitrogen cycle." Oh, yes, and the butterflies rising in golden clouds from the dunes on their way to Mexico, the deer lifting its head on a bluff to gaze down the beach, the silver fish suffocating in the back of the trucks, the very sky would not be subject to anything more. But in that narrower, human sense, of course it can. Malone worried that he had wasted his; and many felt he had. Those smug people who had bought their own houses out here and arrived by seaplane with their Vuitton. Malone only wanted to be liked. Malone wanted life to be beautiful and Malone believed quite literally in happiness—in short, he was the most romantic creature of a community whose citizens are more romantic, perhaps, than any other on earth, and in the end—he learned—more philistine.

He wanted to be liked, and so he ran away to New York —away from his own family—and he vanished on Manhattan, which is a lot easier than vanishing in the jungles of Sumatra. And what did he do? Instead of becoming the success they expected him to be, instead of becoming a corporate lawyer, he went after, like hounds to the fox, the cheapest things in life: beauty, glamour . . . all the reasons this beach had once thrilled us to death. But the parties, the drugs, the T-shirts, the music were as capable of giving him his happiness as this sea I sat beside now was of stinging beneath the whips that Xerxes had his servants turn on the waves for swallowing up his ships.

The rain began to fall as the clouds eclipsed the sun and I got up and went back to the intersection where the suitcases of Malone's T-shirts and Lacostes sat as forlorn as the houses in the sparkling rain, and began dragging them down the boardwalk. The wind came up, the rain thickened, now that the first cloud was over this improbable sandbar—and figures appeared from the dense shrubbery hurrying toward the harbor with their own mementos. "Indian summer is like a woman!" someone yelled to his companion as they scurried. "Ripe, hotly passionate, but fickle!" It was the opening line of *Peyton Place*, the favorite mockery of an aspiring novelist. Witty people came out in autumn; beauties in July.

Our little boat was covered with a tarpaulin when we came to the harbor, with its countless wagons rusting in the rain—a heap of abandoned souls, lying there in the rain till the bodies attached to them came back—and the owner sat in the shelter of the grocery store porch. We dragged our luggage up the stairs of the Sandpiper, and to our surprise found the back door flapping open in the wind. We went inside and shut it behind us, and heard the ghostly murmur of a couple who had already sat down in a far alcove, just where they sat on those blistering, crowded nights to watch the dancers. The room was plunged into a gray-and-silvery gloom, the mirrors and chrome gleaming in an eerie light. We shook ourselves like dogs, and sat down at a table and looked at the empty dance floor where we had spent so many sweaty, ecstatic nights in the past. That blond rectangle of polished wood that had seemed to be at one point the aesthetic center of the universe. It was here I had first seen Rick Hafner glistening with sweat like an idol around which people knelt in a drugged confusion, unconsciously adoring his beauty, assuming the pose of supplicants at some shrine. It was here Stanley Farnsworth would stop dancing with the boy he was seducing that night (for they all ended up with Stanley Farnsworth) in the middle of a song to embrace and kiss him with long, deep, searching kisses that gradually immobilized his prey, like the poison sea corals inject into fish, while everyone whirled like dervishes around them, and the air grew stale with the odor of used poppers, and we danced in our bare feet on their broken cylinders, as ladies had once danced on rose petals in silver slippers at Tea Dance years ago. It was here lovers had come with hollow-eyed, glum faces the first night after breaking up, and here they had desired each other, eyes floating above the crowd, mournful, romantic. It was here Lavalava used to come in sequined helmets and dance with Spanish Lily in a swirl of veils, it was here Malone had been arrested by the police.

"Tell me," I said to a friend who had come into the room and its ghostly light, "where did you first see Anthony Malone?"

"At the Twelfth Floor," he said. "Six years ago this fall."

"Me, too," I said. "I thought Malone was the handsomest man I'd ever seen. But then I was in love with half those people, and I never said hello or good-bye to any of them."

2

_____

LONG before journalists discovered the discotheques of Manhattan, long before they became another possession of the middle class, in the beginning, that particular autumn of 1971, two gentlemen whose names I forget opened up a little club on the twelfth floor of a factory building in the West Thirties. The West Thirties, after dark, form a lunar landscape: The streets that are crowded with men running racks of clothes down the sidewalk during the day, and trucks honking at each other to get through the narrow passageways of factory exits, are completely deserted at night. The place is as still as the oceans of the moon. The buildings are all dark. There isn't a soul in sight—not a bum, a mugger, or a cop. But late on Friday and Saturday nights, around one A.M., flotillas of taxis would pull up to a certain dim doorway and deliver their passengers who, on showing a numbered card, would go up in a freight elevator to the twelfth floor. Everyone who went there that first year agrees: There was never anything before or since so wonderful.

In a town where clubs open and close in a week, no one expected it to last more than one winter. The second year it was too famous, and too many people wished to go. Film stars and rock stars, and photographers, and rich Parisians, and women from Dallas came to look, and it was finished. There were arguments in the lobby about who was whose guest, and there were too many drugs; and toward the end of it, I used to just sit on the sofa in the back and watch the crowd.

The first year contained the thrill of newness, and the thrill of exclusivity—that all these people who might not even know each other, but who knew who each other were, had been brought together in the winter, in this little room, without having done a single thing to bring it about. They all knew each other without ever having been introduced. They formed a group of people who had danced with each other over the years, gone to the same parties, the same beaches on the same trains, yet, in some cases, never even nodded at each other. They were bound together by a common love of a certain kind of music, physical beauty, and style—all the things one shouldn't throw away an ounce of energy pursuing, and sometimes throw away a life pursuing.

Within this larger group—for some of them came but once a month, or twice all season—was a core of people who seemed to have no existence at all outside this room. They were never home, it seemed, but lived only in the ceaseless flow of this tiny society's movements. They seldom looked happy. They passed one another without a word in the elevator, like silent shades in hell, hell-bent on their next look from a handsome stranger. Their next rush from a popper. The next song that turned their bones to jelly and left them all on the dance floor with heads back, eyes nearly closed, in the ecstasy of saints receiving the stigmata. They pursued these things with such devotion that they acquired, after a few seasons, a haggard look, a look of deadly seriousness. Some wiped everything they could off their faces and reduced themselves to blanks. Yet even these, when you entered the hallway where they stood waiting to go in, would turn toward you all at once in that one unpremeditated moment (as when we see ourselves in a mirror we didn't know was there), the same look on all their faces: Take me away from this. Or, Love me. If there had been a prison for such desperadoes, you would have called the police and had them all arrested—just to get them out of these redundant places and give them a rest.

There was a moment when their faces blossomed into the sweetest happiness, however—when everyone came together in a single lovely communion that was the reason they did all they did; and that occurred around six-thirty in the morning, when they took off their sweat-soaked T-shirts and screamed because Patty Joe had begun to sing: "Make me believe in you, show me that love can be true." By then the air was half-nauseating with the stale stench of poppers, broken and dropped on the floor after their fumes had been sucked into the heart, and the odor of sweat, and ethyl chloride from the rags they clamped between their teeth, holding their friends' arms to keep from falling. The people on downs were hardly able to move, and the others rising from the couches where they had been sprawled like martyrs who have given up their souls to Christ pushed onto the floor and united in the cries of animal joy because Patty Joe had begun to sing in her metallic, unreal voice those signal words: "Make me believe in you, show me that love can be true."

(Or because the discaire had gone from Barrabas' "Woman" to Zulema's "Giving Up," or the Temptations' "Law of the Land." Any memory of those days is nothing but a string of songs.)

When the people finally left, the blood-red sun was

perched in the fire escape of a factory building silhouetted on the corner, and the cornices of the buildings were all gold-edged, and they would strip off their T-shirts, in the cold fall morning, and wring them out over the gutter. And the sweat would fall into the gutter like water dripping from a pail, the sweat of athletes after a long and sweaty game of soccer on some playing field to the north, on a fall day as pure as this one; and they would walk up Broadway together, exhausted, ecstatic, their bones light as a bird's, a flotilla of doomed queens on their way to the Everard Baths because they could not come down from the joy and happiness.

They looked, these young men gazing up toward the sky with T-shirts hanging from their belts, like athletes coming from a game, like youths coming home from school, their dark eyes glowing with light, their faces radiant, and no one passing them could have gathered the reason for this happy band.

Toward the end, I used to sit on the sofa in the back of the Twelfth Floor and wonder. Many of them were very attractive, these young men whose cryptic disappearance in New York City their families (unaware they were homosexual) understood less than if they had been killed in a car wreck. They were tall and broad-shouldered, with handsome, open faces and strong white teeth, and they were all dead. They lived only to bathe in the music, and each other's desire, in a strange democracy whose only ticket of admission was physical beauty—and not even that sometimes. All else was strictly classless: The boy passed out on the sofa from an overdose of Tuinols was a Puerto Rican who washed dishes in the employees' cafeteria at CBS, but the doctor bending over him had treated presidents. It was a democracy such as the world—with its rewards and penalties, its competition, its snobbery—never permits, but which flourished in this little room on the twelfth floor of a factory building on West Thirty-third Street, because its central principle was the most anarchic of all: erotic love.

What a carnival of people. One fellow came directly from his tour of duty in the Emergency Room at Bellevue on Saturday nights, and danced in his white coat sprinkled with blood. A handsome blond man whom the nation saw on its television sets almost every day eating a nutritious cereal, came to stand by the doorway to the bathroom, waiting for someone to go in whose piss he could drink. Chatting with him was a famous drug dealer from the Upper East Side who was sending his son through Choate and his daughter through Foxcroft, and who always dressed like a gangster from the forties. They were talking to a rich art collector, who one day had resolved to leave all this, had cursed it and gone to the Orient the next day to live there; within a year he had reappeared standing beside the dance floor, because, as he told his friends, Angkor Wat was not nearly so beautiful as the sight of Luis Sanchez dancing to "Law of the Land" with his chest glistening with sweat and a friend stuffing a rag soaked with ethyl chloride into his mouth.

The art collector walked up to talk to a handsome architect who had also tried to escape this room and the life, and society, which flowed out from it, as a river does from a spring. He had decided one night he was dissipating himself, he had looked in the mirror and decided he was going to waste physically. And so he bought a car and drove west till he found a little shack high in a mountain pass with not a single mirror in the house. Four months of snow, and two of flowers, in the pure mountain air, however, did not arrest the progress of these physical flaws. They were age itself. And so one morning in May, with flowers on the meadows and the valley beneath him, he decided to go back to Manhattan and rot with all the beauties in this artificial hothouse of music and light. For what was this room but a place to forget we are dying? There were people so blessed with beauty there they did not know what to do with it. And so the doctor who came direct from the Emergency Room (whose dark, bearded face was that of a fifteenth-century Spanish saint), the archangelic son of a famous actress, the man who had driven west to leave time behind, breathed now the air of Olympus: Everyone was a god, and no one grew old in a single night. No, it took years for that to happen . . .

For what does one do with Beauty—that oddest, most irrational of careers? There were boys in that room, bank tellers, shoe salesmen, clerks, who had been given faces and forms so extraordinary that they constituted a vocation of their own. They rushed out each night to simply stand in rooms about the city, exhibiting themselves to view much as the priest on Holy Saturday throws open the doors of the Tabernacle to expose the chalice within.

Nevertheless Malone, the night Frankie nearly beat him up on the sidewalk outside the Twelfth Floor (a commotion I was unaware of long after it had occurred, since I had arrived early that night to watch the place fill up with dancers and hear the music that began the whole night, as an overture begins an opera, and that the dancers never heard) and had to be taken off by the police, had by that time come to loathe being looked at; could not bear the gaze of amorous strangers; and the only reason he came out at all, during that period after he left Frankie, when he wanted to go away and hide forever, was the crazy compulsion with which we resolved all the tangled impulses of our lives—the need to dance.

42

Everyone there, in fact, like Malone, was a serious dancer and they were by no means beautiful: Archer Prentiss, who had no chin or hair; Spanish Lily, a tiny, wizened octoroon who lived with his blind mother in the Bronx and sold shoes in a local store—but who by night resembled Salome dancing for the head of John the Baptist in peach-colored veils; Lavalava, a Haitian boy who modeled for *Vogue* till an editor saw him in the dressing room with an enormous penis where a vagina should have been; another man famous for a film he had produced and who had no wish to do anything else with his life—all of them mixed together on that square of blond wood and danced, without looking at anyone else, for one another.

They were the most romantic creatures in the city in that room. If their days were spent in banks and office buildings, no matter: Their true lives began when they walked through this door—and were baptized into a deeper faith, as if brought to life by miraculous immersion. They lived only for the night. The most beautiful Oriental was in fact chaste, as the handmaidens of Dionysius were: He came each night to avoid the eyes of everyone who wanted him (though for different reasons than Malone ignored their gaze), and after dancing for hours in a band of half-naked men, went home alone each night refusing to tinge the exhilaration in his heart with the actuality of carnal kisses. The gossips said he refused to sleep with people because he had a small penis —the leprosy of homosexuals—but this explanation was mundane: He wanted to keep this life in the realm of the perfect, the ideal. He wanted to be desired, not possessed, for in remaining desired he remained, like the figure on the Grecian urn, forever pursued. He knew quite well that once possessed he would no longer be enchanted—so sex itself became secondary to the spectacle: that single moment of walking in that door. And even as he danced now he was aware of whose heart he was breaking; everyone there was utterly aware of one another.

For example: I sat on the sofa watching Archer Prentiss dance with two other men in plaid shirts and moustaches, who looked as if they had just come down from the Maine woods—two people I had seen for years and years, yet never said a word to, as was the case with Archer Prentiss. This technical distance did not keep us from knowing a great deal about each other, however. Although I had no idea who the two strangers on my left were, nor had ever been introduced to Archer Prentiss, I knew, to the quarter inch, the length and diameter of each one's penis, and exactly what they liked to do in bed.

But then so did everyone else in that room.

If one of the figures in this tapestry of gossip woven at the Twelfth Floor vanished—like the man who fled to Cambodia, or the one who drove west—such a disappearance was, in that crowd, less mysterious than most vanishing acts. If a face in that crowd vanished, it was usually for one of three reasons: (1) he was dead, (2) he had moved to another city whose inhabitants he had not all slept with, or (3) he had found a lover and settled down, spending his Saturday nights at home with his mate, going over the plans of the house they hoped to build in Teaneck, New Jersey.

The two strangers in plaid shirts who had sat down on the sofa to my left were discussing at that moment such a move. The big, blond fellow (whose face decorated a dozen billboards on the Long Island Expressway, smiling at a Winston cigarette) said to the dark one: "He wants me to move in with him, after he comes back from Portugal."

"Oh, God, he lives on Beekman Place, doesn't he?"

"Yes, but Howard lives off Sutton, and he wants me to move in, too. Damn, I don't know what to do."

"Marry John! Sutton Place is all Jewish dentists."

And they burst into laughter over their solution to this problem; while at the next instant, the creature who, for a reason I could not put my finger on, fascinated me more than any of the habitués of that place came in the door: Sutherland. He swept in trailing a strange coterie of Egyptian cotton heiresses, the most popular male model to come over from Paris in a decade, a Puerto Rican drug dealer, and an Italian prince. Sutherland was dressed in a black Norell, turban, black pumps, rhinestones, and veil. He held a long cigarette holder to his lips and vanished among the crowd. The dark man began to debate idly whether he should go to bed with Archer Prentiss, who was (a) very ugly, but (b) had a big dick.

In the midst of their deliberations, Zulema's "Giving Up" suddenly burst out of the recapitulations of Deodato, and the two woodsmen got up to dance; at their rising, two other boys in black with tired, beautiful eyes, sat down immediately and began discussing the men who had just left: "I call him the Pancake Man," said one. "*He* doesn't use make-up!" said the other. "Oh, no," the first replied. "The opposite! Because he's the kind of man you imagine waking up with on Saturday morning, and he makes pancakes for you, and then you take the dog out for a walk in the park. And he always has a moustache, and he always wears plaid shirts!"

"I agree he's gorgeous," said his friend, "but someone told me he has the smallest wee-wee in New York."

And with that, as if the boy had snapped his fingers, the big, blond woodsman standing by the dance floor in all his radiant masculinity, crumbled into dust.

"Oh please," said the one, "I don't need that." He covered his face with his hands. "I'm already on downs, why did you say that?"

"Because it's true," said the other.

"Oh, God," the first moaned, in the nasal wail of Brooklyn, "oh, God, I can't believe that. No, he's my Pancake Man."

"They *all* wear plaid shirts, and they all have moustaches," said his friend. "You might as well pick one with a big dick. None of them will look at you, anyway."

He looked out between his fingers at the woodsman, who was now talking animatedly to Sutherland in his black Norell and turban and long cigarette holder, and said, "Who is that woman he's talking to?" And the other said: "Her name is Andrew Sutherland, and she lives on Madison Avenue. She's a speed freak. She hasn't long to live." At that moment, "Needing You" began, buried still in the diminishing chords of "You've Got Me Waiting for the Rain to Fall," and the two boys on the sofa—with hearing sharper than a coyote's, and without even needing to ask each other—bounded up off the sofa and headed for the dance floor. Instantly their seats were taken by an older, gray-haired man and his friend, an even older fellow who because of his hearing aid, toupee, and back brace was known among the younger queens as Spare Parts. "I find him so beautiful," said the man of the boy who had just left, "like a Kabuki, that long neck, those heavy-lidded eyes. He never looks at me, do you think because he's afraid?" They began to discuss a friend on the dance floor who had recently learned he had cancer of the lungs. "No, no," said Spare Parts, "he has cancer of the colon, I think, his mother has cancer of the lungs." "Yes," said the friend, "he used to scream at his mother for smoking too much, and she used to scream at him for eating too fast. And now look." "He flies out to the clinic tomorrow," said Spare Parts. "Do you suppose he wants to go home with someone?" "You know," said the friend, "I would think the fact that he's dying would give him the courage to walk up to all these boys he's been in love with all these years but never had the nerve to say hello to." "Well, he has a look about him," said Spare Parts. "He looks . . . ethereal." At that moment two Puerto Rican boys, oblivious to everything but their own heated discussion, stopped to snuff out their cigarettes in the ashtray beside the sofa.

"And the reason you don't know any English," the one said suddenly in English to his friend, "is because you waste too much time chasing dick!"

And they hurried off into the crowd, the accused defending himself excitedly in rapid Spanish to his friend.

The gray-haired man on the sofa rolled his eyes, sighed a long sigh as he snuffed out his own cigarette in the ashtray, and said: "My dear, whole *lives* have been wasted chasing dick." He sat up suddenly. "Oh!" he said. "There's that song!"

At that moment, "One Night Affair" was beginning to rise from the ruins of "Needing You," and they both put down their paper cups of apple juice and started toward the dance floor.

For a moment the sofa was empty, and two tall black boys wearing wide-brimmed hats eyed it as they moved, like sailing barges, very slowly along the edges of the crowd, but before they could cross the space of carpet to its comfortable cushions, I heard a rustle of silk and a distinctive voice. I turned and saw Sutherland sitting down with a thin, pale young fellow in horn-rimmed glasses who looked as if he had just stumbled out of the stacks of the New York Public Library.

For an instant Sutherland, as he fit a cigarette into his long black holder, and the pale boy in spectacles eyed the black boys in hats across the rug; and then the blacks, seeing they had lost their harbor, turned and continued moving along the crowd like two galleons perusing the Ivory Coast on a hot, windless day.

"I find it perfectly expressive of the whole sad state of human affairs at this moment of history, I find it a perfect *sym*bol of the demise of America," said Sutherland in that low, throaty voice that always seemed breathlessly about to confide something undreamed of in your wildest dreams, "that dinge are the only people who take hats seriously!" And he turned to the boy with the cigarette in its rhinestone holder, waiting for a light.

"Dinge?" said the boy in a cracked, earnest voice as he tried three times to finally get a flame from his lighter.

"Oh, darling, are you one of these millionaires who go around with ninety-nine-cent lighters?" said Sutherland as he waited for the flame to ignite.

The boy—who, we later learned, was the heir to a huge farm implement and nitrogen fertilizer fortune—flushed scarlet, for he could not bear references to his money and was terrified that someone would ask him for a loan, or assume that he would pay the bill. Sutherland puffed on his cigarette and removed it from his lips and said through a cloud of smoke, when the boy repeated his request for a definition of *dinge*: "Blacks, darling. *Shvartzers*, negroes, whatever you like. Why are they the better dancers? For they are. They get away with things here that no white boy could in a million years. And why do they get to wear white hats? And all the outrageous clothes? When gloves come back," he said, pulling at his own long black ones, "and I'm sorry they ever went away, you can be sure they will be the ones to wear them first!"

The boy was not looking at Sutherland as he spoke—his eyes had already been caught by something ten feet away from him; his face had that stricken, despairing expression of someone who has seen for the very first time a race of men whose existence he never suspected before, men more handsome than he had ever imagined, and all of them in this tiny room. He looked as if he were about to burst into tears. He leaned closer to Sutherland who was at that moment just finishing with his gloves and who looked about himself now, with a gossamer cloud of stagnant cigarette smoke forming a double veil over his face. "My face seats five," he sighed, "my honeypot's on fire."

The boy, transfixed and terrified, leaned closer to Sutherland and said, "Who is that?"

"His name is Alan Solis, he has *huge* balls and does public relations work for Pan Am." They looked at him together for a moment. "Ask me about anyone, darling, I know them all. I have been living in New York since the Civil War."

And it was true: Sutherland seemed to have been alive, like the Prime Mover, forever. He had been a candidate for the Episcopalian priesthood, an artist, a socialite, a dealer, a kept boy, a publisher, a film-maker, and was now simply —Sutherland. And yet—behind the black veil his face was still as innocent and wonder-struck as it was the day he arrived in New York; his face, though everyone was waiting for it to crumble—from the speed he took—was open, honest, friendly, and looked, even more than that of the boy on his left, as if it were gazing on all of this for the first time.

"I used to be in love with Alan Solis," he said in his low, breathless voice, "when I came to New York. I was so in love with him, with him," he said (for he stuttered, and repeated phrases, not through any impediment of speech, but for effect), "that when he used the bathroom on the train to Sayville, I used to go in right after him and lock the door, just to smell his farts! To simply breathe the gas of his very bowels! A scent far lovelier to me than Chanel Number Nine, or whatever the ladies are wearing these days."

"You know," said the boy, bending over as if in pain, his eyes on Alan Solis with all the intensity of a mongoose regarding a snake, "if I can only find a flaw. If I can find a flaw in someone, then it's not so bad, you know? But that boy seems to be perfect!" he said. "Oh, God, it's terrible!" And he put a hand to his forehead, stricken by that deadliest of forces, Beauty.

"A flaw, a flaw," said Sutherland, dropping his ash into the ashtray on his left, "I understand perfectly."

"If I can just see a flaw, then it's not so hopeless and depressing," said the boy, his face screwed up in agony, even though Solis, talking to a short, muscular Italian whom he wanted to take home that night, was completely oblivious to this adoring fan whose body was far too thin to interest him.

"I've got it," said Sutherland, who turned to his companion now. "I remember a flaw. His chest," he said, "his chest is so hairy that one can't really see the deep, chiseled indentation between the breasts. Will that do, darling?"

The boy gnawed on his lip and considered.

"I'm afraid it will have to. There isn't a thing else wrong with the man, other than the fact that he knows it."

"You know," the boy said, "when my family was living in England and I came home from school on vacation, there was a boy who worked at our butcher's in the village. And he was astonishing! He had white, white skin, and rosy cheeks, and the most beautiful golden hair! He was as beautiful as an angel! I'm not exaggerating. And all that winter I used to dream of him, walking over the fields, at home at night. And at Princeton, a boy who used to dive at the pool. I was in love with him, and I used to ache walking home in autumn from the gym and think of him for days! And that's why I'm here, I guess, I'm looking for the English butcher boy, the diver at Princeton," he said as Alan Solis wandered onto the dance floor, "because I'm so tired of dreaming of faces and bodies. I want to touch one this time," he said, his voice suddenly choking.

"Well, how about that one over there?" said Sutherland, waving his cigarette holder at a tall, square-jawed fellow who taught English to children of the Third World in Harlem. "Greg Butts. I've always found him very Rupert Brooke; however his cock is very small, they tell me, and would hardly sustain a major fantasy on the scale of yours."

"You know, I hate being gay," said the boy, leaning over toward Sutherland, "I just feel it's ruined my life. It drains me, you know, it's like having a tumor, or a parasite! If I were straight I'd get married and that would be it. But being gay, I waste so much time imagining! I hate the lying to my family, and I know I'll never be any of the things they expect of me," he said, "because it's like having cancer but you can't tell them, that's what a secret vice is like."

Sutherland was speechless at this declaration; he sat there for a moment, with the cigarette holder to his lips, perfectly still; and then he said, "Perhaps what you *need* . . . perhaps what you need," he said, in a speculative tone, "is a good facial." He turned quickly to his friend and said: "Oh, darling, for heaven's sake, don't take it so seriously! Just repeat after me: 'My face seats five, my honeypot's on fire.' "

"My face seats five, my honeypot's on fire," said the boy with a constipated smile.

"That's right, that will get you into the spirit of things!

51

And please don't feel you have an obligation to be secretary of state!" he said, as his two Egyptian heiresses came by. "Their great great great great great great grandfather was a Pharaoh, while yours was just a potato farmer in Würzburg!" And he waved at his two Egyptian women, who were wandering around the French model, wreathed in the happiest of smiles. The floor had cleared momentarily to watch a tall, thin girl dance who came dressed each night in the latest work of a famous designer, and who prided herself on sleeping with all the handsomest homosexuals in New York. "Perhaps what you need is this."

He held out his black-gloved arm, and a little red pill sat in the center of his palm.

"What's that?" said the boy.

"Oh don't ask, darling," said Sutherland. "If it's a pill, take it."

The boy looked askance at the rosy pebble in Sutherland's palm, glowing like a ruby on black velvet in a vault at Bulgari. "I don't . . ." he said.

"Don't you trust me?" said Sutherland. "I would never ask you to take anything that does not enhance lucidity."

"But . . . speed kills," blurted the boy, looking up at Sutherland over his glasses.

"And Dial prevents wetness twenty-four hours a day," breathed Sutherland in his lowest tone. "Darling. Don't believe everything you hear. You mustn't for instance read the newspapers, that will destroy your mind far faster than speed. The *New York Times* has been responsible for more deaths in this city than Angel Dust, *croyez-moi*." He put the red pill on the arm of the sofa and said: "There are many drugs I would not have you take. I am not like these queens whose names I wouldn't mention, but who, if you glance at the dance floor, you can certainly pick out, and who are on *hog tranquilizer*. My dear," he breathed, nodding toward a certain Michael Zubitski, a blond man wandering past the sofa now with no awareness of where he was: a sleepwalking queen whom Sutherland had not spoken to since he alienated a boy with whom Sutherland had been in love. "I do not pickle myself in formaldehyde or drench my brain pan in a drug used to tranquilize pigs, I have no desire to be turned, like Ulysses' men, into beasts, I am not envious of the profound ease felt by a Nebraska hog about to be castrated and bled to death," he said, straight into the face of Michael Zubitski, who, trying to see who this person was, had stopped and bent down to stare into Sutherland's black veil, five inches from his forehead, and hung there now like a huge sea gull poised above a swimming fish, "for the tables of all-American families in Duluth and Council Bluffs, no, you'll have to forgive me, darling, I am old-fashioned, I believe in General Motors and the clarity of the gods . . ."

And here, raising his ponderous blond head, Michael Zubitski withdrew from Sutherland's face and began moving, like a zombie, across the rug till he came to rest against the wall beside a potted plant.

"Who was that?" said the boy, ogling.

"A woman of no importance," said Sutherland, expelling a stream of cigarette smoke. "A vengeful queen. For that great blond beast, that Nazi storm trooper, has a cock that if it were any smaller would be a vagina, and if people, for whatever reason, go to bed with him, they inevitably leave in the middle of it, saying 'I'm tired,' or 'I've already had sex today,' or one of those classic excuses. The boy became so bitter about his fate that when he developed a case of syphilis he went to the Baths and infected everyone he could who sported an enormous organ. Well, darling, I

53

guess it's better than assassinating a president." He expelled a long stream of smoke. "For don't you see, even after the dinge are taken care of and the amputees and Eurasians and the fags, even after all of them are provided for, who will ease the pains of that last minority, that minority within a minority, I mean those lepers of New York, the queens with small cocks? Truly Christ blessed the lepers and the whores, but there is *no* comfort in the Bible for boys with small winks, and they are the most shunned of all. People go to bed with me once, and I never hear from them again!" he said with the bright eyes of a koala bear, confessing what others in his situation spent a lifetime concealing. "What will the government do for *them*? Ah well, no matter," he sighed, "it's certainly not your problem." He squeezed his hand and smiled. "There are three lies in life," Sutherland said to his young companion, whose first night this was in the realm of homosexuality and whose introduction to it Sutherland had taken upon himself to supervise. "One, the check is in the mail. Two, I will not come in your mouth. And three, all Puerto Ricans have big cocks," he said. And with that he leaned forward and cupped the young man's hand in his long black gloves and said to him in that low, breathless voice: "You are beginning a journey, far more bizarre than any excursion up the Nile. You have set foot tonight on a vast, uncharted continent. Do let me take you as far as I can. I shall hold your hand as far as we can go together, and point out to you the more interesting flora and fauna. I will help you avoid the quicksand in which you can drown, or at least waste a *great* deal of time, the thorn-thickets, the false vistas—ah," he sighed. "We have many of those, we have *much* trompe l'oeil in this very room!" he said ecstatically, cocking his cigarette holder at a sprightly angle. "So let us go upriver together as far as we may," he resumed, once more cupping his charge's white, slim hand, "and remember to ask questions, and notice everything, the orchids and the fruit flies, the children rummaging for food in piles of shit, and the ibis that flies across the moon at dusk. Let us go at *least* as far as the falls. What a journey! If only I can help you avoid the detours, culs-de-sac, fevers, and false raptures that *I* have suffered." He squeezed the fellow's hand and said, echoing the signal phrase of a Bar Mitzvah he had once attended in the guise of a Jewish matron from Flatbush: "For tonight, my dear, you are a homosexual!"

And with that he returned his attention to the men coming through the doorway, of whom they had the only unobstructed view from that sofa by the coat check. In the midst of this late-arriving throng (for the desire of everyone to arrive after everyone else had created a ripple effect so that no one could go out anymore before two A.M. at the earliest), in a kind of rest between the arrivals of two of the larger "families," a young man appeared in the doorway by himself; and the fertilizer heir said, 'Oh, who is *that*? Find a flaw, I can't find a flaw."

"That is Malone," said Sutherland in his lowest, most dramatic voice, "and his only flaw is that he is still searching for love, when it should be perfectly clear to us all by now that there is no Mister Right, or Mister Wrong, for that matter. We are all alone. He used to be a White House fellow, darling, and now he talks of suicide, if a certain Puerto Rican maniac doesn't kill him first."

I watched as this individual walked into the room and was immediately greeted by several of the handsomest boys there, the ones so handsome they never looked at anybody, but went to the darkness of back rooms merely to piss on perfect strangers and have their asses licked. They were the first to go over to Malone. He put an arm around their shoulders or shook their hands, with his almost old-fashioned manners. He put his head close to theirs when they spoke to him, as if he didn't want to miss a word, and when he replied he spoke almost against their ear: a charming gesture ostensibly to defeat the noise of the room, but one that made you feel you were being winnowed out, selected, for some confidential revelation. The courtesy with which he moved on through that crowd of zombies who stepped on one another with the oblivious brusqueness of a crowd in a subway, and stopped to talk to whoever tugged at him, was reflected in his smile. He had a face you liked with the certainty that, though you had no idea who he was, he was a good man. He introduced his admirers to one another and then left them new friends and vanished in the crowd. I had no idea who he was, he was just a face I saw in a discotheque one winter; but he was for me the central symbol on which all of it rested.

"He had the misfortune to fall in love with a thug," said Sutherland when the fertilizer heir asked him again about this man, "who has threatened to kill Malone simply because Malone no longer loves him and was foolish enough to say so. Another rule, *caro*, which may help you—if blacks are the only ones who wear hats anymore," he breathed, raising his cigarette holder to his lips, "then Latins, my dear, are the only ones who take love seriously. Malone is now being chased around Manhattan by knives and bullets. He *never* has sex."

The two Egyptian women came up to Sutherland, leaned down, and spoke rapidly in French to him for a few moments; they shrieked with laughter and went on their way. When the fertilizer heir asked what that was all about, Sutherland replied: "They want to know if they should paint their cunts. What do *you* think?"

"Me?" said the boy, his face alarmed.

"Does the thought of cooze make you vomit?" said Sutherland, blowing out a stream of smoke. "Well, to be dead-honest, I find it, the very thought of it, loathsome beyond words! However, I love my girls! They are being driven mad by the presence of so many handsome young men—so many handsome young men who have absolutely no interest whatsoever in dining between their legs this evening. But, *croyez-moi*, my friend, there is steam rising from those pussies!"

The boy sat back, white as a sheet, and Sutherland proceeded to greet a group of five who had come up to talk to him, among them the blond man being pursued by the Puerto Rican maniac, the Egyptian heiresses, and the model who had come over from Paris. For a second, in glancing over, I found myself looking straight at Malone. Our eyes met. His were blue-gray and calm. It was, I noted much later that morning in my journal, like that melodramatic moment in historical novels: when the protagonist, in a crowded marketplace, on a dusty road, on Golgotha, suddenly meets the eyes of Christ, and he is forever changed. Well, I was not changed, but I was singled out—enough to write about it for a while later that day, to record that moment when I looked at Malone and thought: His eyes are like Jesus Christ's.

But at that moment Sutherland turned to the fertilizer heir and said: "Darling, come, we're going uptown! A small Crucifixion at Park and Seventy-fifth, nothing heavy." The boy, pale and stricken, got up and followed the Egyptian women, the French model, and a couple of Halston assistants out of the dim room with Sutherland in his black Norell and turban, leading the pack. With them went Malone, and with him went the magic of the room, which consisted, I realized then, not of the music, the lights, the dancers, the faces, but of those eyes, still, and grave and candid, looking at you with the promise of love.

3

IN the years before Malone arrived in New York City he had done all those things a young man was supposed to do— a young man from a good family, that is, a family that had always had in every generation since it transplanted itself in Ohio from a rural town in Germany, a doctor or two, a judge, and a professor. This Germanic family of his father's worked hard, prospered, and gradually scattered all over the globe, even though they retained a certain love for the small town in Ohio in which they had grown up. As a child Malone had been allowed to read the round robin family letter they circulated among themselves: The news was usually about the vegetables they had planted, the weather, the seasons, and those events another family might have considered primary were mentioned almost as an after-thought—Sally was going to Korea to serve in the medical corps, Andrew was going round the world on the ship "Hope," Martha had discovered she had TB while examining her own sputum in the lab one afternoon, Joe was drinking. Pete had been promoted to treasurer of Sears International, Harry had died. "We had a good year for squash, though the rutabagas didn't come up nearly so fast as we expected. You know how Lawrence loves his squash. It looks like the corn may be a bit late, too . . ." and on and on and on. Malone loved to read these letters as a child; they seemed so friendly and so calm to him, how peaceful to care only about the weather and the fruit. And as he grew older he came to see how modest they were, too, finding the fate of their vegetables of more interest than the fate of those human plants who were growing, in the background, to even greater glory than the squash—for the family letter, if it sounded like a garden club newsletter, also resembled to Malone's mind those glossy annual reports that corporations his father held stock in sent him every spring: listing debts and assets, profits, and future plans of investment. That was the family on his father's side: dispassionate, sensible, hardworking, and generous with one another.

His father had married a city girl, however—from a big, witty Irish family in the suburbs of Chicago—and she had found these Germans sometimes too dispassionate for her tastes. She left Chicago with her new husband, left her friends, her skating parties, rides down Michigan Boulevard, and resorts in Wisconsin, and moved to a small town in southern Indiana; and it was there Malone spent the first few years of his life, chasing rabbits, hunting in the woods, spoiled by his paternal grandmother until his parents went abroad to work for an international engineering firm. It was the golden age of the American corporation, it was the flush of victory following World War II, and the family participated in this, too.

The family taught Malone to be a polite fellow, self-reliant, hardworking, and to believe in God. He took piano lessons on Saturday morning and he scrubbed the patio each morning before he went to school. Above the sideboard in the dining room of their bungalow hung a painting of a woman knitting in a grove of fruit trees while her children played about her skirts. "That is how my family should be," his father said one day. After lunch his father took a nap—a custom of the tropics—and Malone sat by the telephone on the porch, reading his ancient history, and guarding his father's sleep. His father rose and returned to his air-conditioned office at one o'clock, and when he returned at five o'clock in the blue, windy twilight, Malone rushed to embrace him on the porch, and pressed his face against the crisp, white shirt that bore, somehow, the odor of air conditioning. His mother, who had often just arisen, having read murder mysteries through the night, had a drink with his father on the porch while Malone sat out back with the maids, who adored him for his curly golden hair.

The events of his childhood were perfectly ordinary, if there is ever such a thing: He wept when his dog got lost, and wept when it was found. On Sunday mornings his mother wore short gloves to church and he held her hand walking up the aisle. He collected coral in his bedroom. A variety of varicolored maids came and went, and he attached his heart to them, in the washhouse behind their bungalow as they plaited their hair and he sat reading his books beside the washtubs fragrant with the blue astringency of bleach. He loved the odor of bleach and the breeze that blew down the hot, empty, baking street and carried the fragrance of the whole island, its thorn trees and cactus; he loved the warm cement, the empty, sunny sky, the maids' laughter. And he gradually over the years forgot those houses that had not only attics, dry and magical, but damp and vivid basements stored with preserves and tools and old toys; he forgot the snows and turning seasons, and became a habitué of the Equator, whose soul loves light and the pleasures of the senses.

For there is no more sensual place on earth. On Saturdays he went to the blazing white movie house in whose dark womb he watched Errol Flynn jumping onto burning decks to rescue Olivia de Havilland, and when he came outside into the dazzling sunlight, there were the cocoa palms, the lapis lazuli waters of the film itself. At night the trade winds moaned in the louvers as he lay in bed; a dog barked far away under the huge moon, the almond trees creaked in the breeze; and Malone dreamed the usual dreams of a boy his age—of cowboys, and Superman, and pirates—but with this difference: that outside, under the date palms, by the lagoons, was the setting for those dreams, as real as the shoes lying beside his bed on the floor. When he was twelve he gave up the dream of being a pirate, and replaced it with being a saint. He began coming home after school in the afternoons, and the catechism class that followed it, not to play ball, but to sequester himself in his room, kneeling, to pray to a statue of the Sacred Heart of Jesus and hope Christ would manifest Himself. His family said nothing as he prayed a Grace over his soup which lasted so long that by the time he lifted the first spoonful of cold liquid to his lips, they were eating dessert.

His beautiful mother went to parties at night in perfume and necklaces; took Malone to mass in the village and made him light candles for his aunts and uncles in America; drank some evenings, and insisted he sit with her in the cavernous lighted living room of their bungalow as she talked about the snow and Christmases in Chicago. Then she would rise and dance to the Victrola—dance about the room, with or without him, as the moths beat against the screens. "Whatever you do," she said, "never lose your sense of humor. And dance! I hope for God's sake you can dance!" And Malone got up and danced for her. Afterward he dreamed of sleighs and snowy nights, of his mother always loving him, of his being the best dancer, of mittens and blankets, and falling snow. On the hottest nights, as the trade winds blew through the bungalow, he dreamed of snow; on the endless afternoons, of being a saint; but he was always dreaming.

Malone had one of those sweet, receptive natures that take impressions like hot wax: Years later, when he had been sent away, he would remember the oil-black shadows the date palms cast on the patio floor in the moonlight; or his mother dancing in that lighted room; the distressed moan of the wind against the shut louvers; the sunburned faces of the Dutch sailors who came out after showering to sit on the veranda of their hotel next to the church he attended with his mother; the cologne she wore to church and the tendrils of her hair curled behind her ears, damp from the shower; the sunlight slanting across tiles; the shine of granite rocks baking in the sun; the wind in the sea grape trees. But the impressions he took from that lighted bungalow, like the hot days and dreams of northern snow, were contradictory. His mother bequeathed him a loving heart, his father a certain German coldness that surprised him later in life in the midst of his most emotional episodes, like a cadaver suddenly sitting up in its coffin, when he suddenly saw he was cold, too. This duality of his cerebral father and tempestuous mother—of northern snows and tropic nights, of the sailors serenading the girls walking down the street in the hot sunlight and Christ dying on the cross within the darkness of the church—was like some gigantic fault that lies dormant in the earth until that single day when years of pressure cause it to slip. His being homosexual was only one aspect of this. He did not think his childhood any different from others he heard of which produced heterosexuals out of the same, if not worse, tensions—and he finally concluded, years later after the most earnest search for the cause of this inconvenience, that a witch had passed a wand over him as he lay sleeping one evening in Ceylon.

The Bible says, a man divided is unstable in all ways. The child did not know this. The child was dutiful and well brought up, and resolved things by bringing home the first Friday of each month (like the mass devoted to the Sacred Heart of Jesus) a report card that pleased both mother and father. These different people both wanted him to do well in school. This he did. His geography teacher, the Portuguese gardener, his classmates: Everyone loved him for excelling. "Get a degree in law and finance," his father told him one day, "and you'll always be in demand." At the age of fifteen he was shipped off to America like an island pineapple of special quality to be enrolled in a boarding school in Vermont; and thus, with everything unresolved, confused, inchoate, in a young man who thought life's greatest challenge would be in passing a trigonometry examination, he waved good-bye to the man and woman whose own lives, he would later feel, held the key to his. As their figures grew smaller on the dock in Surabanda between the palms and whitewashed houses, the maid weeping beside them, he moved even farther from a mystery that growing up only obscured, by adding further layers of politeness to a relationship already formal. "Get a degree in law and finance," was all he could think of as his father's white shirt was lost in the specks of color that made up that paradisical island.

In New England he found snow—but it was the snow of loneliness, for now he missed his family and felt the first shock that occurs when a heart is sundered from its objects of affection. He studied diligently and postponed happiness to some future time: a habit he would not abandon for years. Though he was never as great a baseball player as his father had been in his youth, apparently, he was elected captain of the soccer team. He loved the vivid falls—the wildness in the air that singes the soul—and made a few good friends. He was what is so important to Americans: popular. He graduated in a shower of gold. He was ambitious and went to Yale, and from Yale he entered law school, and from law school he enrolled at the University of Stockholm for graduate work in shipping and banking law. He joined a large firm in New York on his return and was immediately assigned a crumb of that enormous banquet that would feed lawyers for decades to come: the Penn Central case. He was considered for a post as White House fellow. He was then a handsome young man in a dark suit with a vest and tie from J. Press in New Haven, wearing glasses to read, and you might have seen him on the shuttle to Washington, reading a novel of Henry James, or on a summer dusk in Georgetown, lingering outside a bookshop to examine the volume on French cathedrals in the window, before going off to the train station to get the Metroliner back to New York. There are various ways to keep the world at arm's length, and success is one of them: Malone was irreproachable, and something of a snob.

For something had happened to Malone since he'd been sent to America to school. During those snowy New England winters, besides learning to rise at five to study calculus and trudge two miles through the drifts for breakfast down the road, he had suppressed some tremendous element in himself that took form in a prudish virginity. While his life was impeccable on the surface, he felt he was behind glass: moving through the world in a separate compartment, touching no one else. This was painful. He walked in one night to find his proctor standing nude from the shower in the middle of his room: He was unstrung. He wrote letters to girls in Ceylon, but they were just that: letters. He listened to stories of boys from Connecticut who had made love their first night home of vacation, to girls in Chevrolets; he listened to stories about the town whore, and he leafed through the copies of *Playboy* that everyone kept; and he was utterly untouched. This dissociation between his feelings and the feelings of all his friends baffled Malone. He simply suppressed it all, and studied harder, and dreamed of Ceylon. In New Haven he learned to ignore the tie his roommate hung on the doorknob of his room whenever he had a girl in bed with him, but ties remained for him the symbol of the rich erotic life that other men enjoyed. He himself was still a virgin when he took a room in a large house in the Maryland suburbs in 1972. The house belonged to the widow of an ambassador who had been a friend of his grandmother's when they were girls; and he rented a similar one in Brookfield, Connecticut, since his work was in two cities. Like most of his classmates he loathed cities. His married friends lived in North Salem and he visited them on Sundays. He found it touching and curious that they wanted his company; for he assumed, never having been in love, that they would find another person intrusive. It was important to him that they were happily married and when they got divorced a year later, he was stunned. He felt his presence, somehow, had been a jinx. He had other married friends in the suburbs but seeing them made him feel more solitary.

He began to study wines. He joined the Sierra Club. Every time he planned to join them for a hike, he canceled the last moment—ashamed of his loneliness. He was very proud. He hated being a bachelor. He was at the same time devoted to his family. He called his parents once a month.

He sent gifts to his niece and nephew at Christmas. He gave them each a hundred-dollar bond on their birthdays. He began to jog. He ran alone down country lanes in autumns whose beauty left him pained. He ate sensibly, avoided cholesterol, and took brewer's yeast with his morning orange juice. He was a member of his class. The world tortured him: its ugliness, venality, vulgarity. Sundays he spent the afternoon reading the *Times*. When he came to New York City on business, he saw its steaming towers downriver with the eyes of most of his classmates: an asphalt slag heap baking under a brown shroud of pollution. He was the kind of person who telephoned Citizens for Clean Air if he saw black smoke issuing from a building smokestack on Manhattan longer than the legal limit of ten minutes. He considered wearing a mask when he bicycled to his office from the Yale Club, but thought it would look silly. Bus fumes infuriated him. Architecture he anxiously judged. Its mediocrity, the absence of beautiful avenues, lovely squares, pained him. He lay awake nights replanning the city. He joined the Committee to Reforest Fifth Avenue, thinking it could all be saved with trees, but eventually he despaired that this would ever happen and dropped away from their fund-raisers and dinner dances.

He felt impotent, he felt doomed. He despaired of politics; the world, like the city, seemed an unmanageable mess, filled with squawling, venal babies—a vast kindergarten of infantile delinquents who had to be supervised. He got lost on freeways late at night in the amber glare of the Jersey refineries, and he felt sure he was in hell. His wines, cross-country running, excursions to the theater left him as miserable as the moments of indecision in health food stores, when he felt his life had come to a complete halt over the choice of two brands of vitamins. One night going home on the train to Connecticut he found himself in the air-conditioned car staring at a page of *The New Yorker* on his lap. His mind stopped. The page gleamed with a high, cold gloss in the fluorescent light: He stared at its shining surface, the pale gray pinstripe of his dark pants leg. Eventually his stop appeared. He got off in a somnambulistic daze. No one met him at the station. He felt he should call someone for help—but who?

I saw Malone earlier that night, at a party at Hirschl & Adler, the gallery on East Sixty-seventh Street. It was a preview of an exhibit of portraits by John Singleton Copley. It was crowded with corporate lawyers like himself, their wives, and the older men whose tuxedos had been their father's and grandfather's: They continued to exist as a class, impervious to the disintegration of the city. Malone fitted right in and except for his golden handsomeness, I would never have picked him out—but I did, as I walked through their midst with the tray of cookies and champagne. He talked even then in that animated, electrifying way, but it seemed out of place there, out of proportion even to the surroundings. The smile, so dazzling, seemed brittle—almost like a shriek when viewed from a certain angle. But then a smile is often a shriek: a soul screaming at you. Malone left early to get the train back to his room in the country—and I saw him say good-night, in his affectionate way, to friends and then disappear in a Chesterfield and scarf from Sulka's, to hail a cab . . . a very handsome man I should never see again, since those people were seen in New York only by one another; they lived otherwise an invisible existence.

He moved furthermore to Washington for a while and lived an even more monastic existence, going home after a long day with the Penn Central accountants to the house of the widow in the Maryland suburbs. The widow always had about her the faint odor of cold cream. She sat in a wheelchair on the veranda and when Malone came home in the evenings, he sat with her sometimes drinking tea. She talked about her husband as Malone watched the light in the garden change, she talked about the loveliness of Saigon in the twenties. She talked of the beaches they had found on little islands in the Seychelles, as the dusk gathered in the deep garden shaded by towering oaks, embalmed with the scent of gardenias and crape myrtle. He felt as if he were a character in Henry James; he began to suspect he was to be that man to whom nothing whatsoever was to happen. "When you find the right girl," she said to him putting her hand on his affectionately, "you must take her to Sadrudabad in April and see the flamboyant trees in bloom. There is nothing so wonderful as seeing the wonders of this earth with someone you love!"

It was a phrase that might have appeared in an article in the *Reader's Digest*, but Malone believed it completely. He was depressed by the thought that he should never do this. But he was a disciplined fellow and he rose the next morning, obedient soul, and went to work as usual, and played squash at one with a fellow associate who had recently been married because, as he told Malone, he thought everyone should be married by the time they're thirty. Even his favorite game now struck him with melancholy, for his partner, an old friend from school, was always saying, "Anne this," and "Anne that," and "Anne and I are going to drive to Salzburg this summer," and he felt even gloomier when he came off the court. He stopped visiting married friends. Married friends, he decided one evening after returning from a visit, depress me.

The gloom he felt then was nothing, however, compared

to the terrifying loneliness that assaulted him on Sunday evening around eight o'clock; for then he had spent the whole day by himself, or driving around shopping for antiques with a fellow bachelor, and as he sat in his room looking down into the beautiful garden—the widow having already gone to bed, slathered in cold cream whose scent clung to the air of the hallway—he felt himself so utterly alone, he could not imagine anyone being sadder. Tears came to his eyes as he sat there. This day, Sunday, was his favorite of the week; this day, Sunday, a family always spent together in the evening as they came home from their various errands for a cold supper and a perusal of the Sunday paper; this day, Sunday, the softest, most human, tenderest time, found him sitting bolt upright at his little desk by the window, hearing around his ears the beating of wings —the invisible birds assaulting him, beating the air about him with their accusing presence. He was alone, like Prometheus chained to his rock. Tomorrow the rush of men, all working for a living, would drown him; but now, at this moment, in this soft green twilight, this soft green Sunday evening, when the heart of the world seemed to lie beating in the palm of his hand, he sat in that huge house upstairs terrified that he would never live.

He resolved to do anything to avoid solitude at this particular moment—which he regarded with the same fear an insomniac does the hour he must go to bed. He began seeing a girl he had been introduced to by a fellow in his firm at a concert of Bach cantatas, a graduate student at the American University whose father was an undersecretary of state for the Far East. She would come up the drive in her little white sports car on Sunday afternoon, tooting the horn, and the widow smiled at what she was sure was a romance—but the romance consisted of discussions of

Henry Adams's *Mont-Saint-Michel and Chartres*—and when he said good-bye to her, and her little white Triumph disappeared down the drive in the shadow of the big oak trees, he felt more depressed than he did when he spent the evening alone; depressed with all the genteel talk on stained glass, the ache of too many smiles with too little feeling, the kisses they did not say good-night with, and the seduction that had not occurred in his room upstairs beneath the eaves. What is wrong with me, he wondered.

And then Michael Floria came to work for the widow after school. Malone had given up by this time his swim after work, his browsing through the bookstores in Georgetown, the chamber music concerts he had taken the girl to, as a ridiculous pretense, all of it. He drove straight home in the evenings now to work in the widow's yard and wipe out the strains of a day of intellectual effort with the cold comfort of the dark earth that clung to his hands as they scooped it up to make room for a new plant. She had in rows and rows of rusted tin cans plants whose seeds she had brought back with her from the highlands of Asia, and the Vale of Kashmir, and these he began transplanting in wintertime. Seeing his interest the widow hired a local high school student whose father was an agronomist with the Department of Agriculture to help Malone. He was a friendly, dark-eyed Italian-American who swam for his school and was applying to several colleges. As they knelt in the old flowerbeds, turning over the soil and patting it down around the newly transplanted tea plants, Malone gave him what helpful advice he could. He was very happy then: the cold black soil around his hands, the light glinting on the dark magnolia leaves above them, and the dark beauty of this young man beside him. "He's a great help!" Malone told the widow happily. "A really nice kid."

He thought of the deep flush of hysteria that comes at that age when you start to laugh. He loved to make Michael laugh. He laughed so hard sometimes he fell over onto the ground and lay, laughing, like someone wounded, between the rows of tea roses and frangipani trees from Kashmir, on a late winter afternoon. But it was not he who was wounded. It was Malone. But like the man who looks down to see what is sticky on his foot, and finds he has been bleeding, Malone was not to know till sometime later.

His own work kept Malone busy and one night he came home from a long day of writing loan agreements and heard the widow tell him it was Michael's last day there. He had taken a job in Colorado for the summer and would be off to college at Beloit in the fall. Malone could not understand the emotion that suddenly drained the blood from his limbs. He walked down from the house in his suit and tie from J. Press, carrying his briefcase full of his rough drafts, as if to appear nonchalant, and found Michael standing with a bag of powdered insecticide, carefully spooning it into a five-gallon jug. It was then he felt his own wounds. It was very definite, as if he had been stabbed. "The very best of luck," Malone smiled as he shook his hand, hoping only that Mike could not see through the gray cloth of his suit the vibration created by the fact that Malone's knees had suddenly started to shake violently. He did not trust his voice either and so he turned away.

This physical betrayal astonished him, and he went back upstairs to his room under a cloud of blackest anger. He kicked the wastebasket, slammed his drawers shut, cursed out loud as he undressed. It was of course completely wrong, the completely inconvenient sort of love; it was the one thing he—who had succeeded at everything else, who had been so virtuous, such a model—could not allow. It was as if he had finally admitted to himself that he had cancer. He saw in that instant a life he could not conceive of opening before him, a hopeless abyss. Either way he was doomed: He did what was wrong, and condemned himself, or he did what was right, and remained a ghost. He could see himself in twenty years in a house like this in the suburbs, twenty-eight rooms and no one in them. It made him furious that he, who had led so disciplined, so correct a life, was reduced now to helplessness and hot tears over this perfectly oblivious senior going off to Beloit College on the swimming team.

He stood up from his bed and looked out the window at the gardener laboring in the azaleas. He felt in one instant the vast indifference of nature—the perfect chaos, the haphazard character of the universe—as he stared through the window at his friend; for it was obvious that he, bent over the plants, was thinking of the proper composition of the liquid poison he was mixing to kill the red spiders that had attacked the camelia bushes, and he, Malone, was going through an unendurable tragedy at the same time.

A sensible man would have laughed at Malone; would have called him melodramatic, sentimental; would have told him to get on with life, and stop thinking he had been cast into outer darkness—nonsense! But Malone was not this sensible man. Some live more for love than others. And he experienced a death that night, as he lay upstairs in the widow's house, on that vast floor of empty rooms in whose hallway outside his own the odor of cold cream, the sound of a television program being watched downstairs, hovered. At the moment when the organism usually fructifies Malone perished, like the marigolds that had shriveled up the week before in their pots for no earthly reason they could see.

His entire love had progressed, like the growing and

dying of a plant, from indifference to love to extinction, and not one embrace, not one kiss, not one word had been exchanged between him and his beloved. He heard the widow talking to him down below, he heard the door slam as she withdrew into the kitchen, and he heard the gate open and close by which the boy let himself into the adjacent field and began his walk home, while he lay there staring at the ceiling like the effigy on an Etruscan tomb.

That night he got up out of bed and put on his maroon polo shirt, which everyone said he looked so handsome in, and went downstairs and drove off in his car, where he did not know. He just drove. He drove around that wilderness of gas stations and fast-food franchises that surrounds Washington as once the armies of the Confederacy had, drove around in that crimson glow of doughnut shops and new-car showrooms, in which all things, cars, faces, bodies, gleam with an otherworldly light, and he kept driving—never admitting what he was about—until he came to Dupont Circle and there he stopped and got out under the green trees and met a man and went into the park and blew him.

All this occurred in a state both trancelike and sharply conscious; as if another being had momentarily occupied the physical shell that was Malone.

When he got home, and emerged from this dream-play, like a man who has just murdered someone and returns to his apartment and sits down to a bowl of soup, Malone took a shower that lasted over an hour and washed his mouth out with soap. He sat up the rest of the night writing in his journal. He wrote a poem. He wrote of the fact that for the first time he had used his mouth for something other than those two blameless functions—speech and the ingestion of food—and that now he had profaned it utterly. Those lips, that throat, which were stained with milk, and apples, bread, and life-giving things, had been soiled beyond redemption now. For Malone believed in some undefined but literal sense that the body was the temple of the Holy Ghost: the pure vessel. He sat and watched the garden outside emerge from the darkness. It was his first miserable, yet strangely vivid, dawn of that sort and he watched it silently in a white, rigid state of self-condemnation before which any judgment of God would have paled.

A year went by as if that night had never occurred. Malone was chaste. The widow died the following spring, and Malone moved into town and took an apartment in the northwest section of the city; and he lived a quiet life. He played squash with the associate who had married because he felt one should be at thirty. He visited museums and gazed at his favorite Watteau, and drove to sites of Civil War battles in the surrounding hills. But his interest in history now seemed to him an interest in death, and the cold skin of his face as he stood on a tawny hill staring at the bare trees against the pale blue sky no longer exhilarated his soul but made him feel condemned against his will to the company of nature. His mind began to stray over the intricacies of loan prepayments and he could no longer plow through the papers on his desk with his usual celerity. In the middle of the day, he fell into that abyss he carried within him now, the knowledge that he could not live alone forever, or without love. This fact changed his attitude toward his work. It seemed little more than a mercenary exchange for dining out, tennis lessons, and a week in summer at the French cathedrals. The bourgeois arrangement of the world, his own parasitical relationship with a vast, impersonal economy by which he drew off his living, repelled him strangely. He read Heine's remark, "Fame isn't worth a milkmaid's kiss," and thought: Neither is money, nor comfort, nor prestige.

On his most miserable nights he would go out to a public park in Washington and simply sit watching these compatriots of his—these citizens of hell, he thought gloomily, this *paseo* of the damned—till birds began to sing around him and he hurried home at dawn, like a man who stands on a beach a long time at the water's edge and then decides not to swim that evening after all. The water is colder than he thought, the sky forbidding; he loses heart. He sat at his desk and, like a penitent in the confessional, pored over the journal his love for the gardener had impelled him to begin. The brief paragraphs therein did not even contain the young man's name, but referred to him as X (so appalled was Malone by his own emotions). Malone had been raised by a lady both Irish and Catholic, in a good bourgeois home in which careless table manners were a sin, much less this storm in his heart.

"My only hope," he wrote in his hardbound ledger, resembling the account books of store clerks in the early part of this century, "is with those men circling the fountain. They are my fate and if I wish to have Life, it must be with *them*. What is most remarkable, I have no choice. I who have never been constrained by poverty, disease, accident, am now constrained by this. God's joke. His little joke. To keep us human. To humble the proud. And I have been so proud."

It seemed sentimental to think of it as the cross he must bear in life, but if it wasn't that, what was it? The sound of a late-night show drifted down the hall from the television of the woman who lived next door to him, and its very laughter, cold and eerie and distant, made his heart beat faster;

for he himself was dying. He wrote again: "You are doomed to a life that will repeat itself again and again, as do all lives —for lives are static things, readings of already written papers—but whereas some men are fortunate to repeat a good pattern, others have the opposite luck—and you can surely see by now that your life is doomed to this same humiliation, endlessly repeated.

"Imagine a pleasure in which the moment of satisfaction is simultaneous with the moment of destruction: to kiss is to poison; lifting to your lips this face after which you have ached, dreamed, longed for, the face shatters, every time." And with one final stroke he scrawled across the page: "IF THE EYE OFFENDS THEE, PLUCK IT OUT."

But how was he to? The great fault in his character was slipping after all these years, was giving way as he went about the empty rituals of his life in the succeeding weeks. His life was a sham. He hated the law; its Pharisaical quibbling over the division of property seemed another aspect of death-in-life. He wasn't even good at it. He had achieved everything only through the most dogged hard work. He hadn't one of those minds that dealt with contract disputes and the Byzantine innuendos of the tax code, like one of those mechanical devices that slice up a vegetable in twelve seconds. He was more than ever certain that he had a vague romantic destiny. Little wonder that when he looked at strangers on the street now, his unquiet yearning for rescue went out to them. No one came to his aid—till late one night on a visit to New York City he was working in an office on Wall Street, high in a fluorescent cell, on a promissory note for the Republic of Zaire, when a messenger boy came in with a batch of Telexes from his boss in London. Malone, who felt at that moment like a rat gnawing his leg off to get free of a trap, looked up at him. How could he know that his desires, his loneliness, were written on his face as clear as characters on a printed page? For that was his charm, that his feelings were always in his eyes and face. He could hide nothing. The messenger boy, a young Puerto Rican from the Bronx in maroon pants and tennis sneakers, put the Telexes down on the desk and then let his hand fall on Malone's back. The hand drew a circle on his back, and then strayed around to his chest and stomach; and Malone turned to look at him. They kissed. It was the kiss of life. He felt a wild gladness in his heart. Someone entered the outer office, the boy left, and Malone sat there with an expression on his face such as the Blessed Virgin wears in paintings of the Annunciation.

In summer New York is a tropical city—in all seasons, for that matter—and when Malone left the office late that night the streets were thronged with faces that glistened beneath the streetlights. Every street his taxi passed seemed to hold a terrible promise. He went to the Yale Club and wrote a long letter to his parents explaining his unhappiness with the law, and the next day he resigned from Courdet Brothers in order to "pursue a career in journalism." What he wished to pursue was a career in love. One night he had got lost on the subway and had come up in Sheridan Square, which was filled, that summer evening, with young men staring at each other, talking in boisterous throngs. Malone headed there now to find a room nearby. It was the middle of August. He did not wish to be the man to whom nothing was ever to happen. He vanished meanwhile from his former friends and family as if he had gone to Bali, or died in a traffic accident. He was completely free now to pursue with the same passion for success he had brought to squash matches and the law, the one thing that had eluded him utterly till now: love.

For love, he felt as he watched the Puerto Rican boys unloading soda pop for the Gem Spa on his new corner, love was all in life that mattered; without it, there was no point in having lived at all. And so the last Sunday evening of August 1973 found him sitting on his stoop like a monk who comes finally to the shrine of Santiago de Compostela —devoted not to Christ, in whom he no longer believed, but love.

4

HOW vacant, how ghostly some sections of Manhattan are on summer evenings after dark: those cobblestoned streets on whose bluish stones no neon light reflects—at most an isolated bulb above the door of an abandoned factory, on a corner where four deserted warehouses stare blankly at each other—streets resembling New Orleans more than New York, where the dark sidewalks are covered with rusted metal awnings, like the verandas of the South, all deserted under the white summer moon beside the glassy river. If souls whose future has not been decided truly wait in a vacuum between heaven and hell called limbo, then Malone occupied a similar realm on his arrival in New York. That first summer he was a ghost: Sitting in his room late at night, bathed in clammy sweat, he listened to the odd and poignant sounds in the building around him. A woman coughed in the next apartment; someone raised a rotting window in the dark night, a man screamed at his wife, the toilet flushed, a radio chattered an uninterrupted stream of news. By the time he arrived each evening at 245 Wall Street—where he typed up that day's documents for a patent lawyer he never saw—the financial district was as deserted as the floor of a factory after the whistle has blown, and men were scurrying home to their own erotic dreams. By the time he left, there was no one abroad but homosexuals and thieves, and it was with these he wandered.

He wandered—in a very tentative way—through those dark clots of people who coagulate in empty lots, parked trucks, alleyways, worshiping Priapus under the summer moon. Little wonder that he wandered in these ghostly places late summer nights: He was half-waiting to be born. Having vanished from his former life, having shed his previous self with the suits he had left behind in a basement in Washington, he was a ghost, in fact, waiting to come to life through love. He fell in love with people he did not know how to meet. He began carrying around with him the momentary faces of men seen in restaurants, on streetcorners, in the subways, and fed on their imagined loves as a roach feeds on crumbs. He knew from the looks on faces he surprised by looking up, that he too was being stored in other human hearts. Then he might have fallen victim to the great homosexual disease—the sanctity of the face seen and never spoken to—but fortunately for Malone this hopeless romanticism was not given time to develop further, for he met someone and fell in love.

He was standing on a subway platform on the Upper West Side very late one night, at the dead hour of four A.M., when out of the darkness Malone had been watching for the lights of the train, emerged four men, like miners coming out of a shaft. They carried lanterns and coiled wire and brooms, and wore bright orange vests, and one of them caused Malone's heart to lurch; for he looked at Malone with eyes so still, and calm, and grave, it was as if a medieval age lived in them, as he came out of the darkness with his lantern. He looked at Malone once, and Malone looked at him, and then he climbed up onto the platform with the other men—and a moment later, with a low rumble, and the toot of a horn, the train roared into the station. Malone got on, feeling he was in some way avoiding the purpose of his life; with the calm despair of someone who goes to his death, he stepped onto the train and composed himself and stared at an advertisement for lamb chops, and the subway started, and took him hurtling away from the central core of his whole life, the reason he had come to New York.

But what does anyone do in those circumstances, but get on the train? The door slides shut, and you go dashing off away from what in the very interior of your heart means most to you.

He carried this face like a banner in his heart for weeks, and then he saw him again on the sidewalk outside the Bank of Leumi in Union Square and he smiled with relief at this evidence of another existence; for now he would not have to haunt the tunnels of the subway late at night in search of him. The man got in a taxi and drove off before Malone could reach him. A month went by but Malone felt he was above ground now, in the streets, and left it up to God if they should meet again; and with this fatalism, and calm, and pure devotion, he was not at all prepared to walk into the VD Clinic on Ninth Avenue one afternoon for a blood test and find him sitting there in the waiting room, sullenly reading a magazine. He looked up at Malone from his reading. The same timeless pause occurred, as if the world had suddenly stopped its hysterical motion; and Malone stood there for a moment in the middle of the floor, not knowing what to do. To meet their venereal selves in this place! The nurse called, "Mr. Oliveiri," and the man got up and went into the office and Malone sat down, heart pounding, and thought: At least I know his name.

At his own interview with the doctor, in which those physical riots of his soul were so clinically discussed, usually to Malone's amusement, he could only sit on the edge of his chair thinking that all his fornication till now was a blind thrashing about, that he must be healthy this time, for love itself was at that moment in the waiting room. Malone rushed outside to see him on the curbstone, waiting for him. "Hello," he said. "Hello," said Malone. He had wondered what he would say and now as they talked he realized it didn't matter: Anything would serve. They moved into an abandoned building in lower Manhattan. Summer was just beginning, and they were as alone in that part of town as if they had been living in a meadow in Vermont. The rotting factories, cobblestoned alleys, grass growing between the stones, the lots strewn with broken glass and abandoned, rusting fenders had a rural stillness and peace to them under the incandescent clouds floating overhead. Frankie left a wife and child for Malone. He had been living with them in Bayonne, where he had grown up and married. He disliked the city but he moved there to live with Malone. He had the qualities that Malone had learned to notice in boys from New Jersey, who were, somehow, kinder than those who had come to Manhattan to pursue careers. He had a daytime job now, having been promoted in the transit department out of the nighttime crew. Frankie had never gon-to a bar, had never wanted to, had heard of Fire Island but considered it "a bunch of queens" and lived a life that, save for the fact that he slept with Malone, was hardly homosexual.

The place they found was within view of Frankie's former home on the waterfront in New Jersey, across the flat, silver river on those blistering summer afternoons: They lived above the empty West Side Highway, and were utterly alone.

They had a whole floor, which, years ago, had been filled with women in bustles nervously spinning thread for knickers; now Malone and Frankie perched like arboreal creatures high up in the ruins of this city of steel and engineers, naked in the heat, pale forms in a shaft of sunlight swimming with motes of dust between two girders across the dusty floor. High above the deserted streets of that no-man's-land between the financial district and the neighborhoods that eventually become the Village, they lay on a mattress devouring one another till they stopped, merely to wait for the long bout of lovemaking that night.

At the beginning Malone could not even allow Frankie to sit down opposite him without getting up and going over to embrace him. He could not see him standing at the tall window looking out over the harbor without enfolding him from behind in his arms. He could not let him piss without doing this. He sat waiting for him downstairs on the steps at the end of the day, eating an apple or a peach and letting the juice run down his chin and turn to a sticky coating in the breeze. He wore tennis sneakers and blue jeans, and a cross around his neck, like Frankie, a crucifix Frankie had given him on his birthday; and, like all homosexual lovers, they began to look like each other—except for that unmistakable difference, when they lay tangled in each other's limbs by day or night, the pale, golden form, and the swarthy, dark-eyed, one, the northern and southern race joined at last. Each had his right ear pierced and wore a small gold ring in it. They looked like pirates. And Malone, who marveled at the beauty of Frankie's body (which had been given to him like the beauty of his eyes), began to visit a small gymnasium in the afternoon, to make his body as beautiful as his lover's; and there, under the tutelage of an old Sicilian man, who prescribed for him a diet of avocados and ice cream, Malone ignored what he knew already, that his body was beautiful in a natural way. He wished to do something for his lover and so he worked at making it more muscular, till eventually he became exceptional—one of the famous bodies of homosexual New York—sitting on the stoop in that deserted region of Manhattan, still unknown to that world which valued bodies such as his. Malone lived only for Frankie now. He bought soaps he remembered from his childhood, scented soaps manufactured in New Delhi, and soaped his lover's body and smelled his sweet-smelling skin as they lay together afterward; in the morning, when it was still dark, and cool, Malone got up to bathe and then got back in bed so that Frankie would awaken to a fresh, clean lover and they could kiss in the coolness that comes, if at all, before dawn on a summer day. And eventually Malone's happiness was so full he no longer needed to touch Frankie in that same mad, compulsive way, but only to look at him: shaving, stirring soup, standing at the window, lighting a cigarette . . .

And Frankie adored Malone: bought him the crucifix on his birthday, kissed him on the eyelids and neck and held him long hours in their window above the harbor, watching ships sail out to sea; promised him they would go to Rio de Janeiro; and when he said one evening, after they had ruined another lasagne, "When we're fifty, we'll probably be good cooks," Malone was deeply touched; for with those words he had said, "I'll love you till I die." He had assumed they would always be together, and Malone could see them years and years from now, old men, for he still loved Frankie and could not imagine feeling differently. He felt a perfect peace as he lay there on Sunday afternoon in the shadows, his face laid on the cool, smooth depression of Frankie's stomach. "I used to hate Sunday evenings," he murmured as dusk started to descend slowly from the sky and the air of the harbor turned blue. "Do Sundays seem —peculiar to you?" he asked. Frankie shrugged and raised his cigarette to his lips and said in that dark, slow voice: "I hate them 'cause I have to go to work the next day." And Malone smiled, and he said no more, realizing he could hardly expect Frankie to feel exactly as he did about the dove-blue holiness of Sunday evenings. "You think too much," Frankie said to Malone, as he caressed the hairs that clustered behind his ear. "I don't think, I just do . . ." and he bent his face to Malone's and began that thorough investigation of each other's mouth, through which, Malone thought as they kissed, souls actually are sucked out of the body . . .

There was something extraordinarily soft about Frankie's skin; Malone could not understand it, but only ran his hands over his stomach, his limbs, as if trying to discern what material it was made of, like a buyer in Hong Kong feeling silks. The touch of Frankie's body against his own was so soft, so delicate, when their legs were intertwined after making love and Frankie was drifting off to sleep, that Malone would find himself farther than ever from sleep, and he would raise his head in the dark silence and wish to say to someone: "You be witness. I am perfectly happy. This boy is a miracle. That he loves me is a second miracle." And he would listen in the darkness for a clock, a sound, as if the whole world had vanished and only he and Frankie, by reason of their perfect happiness, still existed. When he lay back again and Frankie's dark, soft hair rested against his shoulder, and the wind, coming across the harbor, be- gan to rattle the window gently, he felt as if they were on some high promontory above the world, as solitary as shepherds on a crag in a canvas of Brueghel—all alone in the blue, windy, gentle world. Malone would lie awake all night in wonderment and peace, like a shepherd who keeps watch over his flock, only this vigil was not dull, this vigil was a joy. When later it began to rain, in great sparkling clouds that drifted down into the empty street below past the orange streetlights, Malone had to extract himself from Frankie's embrace to get up, cross the floor, and close a window. He found when he returned that Frankie had awakened. When he climbed into bed beneath the covers and felt the warmth of Frankie's body, the warmth of his legs and stomach and arms that enfolded him immediately, as if Frankie were one of those plants that attaches itself to stone or wrought iron with tiny pale green tendrils, curling and locking so the vine may follow, Malone felt his happiness choke him. He felt he had been embraced, taken in beneath these warm covers, not by Frankie, but by the world itself, by God, and he lay there, listening to Frankie's heart beat against his ear, afraid to breathe he was so happy; till Frankie kissed him, and he looked up and saw, in the faint light of the streetlight, the tenderness and gratitude that had flooded Frankie's eyes, and made them glisten and sparkle like the rain outside, as he looked down at Malone with the faint smile of a man who awakens in the depths of the night to find not only is he safe, but loved. Frankie merely smiled at him, but for that look, those eyes, Malone would have given the world.

And embracing Frankie those hot afternoons, Malone returned to the core of his existence: the hot afternoons beneath the rustling date palms on a green patio, his mother's perfume, the odor of his father's crisp white shirts and the air conditioning that clung to them, the lapis lazuli lagoons, schooners, palm tree fronds glistening in the light as if water streamed down their tips, the hot blast of a factory whistle at one o'clock, naps in the afternoon, the black women in scarves praying the rosary at church; and the false years of dutiful behavior fell away and Malone felt as peaceful as he had sitting by the washtubs with Irene as she sang songs and straightened her hair with a hot iron. Love was the key: The popular songs he heard on the radio, Malone realized now, were in the end perfectly accurate. Each time he ran his lips across the concave depression of Frankie's stomach, he banished further the nights of loneliness, the widow's cold cream, the sterile years of his wasted youth, and he burrowed deeper at the thought of it into Frankie's flesh. He looked up at those moments to find Frankie gazing down at him with an expression of mild curiosity, and wonderment, at Malone's passion.

Frankie wondered about Malone's past: Frankie had left, after all, his wife and child for him. But it made Malone curiously impatient when he detected in Frankie an eagerness to hear about the schools he had attended and the places he had lived, for that aspect of himself he had decided was worthless. Frankie read the papers, asking Malone to pronounce for him the words he had never come across before, and tell him what they meant. Malone no longer read the papers. They meant nothing to him. He was in love. Newspapers only summoned up to him the forlorn Sundays of his past; in the same way Frankie hated tuna fish because he had eaten it so much when he was poor. Frankie was no longer poor, but he still wanted to make more money; he read the want ads, and wrote down the addresses of schools he heard advertised on the radio. He came home with ideas and schemes. "Maybe I should be an electrician," he said, "we could move to Jersey and have a house. Just you and me and all those honkies." He wanted to have a skill, he believed in the unions, he planned for a while to go into the television repair business. He was good with his hands. He was never sick a day at work, even while he discussed his future with Malone, but he wanted to be his own boss. "You need a skill," he said. He blew out a stream of smoke and added: "Even the chicks in the massage parlors have been trained." He said, "Even the hookers." And Malone thought what a fascinating life that would be: the life of a prostitute. For something had happened in him—having renounced the world of work, duty, caution, and practicality, he now wished to live the life of a bohemian. Whores fascinated him, people who lived solely for love, artists, neurotics, and with these the city was filled . . .

"But you've been to school, man," he would say to Malone, holding his head in both his hands, cupping it beneath the ears so that Malone felt as if his skull could be crushed between Frankie's huge hands like a grapefruit; and Malone thought how miraculous the hands and arms of a lover are. "The world is too much with us," he said, and shut Frankie up with a kiss. But Frankie would not be silent; it obsessed him that Malone was better educated than he. Frankie was proud of his Italian past and did not like being taken for a Puerto Rican. He wanted his son to be a doctor, perhaps, he told Malone shyly. For himself? He wanted to improve his lot; he wanted to learn a skill, fix TV's, and move to New Jersey with Malone to a house in the pine barrens. He was a true American. Malone let these words pass, like a summer rain he knew would end.

The two of them were as alone with one another in that building as two apes in a tree. Nothing intruded in this neighborhood, which hadn't even a name, and seemed to be filled with more parked trucks than human beings, this region of grassy lots, huge, faceless warehouses, and the hulks of switching stations of New York Telephone. They lived in an institutional graveyard. They would have gone on living this placid, rural existence had Malone not gone over to Grand Street to buy watermelon one blistering afternoon—and found there a young man as beautiful, as strangely moving, as Frankie. They hardly said a word to one another before making love in his apartment above a hardware store. It was as if he had fallen from a tree, in fact, for going home to that game preserve in which he lived with Frankie high above the ghostly cables of the telephone company, he encountered more dark-eyed stray young men wandering south from the purlieus of homosexuals. He made love with them in the ensuing afternoons. He did not know what would happen, but he knew he would have to lie. What he was not prepared for was the subtle current of knowledge that passed from his own limbs into Frankie's one evening while making love—no more than a brief pause, the mere skip of a heartbeat, a momentary detachment that Frankie felt instantly, and as Malone lay back with a sigh, caused him to look at Malone with his gorgeous, prepossessing eyes and say in a calm voice: "If you leave me, I will kill you."

It was as if the electricity had failed in the entire city, as if suddenly the current had been shut off, and a tremendous stillness suddenly settled down over the echoing avenues beneath them. Malone shuddered. The words were so out-of-the-blue, and spoken in so grave and quiet a voice, that he believed them; even as he watched a fly above them land on the No-Pest strip that dangled from the ceiling, buzz frantically, and then be still . . .

The disembodied hiss of a passing car rose up with the vanishing heat; and later when a cool breeze came through the window, as the refrigerator hummed, they made love again. Making love to Frankie had always been like making love to someone underwater. They were like two swimmers kissing beneath the sea, in slow motion; but this very stillness, this very gravity that Malone had found so wondrous —that medieval calm that his eyes had given Malone the first moment he saw them—now seemed to him not so much medieval calm as a lethargy of spirit. Was Frankie a trap? As viscous as the sticky glue on the No-Pest strip that hung above them like the streamer of a Chinese lantern? He wondered as he lay entangled in his limbs, making love and thinking of a dozen distracting things—the other rooms he had made love in, the death of God, his father's white shirts —how curious it was that he lay there confined in this high tower in the ruins of the city on a summer evening. Through the window, from the lazy perch of his mattress, he saw the snow-white, lighted hull of the S.S. *Canberra* sailing slowly through the harbor to the open sea, and above them another fly buzzed frantically in the glue of the No-Pest strip and then was still. Malone lay beside Frankie in a state of white, cool, dumb confusion; he was not sure himself what had happened, and he resolved the issue by staring finally at the sky, the blue, empty sky through the tall window, and letting his soul float out into the limitless space there.

"Oh man, oh man," Frankie would say when he came home from work that week, stripping off his tie and lighting a joint. He kissed Malone and he tried, not understanding why an estrangement had occurred, to bring things back to what they were. Malone was touched by this. He asked Frankie how his day was, but they had little, in fact, to talk about. Before it had never mattered, now the silences ached. Frankie liked to watch TV, Malone could not bear it. And now Malone had to look at him in the middle of the long, dull evenings in which the comedies of the television set spilled out into the air, and Malone asked himself why he was there, with someone who watched TV and got stoned each evening and hated his boss and had a temper; but then Frankie, turning from the refrigerator with a glass of wine, would look at Malone with those cloudy eyes, and Malone would remember . . .

One Sunday afternoon—aware that Malone could no longer bear what had been his favorite day in their sunny perch above the harbor—Frankie bent down and kissed Malone and then, lying beside him as he held his hand, asked if he would come to New Jersey that day and take Frankie's son for a walk. Malone felt something churn within himself. But he went, and hand in hand with Enrico between them, they went to gaudy amusement parks and sat in ice-cream parlors under the blistering sun, and Malone felt sadder and sadder.

It was the habit of recording his thoughts, his days, in his journal that ended Malone's affair. He came home from work one night and found Frankie standing silent in the middle of the floor. The television was dead. Malone looked at Frankie's face and knew instantly what had happened. His journal lay open on the mattress. "What's wrong?" gasped Malone. "So where were you on Monday afternoon?" Frankie said in the furious, hard voice of an interrogator. "And where were you Wednesday afternoon when I called? And who is George Dillow and Stanley Cohen? You fucking bastard!" he said, and slapped Malone on his cheek and pushed him back against the wall. And Malone thought to himself, with the cool detachment of a man who has just been hurled from a car wreck and sits on the hillside wondering why he isn't in his bed at home: Ah, this is how it happens. They beat you up, they are jealous. Love-nest slaying . . . For he had always wondered what would happen if Frankie ever turned on him the temper he had shown the day a grocer refused to cash his check, or the afternoon he learned on the telephone that a friend in New Jersey had turned other friends in to a narcotics agent. "Man, he is dead," Frankie had said. "He is going to find himself in the river by tomorrow," and Malone had listened, in disbelief. But here was Frankie now, slapping him again and again on the face, shoving him against the wall and kicking him and punching his ribs. He beat Malone up and Malone, realizing an explanation was impossible, and so heartsick he could not, would not strike back, ran. He ran downstairs into the warm, empty streets, and kept running as best he could with a cracked rib till he stopped in a dark alley near Bond Street and sat down and coughed, and wept, and waited till he had stopped shaking. Then he got up and continued walking north, until he came to a crowded part of the Village, with movie houses, stores still open, and restaurants filled with smiling people behind plants and plate glass windows. He sat down on a stoop. He had no place to go, and he ached in several places. He sat there oblivious to the throngs walking past him on West Tenth Street.

And then someone caught his eye: a wigged duchess emerging from the back door of a warehouse in which the Magic, Fantasy, and Dreams Ball was just breaking up. "Help me," said Malone. "My dear," said Sutherland after taking one look at his terrified face, "the house of Guiche shall never refuse the protection of its manor to the poorest of its subjects," and he assisted Malone into a cab pulled up at the curb. They rode in silence for some time as Malone panted beside Sutherland, his legs vibrating like windshield wipers. Neither spoke. Sutherland offered Malone a cigarette, Malone shook his head, and Sutherland smoked in silence, glancing at Malone from time to time in the light of passing streets as they floated north. Time had passed since he had stood outside the bookstore in Georgetown, peering in at volumes on the French cathedrals, and Malone no longer looked as if he were a young man peering into a bookstore in Georgetown on a summer night; he looked more like the fellow who had just run in off the playing fields in New Hampshire, his eyes brilliant—a rather exhausted soccer player now, his face scratched from the fray—the earring hidden behind a cluster of golden curls. Malone would always have that ambiguous look, half-fine, half-rough, and it so intrigued Sutherland that when the taxi slowed at his block of Madison Avenue, he turned to Malone and said: "Forgive me for inquiring, but—are you for rent?"

And Malone, as polite as this stranger who sat smoking a Gauloise beside him under a white wig of the seventeenth century, in brocade and rhinestones, smiled weakly and said: "Thank you, no." For he was so softhearted he hated refusing anyone. Rejecting another person upset him far more than being refused himself—and he was one of the few homosexuals in New York who went home with people because he did not wish to hurt their feelings. "I'm recovering from a lovers' brawl," he added. "Unlucky in love."

"Then come to the Carlyle," said Sutherland, extending his arm, "and let's have a drink. I always go to the Carlyle to rub an ice cube, bathed in Pernod, on my bruises. And then go dancing at the Twelfth Floor."

After the Carlyle they went to Sutherland's room above a little gallery on upper Madison Avenue, since one could not arrive at the Twelfth Floor before two A.M. and it was just past one. Sutherland pushed off his bed the manuscript on the history of religion that he had been writing the past five years, and lay Malone down, to wash his bruises— and it was this, years later, he never forgot, as Christ's definition of charity is the simplest and truest: You took me in when I was wounded. He made Malone tell his story again, as he washed his face with Germaine Monteil astringents, gasping at different parts and saying, his eyes very bright, "*Ah!*" For Sutherland, like the emperor with Scheherazade, could listen for hours to love stories. He knew perfectly well what Malone had run from. "Of course he beat you up," said Sutherland, dabbing with a cotton swab at Malone's lavender temple. "Latins are the last egocentrics on earth! Enslaved as you are to dark beauties, I see only dolors ahead for you—heartbreak *dead* ahead," he said. "Couldn't you, wouldn't you, love someone like me instead?"

But this very question was rhetorical, an invitation that Sutherland himself no longer believed in. He looked at Malone even now and said: "God! There are so many people I'm going to have to introduce you to!"

And then, as if preserving in wrapping paper a fine piece of bric-a-brac he had found on the street, he covered Malone in a blanket and said, "Of course he beat you. Let it be a lesson. This ethnic gene pool in which we sit, like children in their own shit."

He poured Malone a glass of Perrier, "The mineral water of aware French women everywhere," he mumbled.

"God knows I looked for it," he resumed when he had sipped his own glass, sighed, and handed Malone a Cuban cigar. "Uptown, downtown. I used to even go out to the boroughs on Saturday nights because there were so many dark-eyed beauties out there. For a while I was commuting to Philadelphia. To Rhode Island. But let's be honest. As divine as they are in bed, a guinea hasn't got a heart! They are ruined by their women from the crib, adored, coddled, assumed to be gods. Sad they happen to be so handsome. The real lovers, alas, are Wasps like you and me, even though *we're* supposed to be the ones who are emotionally stunted—well, of course, we are cold as fish in one sense. In another, we are the only true lovers. Let the Italians and the Jews wave their arms about and claim to be passionate, but they understand nothing, but nothing about love! They are show girls, my friend, and don't forget it! It takes a northern European to really suffer the pangs of heartache." And here he blew out a stream of smoke and stared at Malone; for he was looking at himself ten, even fifteen years before, as he saw Malone sitting there with his bruised ribs and blotchy face in the lamplight on that late-summer evening in Sutherland's room on Madison Avenue. He was Sutherland those many years ago, his visage still capable of registering that romantic hopefulness with which so many came to this city; and Sutherland took pleasure in the spectacle. "My God," he murmured again, in a low voice, "there are so many people I have to introduce you to." Malone sat there amused and fascinated by this strange wisdom pouring from this man and conscious that he had no other place to go. It was half-past midnight and he knew no one in the city but the lover he had just fled.

"We live, after all, in perilous times," Sutherland went on, lighting another cigar, "of complete philosophic sterility, we live in a rude and dangerous time in which there are no values to speak to and one can cling to only concrete things—such as cock," he sighed, tapping his ashes into a bowl of faded marigolds. He stood up and walked over to a closet and opened the door to reveal, like the Count of Monte Cristo his fabulous treasure, the accumulated wardrobe of fifteen seasons on the circuit. They stared silently for a moment at the stacks of jungle fatigues, and plain fatigues, bleached fatigues and painter's jeans, jeans with zippers and jeans with buttons, tank tops and undershirts, web belts, plaid shirts, and dozens of T-shirts in every color; nylon bomber jackets hanging beside leather bomber jackets, brown and black; and, on the floor in rows, work boots, engineer boots, cowboy boots, work shoes, hiking shoes, baseball caps, coal miner's caps, and, in one wicker basket, coiled like snakes, the transparent plastic belts that Sutherland found one day in a store on Canal Street and that he had introduced to gay New York, which meant, eventually, the nation, several seasons ago. Whistles, tambourines, knit caps, aviator glasses, aluminum inhalers, double-tipped dark glasses in both Orphan Annie and aviator styles, and huge mother-of-pearl fans occupied another basket that testified to the various accouterments Sutherland had considered necessary when he went dancing in winters past.

"But after a while you realize," sighed Sutherland, in a dejected mood because he had been rejected that evening at the party by someone he had been waiting to talk to for two years, "that there is nothing but these," he said, picking up a pale orange-and-red plaid shirt from Bloomingdale's and letting it dangle onto a pile of pastel-colored T-shirts from an army-navy surplus store on Canal Street and the basket filled with transparent plastic belts. He put a baseball cap on and left the closet. "Is there anything here you'd like to put on?" he asked. "You must get out of those tennis sneakers."

He tossed Malone a pair of Herman Chemi-Gums from Hudson's on Thirteenth Street. "They're far more sturdy. So what remains for us?" he said, as he sat down beside

Malone and lifted his glass of Pernod to his lips. "What, we may well ask, is there left to live for? Why get out of bed? For this dreary round of amusing insincerity? This filthy bourgeois society that the Aristotelians have foisted upon us? No, we may still choose to live like gods, like poets. Which brings us down to dancing. Yes," he said, turning to Malone, "that is all that's left when love has gone. Dancing," he said, indicating with a wave of his hand the stacks of tapes and records in another corner of the room. "There is no love in this city," he said, looking down at Malone with a cool expression, "only discotheques—and they too are going fast, under the relentless pressure of capitalist exploitation . . ." He looked at Malone a moment more and then said quietly: "And what more appropriate way to begin your education than to take you to the Twelfth Floor?"

Malone slept instead that evening, and slept a lot more those first weeks of autumn—for when we have nothing in our lives, we simply stay in bed—and he would hear, vaguely, through his sleep, or see, through half-opened eyes, the tangle of eyelashes, strange figures slipping in and out of the room, doing their best to keep the silence: It was Sutherland (and friends he brought by to simply look at Malone, sleeping like a Norman prince on a stone tomb) in huge constructions of papier-mâché—monstrous heads, birds of paradise, courtiers of France and Padua, figures from Fellini films—going to the costume parties of that season. Malone missed, that year, the Fellini Ball in the Rainbow Room, the Leo Party at the Armory, the Illusions and Nightmares affair in the Automat on Forty-second Street, while he lay in bed, hearing, as at the bottom of the sea, the distant, reverberating echo of taxicabs honking

in the street—a sound that came up to him from the depths
as a memory of childhood, when he had come through
New York on his vacations from school. Sutherland had
fallen in love with the city in the same way—if New York
was to Malone that distant quaver of a taxi horn, deep in
the chasms of mid-Manhattan, it was to Sutherland the
curious taste of an egg-salad sandwich sold in hotel coffee
shops, where he'd sat wide-eyed and wondering as he waited
for the bellhops to bring down his mother's luggage before
they got a taxi for Pier Forty-seven, where a stateroom on
the S.S. *Rotterdam* waited to take them to Europe. He had
fallen in love with New York City passing through it as a
child, and the distinct smell of its damp, vivid air, the sea
gulls circling the masts of his ship as it pushed up the
Hudson River to its berth. He had fallen in love with the
city then, and even though it was now a different city, this
residue of affection remained, overlaid by the loves of his
adolescence and manhood. At five o'clock now, the hour
at which he had wandered down into the streets with his
mother to visit a museum, a department store, a restaurant,
and the theater, he awoke from the party of the previous
night, doused his face, and rushed downstairs to meet the
handsome men coming home from work, and have, if not
sex, at least cocktails.

Sometimes Malone would awaken and find Sutherland
in the uniform of Clara Barton, washing his face with a
bottle of Ernst Lazslo and saying: "You must get well,
dear, there are so many people who can't *wait* to talk to
you! I've had to turn down so many invitations, from the
Vicomtesse de Ribes, Babe Paley, that dance maven on
Second Avenue with the Art Deco bathroom, you know,"
he said, putting the cotton swab drenched in cleanser to
his neck before returning it to Malone's forehead. He awoke

at other hours to find Sutherland trying to perfect his quiche, or sitting in a pinstripe suit beside a lamp reading aloud Ortega y Gasset on love.

Malone lay on the sofa like a convalescent, listening to the words as he watched the lamp's shadows on the ceiling. As for Sutherland, he could not have been happier having a new charge both handsome and willing to listen. It was always a joy to sponsor a new face in the crowd he ran with—among the most bored and frenetic on earth—and it was moving to see someone as charmingly lost as Malone.

Still there were enormous differences between them and as Malone watched Sutherland move through his mottled days he found much that appalled. Why then did he stay? Years later he would wonder why he remained with Sutherland that evening, and the next seven years. He never knew. As he listened to Sutherland's tales, as he spent the afternoons reading the volumes of Santayana, Plato, and Ortega y Gasset with which Sutherland left him alone, he began to think that the city is the greatest university of all, the real one, and all his education until now had been a mime. He who had spent hours poring over the history of the Supreme Court, the rise of the Protestant Ethic, the religious credo of Herman Melville, lay there now through the first crisp days of autumn as immobile on his sofa as a man recovering from some radical operation. And then one day he got up and went downtown in the early afternoon, when he knew Frankie was at work, to get his things; and he walked into their old factory building to find their home stripped bare . . . only a small pile of jeans huddled in one corner, and his journal, open still to the very page on which Frankie had read of his adulteries, on the mattress. Malone went to the window and looked down on the sparkling blue harbor and remembered how they had stood there in the hot breezes of July, embracing; he looked at the refrigerator, where Frankie seemed to be always standing with a tray of ice cubes; at the mattress, now dusty in a shaft of sunlight—and he suddenly bolted from the room. It was all over: dead. He had no idea where Frankie had gone.

But what was worse, he was everywhere: Going back uptown to Sutherland's room, Malone saw, in the subway, on the streets, half a dozen boys whose grave expressions and dark eyes invited him to turn back, his heart racing. This was his first taste of despair. He got to Sutherland's and closed the door behind him like a man fleeing the police.

And so Malone was grateful to remain behind, shut away from the city, on the most splendid afternoons of autumn when Sutherland would spend the day in the men's rooms of subways, or the rush hour at Grand Central Station, catching the explosive desires of insurance brokers trapped between a day at the office and an evening at home with the wife. Malone read and sighed and reflected, but he seldom spent the day alone; for people were constantly running up the stairs to Sutherland's room.

"How do you live?" Malone asked Sutherland one day, and he replied: "Hand to mouth." The usual exigencies didn't seem to apply in his case; people sent him plane tickets, and the latter half of October Sutherland spent in Cartagena playing bridge. Malone lay there and watched a whole race of handsome men come through the apartment, men he had never seen before. They were the faces that helped sell cereal and gin to the masses, and they came by at all hours of the day and night until finally Sutherland, on his return from Colombia, established "office hours" and sat at his desk in a big black picture hat, with painted nails and a gardenia on the lapel of his Chanel suit, ringing up sales on an office calculator. "Ignore them, darling," he breathed to Malone. "They are simply people who will take anything in pill form. Does the sight of a syringe bother you?" he asked in a solicitous voice. "If so, we can go downstairs . . ."

It was a rainstorm rather that drove Malone downstairs; a storm that drifted down from Boston and stayed for two days in late October made Malone put on a pair of tennis sneakers, take an umbrella, and flee the apartment. Lovers were everywhere: waiting for each other outside grocery stores with lost, annoyed expressions till the mate emerged with a sack of groceries, and hand in hand, they walked off together to cook dinner. Bearded students and their girl friends standing in the subway close together mesmerized Malone, staring at the man's white, veined hand resting lightly on the girl's neck. He tramped around the streets for hours and ended up lost in the Chambers Street station at three in the morning, all alone in the damp, chill, fluorescent light, thinking as he waited for the uptown train that he had first seen Frankie walking down one of these tracks with a lantern in his hand at about this hour one night long ago. Later he found himself walking home on Madison Avenue, having massacred, walked to death, the night whose gentle rain undid him. He saw a man he'd seen earlier lurch into a doorway for protection from the storm walking unsteadily toward him now. The man suddenly stopped on the sidewalk, in the slanting clouds of rain, looked at Malone, his face etched in the garish glow of the streetlight, and said: "Take me home with you. Please." Malone said nothing and walked on, just as he had learned to walk by lunatics giving speeches and beggars asking for money, horrified.

He went home to Ohio at Thanksgiving on the train along the Susquehanna, in the early darkness filled with snowflakes at bends in the dark woods. He took the slowest way home, like a diver who must allow himself time coming up from the depths in order to avoid poisoning. He was so sad he felt ill. He sat beside an anxious college student whose problems were maintaining an academic average good enough to secure him a place in medical school; Malone listened to him talk about his fears with a certain relief. He watched this fellow being greeted by his parents on the train platform, and felt suddenly that he could not face his own family. But when he arrived at his sister's house, the slamming of car doors, the screams of nephews and nieces flocking around him in the thickening snow flurry with the new puppies the family had acquired, the terror he had felt evaporated. "When are you going to get married?" chirped his youngest niece as she leaned against him at the Thanksgiving table. "Why don't you have a car?" These were the two things in her five-year-old mind that constituted—and was she wrong?—adulthood in America. He made some excuse as his parents, who had returned to Ohio that fall, hung on every word; even though they, out of that austere respect for one another's privacy peculiar to his family, had never asked the question themselves. They thought he was writing a book on jurisprudence. Later in the evening, dozing beneath a coverlet of newspapers in the den, the fire crackling beside him, the house filled with the faraway shouts of children playing in rooms upstairs, of adults playing cards in the dining room, he looked up once at the dog—and the dog looked up, inquiring, at him. "I'm gay," he whispered to the dog. The snow was falling lightly through the delicate branches of the fir trees pressed against the windowpanes, and he thought of it falling on all the shopping centers in the hills around that town, filled with families just like this one, and he heard the hiss of station wagons passing on the road outside, filled with children in Eskimo hoods, dozing in each other's laps. He smiled at the quirk of fate that kept him from it all like a prisoner being escorted down the corridor of a hospital in handcuffs, past the other patients, and then he fell asleep. When he awoke, much later in the night, the fire embers, the house suddenly chill and silent, his lips were damp with spittle and he thought, I was dreaming of Frankie, and he had, for an instant, a desire to rush down to the airport on some pretext and fly back to New York because he could not bear to be without what now seemed the source of his being: those dark-eyed, grave young men passing in the light of liquor stores on dingy streets, their eyes wide and beautiful, in the early winter darkness of that hard, unreal city.

When he did return to New York a week later laden with good wishes and fudge, he found Sutherland standing in the middle of the room with a mudpack on his face, round earrings, and a red dress pulled down to his waist—all that remained of the costume in which he had gone to a dinner dance as La Lupe—and the twenty-five-foot telephone cord wrapped around his body. He squirmed, like Laocoon trapped by snakes, and made an anguished face at Malone. "I simply must get off," he said into the phone, "the bank beneath us is on fire and we're being evacuated." He hung the telephone up and said, as he shook Malone's hand gravely: "My sister, in Boston. Our brother just cut off three toes in the lawn mower, after defaulting on a bank loan, our other sister has hepatitis and will have to finish school in Richmond, Mother is drinking, Father refuses to see anyone, and the woman across the street went into her garage yesterday and turned on the automobile and asphyxiated herself. What is wrong with this country, for God's sake?" he said, pulling off the red clip earrings. "Americans, for my money, are just too damned sophisticated!" He waved his arms in the air. "But, darling, how was the Heartland? So good to go home," he said. "So good to be with the family after a divorce. Who else will comfort?" But when he handed Malone a glass of Pernod, he saw his melancholy face and said: "I told you, dear, you shouldn't go."

They sat down and Sutherland began removing his facial with a warm washcloth, and Malone, feeling more depressed than ever, could not refrain from asking: "Do you sometimes not loathe being—gay?"

"My dear, you play the hand you're dealt," said Sutherland as he examined his face in the mirror. "Which reminds me, I'm due for bridge at Helen Auchincloss'."

"What do you mean?" said Malone anxiously.

"I mean," said Sutherland, who turned frosty at the slightest sign of complaint, self-pity, or sentimentality on this or any subject (for beneath his frivolity, he was hard as English pewter), "that if Helen Keller could get through life, we certainly can."

"Oh," said Malone weakly, leaning back in his chair.

"You, however, may be a homosexual *manqué*," said Sutherland, turning back to the mirror. "Oh God," he said, "I'm late again."

"Where are you going?" said Malone sadly.

"I'm supposed to be at the opening of Teddy Ransome's gallery on Seventy-eighth Street, I'm supposed to be playing bridge with Helen Auchincloss, I'm supposed to be reading to the blind, and going out to East Hampton at eight, but you see I'm stuck right here," he said, sitting down with a sigh and the bright eyes of a koala bear, "because the exterminator is coming."

"The exterminator?" said Malone.

"Yes," he said. "He exterminates the roaches with his insecticide, then exterminates *me* by tugging at his crotch to adjust his scrotum. He is the most *divine* Puerto Rican you've ever seen. The most beautiful Puerto Rican in New York—and God assigned him to *this* building," he said, spilling some wine on the rug as a libation. "Now that's an accolade!" he said, picking up the phone to dial his regrets to four different people and cancel his dates because of the imminent arrival of this exotic visitor. "Don't you love these winter nights," he said, turning to Malone as he dialed a number, "and the possibility of so much dick?"

All winter long Malone declined the many invitations to parties and dinners that Sutherland gave him; till one crisp February night he met Sutherland in the Oak Room, where Sutherland often went after an hour or two in the men's room at Grand Central, and had drinks while he read the notes he and strange men had passed to one another from stall to stall on segments of toilet paper. "The trouble with this one was," said Sutherland in a cloud of cigarette smoke as he raised his martini to sip, "his shoes. Cheap shoes, you see. American men will not spend money on their footwear, whereas in Europe it is crucial. I found his notes quite dreamy," he said, expelling another stream of smoke, "but the shoes were out of the question. Don't look now," he murmured, lowering his eyes demurely, "but the most handsome man in Brookfield, Connecticut, has just walked in the room. He's married now and has two kids, but we were once very much in love. Like a young Scott Fitzgerald, don't you think? Almost a Gibson boy, no, don't look yet, I'll tell you when," he said to Malone, who could feel someone sitting down behind him. "I must only add as a brief footnote that besides the hyacinth hair, the classic teeth, he sports one of the greatest schlongs in the Northeast Corridor. Try catching him on the shuttle to Washington sometime," he said, and finished off his drink. "We were deeply in love."

When they finally left, the twilight was filled with men hurrying on errands, handsome, dark-eyed messenger boys disappearing into the vaulted, steel-gray lobbies of tall office buildings; businessmen hurrying to catch a taxi to the airport; pale proofreaders going on the night shift at law firms on Park Avenue; waiters going to the Brasserie; students returning to the boroughs; and Malone began to feel the promise of the city once again. He did not go off like Sutherland with cashew nuts and dried apricots in his pockets to spend the day in the men's rooms of the BMT and IRT, but he began to meet him more often in the evenings, to linger on the boulevards and watch the throngs of people rushing past: a messenger boy from Twentieth Century Fox, a researcher at Sloan-Kettering, a public relations man hurrying about the business of Pan American Airways. "He lives with his parents in Forest Hills, he subscribes to the *Atlantic Monthly* and *After Dark*, his bedroom is all wicker, he falls in love with boys on the tennis courts," Sutherland would say. "Have you met him?" asked Malone. "No," said Sutherland as they watched the handsome figure disappear into Rizzoli's. "That would be quite superfluous." They strolled on, peering, like cupids, not at the Beatific Vision, but the windows of Bendel's.

And then out of the evening would materialize a pair of eyes that would lock with Malone's eyes with the intensity of two men who have reduced one another to immobility as wrestlers. It happened one evening entering a church on Fifth Avenue to hear a concert—a young man handing out programs, a dealer named Rafael who had come in fact to deliver cocaine to a priest. It was with a heavy heart that Malone whispered to Sutherland as they paused to anoint themselves with holy water after the concert, staring even then at Rafael's dark eyes with the dumb helplessness of an animal poisoned by a scorpion: "Can I call you later at the apartment?"

"The heart is a lonely hunter," sighed Sutherland, who understood perfectly that either one of them could disappear at any moment, alone in the end, to pursue the superior call of love . . .

And Malone would go off to the Upper West Side with Rafael, or Jesus, or Luis, and lie in a room, a prisoner of a pair of eyes, a smooth chest, enveloping limbs. But love was like drinking seawater, Malone discovered. The more he made love the more he desired the replicas of his current lover he inevitably found on every corner. Malone was love-sick, he was feverish, and it glowed in his eyes so that other people only had to look at him to realize instantly he was theirs. Yet each time he looked at someone tenderly, he felt he was seeing a double exposure in which the face behind the one in front of him bore the outlines of Frankie—and the half an inch between his lips and these others was a crevasse he could not cross. Then Malone would walk back across the park with a miserable heart to find Sutherland hanging out his window in an orange wig, frilly peasant blouse, and gas-blue beads, screaming in Italian to the people passing on the street below to come up and suck his twat. The mask of comedy was sometimes difficult to put on; and Malone might linger in the doorway of the Whitney Museum for an hour or so, watching Sutherland finger the avocados in his blouse, throw out his arms, pat his hair, finger his beads, wave coquettishly like a marionette, before he felt himself able finally to cross the street. Sutherland was happy without love. So could he be. He waited till this lady who had just put out her wash, chattering happily as she drank in the life of the street and waited for Mario to come home, spotted him and then he went upstairs, with the melancholy heart of a sailor who is returning from an unsuccessful voyage. "Darling!" Sutherland gasped, at the sight of Malone coming into his room after so long an absence. "Is he playing poker? Did he give you the afternoon off?"

And Sutherland gave him the elaborate parody of a cocktail kiss, which he was fond of: missing, by a foot, at least, both cheeks.

"Entre nous," Malone said, "it's over."

"Ahhhhh," said Sutherland in a melancholy tone, fingering his beads, *"l'amore non fa niente."* He collapsed on the sofa in a cloud of perfumed powder. "There have been so many parties while you were away," he sighed. "There have just been too many to respond to. Does love mean never having to say you're sorry," he said, dabbing his upper chest with a bit of perfume, "or too sore to get fucked again?" He threw more cologne on the inside of his thighs. "I've been sitting home all afternoon hoping to receive the stigmata," he said, closing the autobiography of Saint Theresa, which he had been reading when he began his impersonation of a Neapolitan whore, "but all I got were invitations to brunch this weekend. No more quiches, please! One could die of quiches!"

He looked at Malone, tender and serious for a moment. "It's not like Plato, is it?" he said, taking down a volume of the *Symposium* from his bookshelf. "It's not like Ortega y Gasset, or even Proust, is it?" he said. "Or, for that matter, Stendhal. It's so hopelessly ordinary—I don't even think people have souls anymore. And not having souls, they cannot be expected to have love affairs . . ."

108

He removed the avocados from his blouse and mixed daiquiris for himself and Malone. The telephone rang and Sutherland picked it up and said: "I'm sorry, I have to keep this line open for sex." He hung up, for he was, once again, waiting for a boy he had met in the street the previous night to call. "Oh, God," he sighed to Malone as he regarded his gleaming refrigerator—which contained a kind of emblem of life on the circuit: a leftover salmon mousse and a box of poppers—"the young ones are so cruel. Such oblivious assassins! He was so wonderful, such huge dark eyes, such a long-limbed body, such good sex, and this morning he can't even remember my name." He went to the window and said: "He's out there somewhere, that perfect beauty!" He turned, handed Malone his daiquiri and plate of salmon mousse and said: "The cruelty of people is beyond measure. Well," he sighed, "though it is very soon after the divorce, could we twist your arm to go dancing tonight? After, of course, we take a beauty nap. One can't go out dancing anymore before four. And hope to make an entrance, I mean."

And he sighed and grew drowsy as the light turned blue in the street, and murmuring a request to Malone to pass the vial of Vitamin E to him, Sutherland applied the oil to the area beneath his eyes—with the gentle, upward strokes of the weakest finger of his hand, the fourth—and then fell into a deep sleep. His body began discharging whatever drug he had taken that morning, and refreshed itself for the next endeavor. He would awaken at three and take another drug and begin to dress for the evening at the Twelfth Floor. Malone, who could not sleep, left a note that said he would meet Sutherland there, and went downtown. A sliver of a moon floated in the sky above the West Side Highway. Malone walked down the cobblestoned street to the old factory building where he and

Frankie had lived that summer. He walked up the riverside till he came to that forlorn neighborhood whose awning-covered sidewalks, and meat-packing plants, and air of rural desertion he loved. He saw the dark figures crossing the piazzas far ahead of him; he paused to see the carcasses of pigs, blue-white and bright red, slide on steel wire from the trucks into the refrigerated depths of the butcher's, while at his back homosexual young men trod that Via Dolorosa searching in a dozen bars, a string of parked trucks, abandoned piers, empty lots, for the magician of love. Malone paused beneath the pale, chaste moon and watched the dark figures vanish and appear again; he drew in the silvery air with one hand the Sign of the Cross and then he went dancing.

He danced till seven that morning, and he danced for three winters after that. He was a terrible dancer at first: stiff and unhappy. I used to see him standing on the floor with a detached look of composure on his face while Sutherland danced brilliantly around him. Sutherland danced with a cigarette in one hand, hardly moving at all, as he turned slowly around and surveyed the other dancers for all the world like someone at a cocktail party perusing the other guests. He always danced with a cigarette, with very subtle movements, loose, relaxed, of the shoulders and hips; except when a song came on he loved from the old days—for Sutherland had been dancing long before any of us—such as "Looking for My Baby," and then he would cut away and leave Malone standing self-consciously on the floor while Sutherland cut back and forth across the room in a choreography only a natural dancer can improvise. Then he would calm down again and stand there with his cigarette, barely moving to the music. I was once in a place with Sutherland when, over the din of the music, I became aware of a single high note being sustained, and, deciding it was in the record, thought no more until I heard it again in another song and realized finally it was Sutherland, singing a piercing, high E-flat as he danced to Barrabas.

The two of them began to dance the winter the Twelfth Floor opened, the year we returned from Fire Island in September distressed because—what with the demise of Sanctuary—there was as yet no place to dance. Such was our distress at that time: We would not stop dancing. We moved with the regularity of the Pope from the city to Fire Island in the summer, where we danced till the fall, and then, with the geese flying south, the butterflies dying in the dunes, we found some new place in Manhattan and danced all winter there. The composition of our band of dancers changed, but it usually included one doctor, one hustler, one designer, one discaire, one dealer, and the assorted souls who had no idea what they were doing on earth and moved from disguise to disguise (decorator, haircutter, bank teller, magazine salesman, stockbroker) with a crazy look in their eyes because their real happiness was only in music and sex.

We danced the fall of 1971 in a dive off Times Square, living on rumors that the Twelfth Floor would open soon after Thanksgiving; and that is when we first saw Malone with Sutherland. Sutherland we all knew, or knew of: even among us, he was thought to come from another planet. Now of all the bonds between homosexual friends, none was greater than that between the friends who danced together. The friend you danced with, when you had no lover, was the most important person in your life; and for people who went without lovers for years, that was all they had. It was a continuing bond and that is what Malone and Sutherland were for years, starting that fall: two friends who danced with one another.

The bar we saw them in that first season was frequented by a mean crowd, messengers and shop-girls and dealers by day, conceited beauties by night. The first evening we stood behind Malone waiting to go in, and heard the Mafia bouncer ask him twice (for Malone hadn't heard the first time) if there were a "gun, knife, or bottle" in the bag he was carrying, Malone bent forward politely, and when he finally understood, said, "Ah! No," and then was ushered into paradise. It was extraordinary, the emotions in those rooms: At the beach, the music floated out of open windows, wandered over the bay, lost itself in the starry night, just as sexual desire on summer evenings in the city rose into the sky with the pigeons and the heat itself. But in winter, in those rooms in the city, with the music and the men, everything was trapped, and nature being banished, everyone was reduced to an ecstatic gloom. How serious it was, how dark, how deep—how aching, how desperate. We lived on certain chords in a song, and the proximity of another individual dancing beside you, taking communion from the same hand, soaked with sweat, stroked by the same tambourines.

Malone was appalled the first night he went to that particular bar, by the music (the likes of which he had never heard before, and hadn't the ears to hear at first) and the rudeness of the crowd, while Sutherland loved the very sordidness. Later that night, a queen spun around and embraced Malone at the waist and threw her head back and began dancing to him as if to some idol in the jungle— pulled him out onto the floor, where he tried to dance because even then he could not bear to reject anyone. He was wise to do so. Egos were huge and tempers quick in that place; the slightest insult could set off a fight with hidden knives. The queen spun around Malone, some Rita Hayworth in a movie that was never made, until the song ended and then Malone smiled, murmured something, and drifted unobtrusively back to Sutherland, who was shaking with laughter. Malone still had only one set of manners, for all people, and they were somewhat too polite for this place. In fact he was abducted many times that way until he began standing in the corners, behind several lines of people, for he was shy and did not want to be out there on the floor. Furthermore, he was not a good dancer. They were all good dancers in that place. It was a serious crowd—the kind of crowd who one night burned down a discotheque in the Bronx because the music had been bad. As Sutherland murmured one night when he began to look around for an emergency exit (we all would have been snuffed out in a minute had that place caught on fire, as was the case with nearly every place we went, from baths to bars to discotheques): "If there were a fire in this place, darling, no one would be a hero." We stayed until closing anyway, because the music was superb, dancing beside those messenger boys so drugged they danced by themselves in front of mirrors (with their eyes closed), and when we finally emerged, it was in time to see the sun come up from the empty sidewalks of Times Square, which at that hour was as empty, as clean, as ghostly as the oceans of the moon.

We had all seen Malone, yet going home on the subway no one spoke of him, even though each one of us was thinking of that handsome man—and he had seen us. What must he have thought of us at that time. What queens we were! We had been crazed for several years already when we danced at the Bearded Lady that winter. We lived only to dance. What was the true characteristic of a queen, I wondered later on; and you could argue that forever. "What do we all have in common in this group?" I once asked a friend seriously, when it occurred to me how slender, how immaterial, how ephemeral the bond was that joined us; and he responded, "We all have lips." Perhaps that is what we all had in common: No one was allowed to be serious, except about the importance of music, the glory of faces seen in the crowd. We had our songs, we had our faces! We had our web belts and painter's jeans, our dyed tank tops and haircuts, the plaid shirts, bomber jackets, jungle fatigues, the all-important shoes.

What queens we were! With piercing shrieks we met each other on the sidewalk, the piercing shriek that some-times, walking down a perfectly deserted block of lower Broadway, rose from my throat to the sky because I had just seen one of God's angels, some languorous, soft-eyed face lounging in a doorway, or when I was on my way to dance, so happy and alive you could only scream. I was a queen ("Life in a palace changes one," said another), my soul cries out to Thee. The moon, which already floated in the sky when we awoke, above the deserted buildings on the Bowery was more beautiful to me than any summer moon that I had seen hanging over the golden walls of the city of Toledo. Some strange energy was in the very air, the pigeons fluttering to rest in the gutters of the tenement behind the fire escape. In the perfect silence the telephone would ring, thrilling, joyous, and we would slip into the stream of gossip as we would slip into a bath, to dissect, judge, memorialize the previous night and forecast the one to come.

The queen throws on her clothes, discarding at least

ten shirts, five pairs of pants, innumerable belts before she settles on her costume, while the couple next door throws things at each other. She has her solitary meal, as spartan as an athlete's before a race (some say to avoid occlusion of the drugs she plans to take), as they scream drunkenly. And then, just as the Polish barbers who stand all evening by the stoop are turning back to go upstairs to bed, she slips out of her hovel—for the queen lives among ruins; she lives only to dance—and is astride the night, on the street, that ecstatic river that flows through New York City as definitely as the Adriatic washes through Venice, down into the dim, hot subway, where she checks the men's room. An old man sits morosely on the toilet above a puddle of soggy toilet paper, looking up as she peeks in, waiting himself for love. The subway comes; she hurries to the room in which she has agreed to dance this night. Some of the dancers are on drugs and enter the discotheque with the radiant faces of the Magi coming to the Christ Child; others, who are not, enter with a bored expression, as if this is the last thing they want to do tonight. In half an hour they are indistinguishable, sweat-stained, ecstatic, lost. For the fact was drugs were not necessary to most of us, because the music, youth, sweaty bodies were enough. And if it was too hot, too humid to sleep the next day, and we awoke bathed in sweat, it did not matter: We remained in a state of animated suspension the whole hot day. We lived for music, we lived for Beauty, and we were poor. But we didn't care where we were living, or what we had to do during the day to make it possible; eventually, if you waited long enough, you were finally standing before the mirror in that cheap room, looking at your face one last time, like an actor going onstage, before rushing out to walk in the door of that discotheque and see someone like Malone. Through those summers, at the beach, and those winters, in the city, we seldom lost him for very long. He was at the huge parties in the Pines, one of which Sutherland arrived at by helicopter, lowered on a huge bunch of polyethylene bananas, dressed as Carmen Miranda, and he was at the most obscure bars in Hackensack where we sometimes went because we heard a certain discaire was playing. In fact, as it all became a business and the public began to dance, we had to abandon places when they became too professional, too knowing, too slick. Places we had loved—such as the dive off Times Square we often saw Malone in—were written about now in *New York* magazine, *Newsweek*, and *GQ*, and then, the final stage of death, we would pass their doors one evening and see, where we had once thronged to begin those ecstatic rites of Dionysius, a mob of teen-agers and couples from Queens whose place it was now. And so we would go out to New Jersey on those perfumed Saturday nights of summer, against the river of young Puerto Ricans in flowered shirts and thin leather jackets, taking their girls into the city to dance, crowds of people drenched in sweet cologne. But every time we got to this obscure bar in Queens or Jersey City, who was there already? Sutherland (and Malone), for Sutherland, as far as being jaded was concerned, was way ahead of any of us; Sutherland had danced at Sanctuary, the Alibi, the Blue Bunny, for that matter, when places never lasted more than a month and gay life was a floating crap game that moved about the city as nomads pitch and strike their tents, before we had even come to this city. So we traveled in parallel careers, and Malone eventually became a very good dancer, and it was wonderful to dance beside him, on Fire Island, in Jersey City, in those hot, hot rooms, or at the beach, his shirt off, his chest silver with sweat, his face as serious as ours, enveloped in the same music.

We danced near one another for several years and never said a word; even at the very end of an evening, when everyone converged at an after-hours club on Houston Street where the people who could not stop went, who artificially extended the night by remaining in rooms whose windows were painted with black paint, where the dregs of night, the bartenders, the discaires themselves, all tumbled down into one room in which pretensions were impossible. The bathroom was jammed with people sharing drugs, drag queens danced with designers, hustlers played pool, sharing another kind of communion, till, hours later, I would look up to see Malone standing with a drink on the edge of the crowd, and above him the light glowing in the ribs of the ventilating fan over the door—which gave away the whole fiction, the pretense that it was still night, and proved not only that day had come, but it was maturing rapidly— and I would wonder in the sudden stillness why I did not speak to him. It was not simply his beauty—having danced with these people as long as we had, that was no bar to introducing oneself; it was the expression on his face. It was deeply serious, and more, it seemed to promise love. But how could that be? We were too smart to believe in that. We wished to keep him at a distance, as a kind of untried resource, a reward we should have in our secret hearts. We wanted to be loved by Malone, with this egotistic detail: that it would be an exclusive love. At first we thought he was a medical student; then we heard he worked on Seventh Avenue for Clovis Ruffin; besides that, he was dying of an incurable bone disease. Then someone said he didn't work at all and was being kept by an Episcopalian bishop; and so Malone went through as many guises as the discotheques we danced at. But that look never vanished from his eyes. Sutherland—who looked like a lumberjack one night, a Gucci queen the next, a prep school swim star, or an East Village dropout—dressed Malone like a doll each night and ushered him out into the city to be a fantasy for someone. How much was Malone aware of what he was doing? At that time he didn't know he was the object of so many eyes; he didn't care that we possessed each other through the medium of gossip.

And then Malone would vanish for a while, in love with one of the young Latin beauties who made up half our crowd (the other half being the doctors, designers, white boys who loved to dance), and of whom Frankie had been the first. But there were so many Frankies—that was the horror—and eventually Malone would return to find Sutherland hanging out the window of his apartment, swinging his gas-blue beads and talking in Italian to the passersby. Sutherland would see Malone, clutch the avocados in his blouse, and scream, "My son! He is back from that bitch he married!" and Malone would walk into the apartment with a rueful smile and sit down and tell Sutherland what had gone wrong with his latest marriage. Then they would go out dancing. Seeing Malone, we would realize how much we had missed him.

One night he ran into the real Frankie in a bar in Hackensack where Luis Sanchez was playing (our favorite discaire who eventually went off to Paris to play for a count and who seemed to take the best music with him). Frankie was, after all, Malone's first love. Malone was a sentimental soul and when he asked to meet him the next afternoon to talk, Malone agreed. They met in Central Park. Frankie had since been promoted at work and was even wearing glasses to appear more intellectual (though his vision was perfect, and the glass clear), and as they sat by the pond near Seventy-second Street, the conversation was polite. Then Frankie began to query Malone on the crowd into which he had disappeared as totally as a mermaid returning to the sea who leaves her human lover staring blankly at the waves, and of which Frankie disapproved utterly. Frankie was a Latin, Catholic, a conservative soul who hated queens. He had no use for them. He had one dream in life: a home, a wife, a family, and if Nature had made a joke of this, he was not about to smile with her; he would have it anyway, with Malone, in a room somewhere. For such a handsome boy, his soul was a dead weight; the very seriousness Malone had loved at first now seemed to Malone lugubrious, and in fact, as they continued sitting there, Frankie began to cry. Then he lost his temper. He hit Malone twice in the face and stopped only when a policeman came up, at which point Malone fled without a word.

He ran all the way back to Sutherland's apartment, where he found Sutherland in a black Norell standing beside the baby grand piano and singing in a velvet voice: "This time we almost made the pieces fit, didn't we?" He held out his long-gloved arm to Malone and said: "Were you a model of propriety? Did you conduct yourself with dignity?" And then, seeing Malone was distraught, he took off his long gloves, made him a cup of tea, and sat with him on the sofa and listened to his tale of regret and loss until it was time to go to the White Party.

The next afternoon when they awoke with the empty heads of angels being born, pushed their costumes off their limbs, and walked to the window to see if it was day or night, Malone saw Frankie on the corner opposite. Malone drew back; he was convinced, once again, that Frankie was mad. "To take love so seriously!" said Sutherland in a thrilled voice as he came to the window. "Only Latins take love seriously, and he is *so* beautiful. We northern Europeans are cold as fish," he smiled, and wrapped his robe around him as he sat down with a bottle of Perrier. But then Malone looked out at him and felt a vague melancholy: He was crazy, but at least he valued love more than anything, and had adored him. And his very seriousness, his very earnest fury, as he stood there on the corner looking across the street at Sutherland's windows, took Malone's breath away. He knew nothing of discotheques and gossip, body-building and baseball caps, bleached fatigues and plaid shirts, the whole milieu of trends on which the city, and the society that revolved around the Twelfth Floor, thrived, even originated. He stood there in his jeans (the wrong kind, cheap knock-offs from a discount house in Jersey City) and windbreaker (shapeless and green), frowning at Sutherland's window, his dark eyes cloudy as the sky filled that afternoon with an impending thunderstorm, and dark hair blowing about his ears, a creature from a different planet, unfashionable, unself-conscious, unknowing. Yet vain in his own way, Malone reminded himself as he put down the binoculars and turned from the window with a feeling of sadness.

"I don't know if he's waiting to take me to lunch," Malone said, "or stick a knife in my ribs."

"I ask myself the same question every time I go over to Ceil Tyson's for dinner," said Sutherland, peering out the window. "Perhaps you should go to Rome until we clear this up."

"But I can't leave the city," said Malone miserably, "as long as he's in it."

"Poor baby," said Sutherland, withdrawing from the window. "Then what do you plan to do?"

It began to rain and Frankie stepped under the portico of the museum as Malone said: "I want to disappear. Can I leave Manhattan without leaving Manhattan? I'd just better vanish in the metropolitan equivalent of one of those holes scientists have discovered in the universe."

"Well," said Sutherland, putting a finger to his lips judiciously, "you could move to Harlem. One hundred thirtieth Street? But then, northern blacks are so rude. No, I think you should go in the other direction," he said. "I think you should go to the Lower East Side."

That day friends found for Malone—who had little money now—a small apartment on St. Marks Place in which to hide till Frankie went home himself. "They forget *me*," said Sutherland enviously, "within five minutes after leaving the apartment. But then I have such a tiny wink," he sighed.

And so late one night a caravan of taxicabs rolled down Second Avenue south of Fourteenth Street—where Sutherland had once lived as part of Warhol's stable—down the sordid streets of the East Village, bathed in the orange glare of the latest streetlights designed to prevent street crime, and which made each street into a Gaza Strip lacking only barbed wire to prevent the pedestrians on one block from migrating to the one opposite. The whores watched them rumble past; the bums were already sprawled in the doorway of the Ottendorf Library, and the bag ladies were asleep on the sidewalk beside baby carriages heaped with trash. "So much local color!" said Sutherland as the three yellow cabs rolled down the bricks of Second Avenue. "So much raw life. Very Hogarth. Very pretty!" he said, as a man stood shaking his penis against the windshield of a car stopped for a red light, whose driver, a young woman, stared bravely off into the distance, ignoring its presence. "Do you know who used to live along

Second Avenue in all these buildings in the twenties?" he said, leaning forward on the seat to look up at the big stone apartment houses in which lighted windows glowed. "Jewish gangsters! Yes!" he said excitedly. "The famous Rosy Segal lived here, and Bugsy Levine and all the boys who used to hang around the Café Metropole. They kept mistresses in these buildings, just like me," he said, for he still got occasional checks from his Brazilian neurosurgeon and his Parisian art dealer. "The biggest Jewish gangsters of the twenties, this was their block," he said, as the pale cornices went by beneath the radiance of a yellow summer moon. "They are huge apartments," said one of the friends who were accompanying them downtown, an urban planner from Boston, "as big as the ones on the Upper West Side."

"And who lives in them now?" Sutherland said. But before the friend could answer, Sutherland replied himself. "Faggots!" he said. "Faggots where the Jewish gangsters used to keep their mistresses! Ah, this avenue has never been anything but déclassé, it is the perfect place in which to disappear," he said, turning back to Malone. "The perfect place for social oblivion. Not only will nobody know where you are, but when they do find out, they won't visit you after four o'clock in the afternoon!" he said, as they got out of the cab and stepped over the supine body of a man sleeping in the gutter. "*Mira!*" he said, pointing to a young Puerto Rican man bent at the waist, as he reached for something on the sidewalk at his feet—but as they gazed at him, he remained in that impossible pose, immobilized by a drug he had taken earlier that evening. "I believe," said Sutherland breathlessly, "I believe he is trying to pick up his comb! Welcome," he said, turning to Malone. "Welcome to Forgetfulness!"

5

THE Lower East Side reminds some people of photographs of Berlin just after the war. And in fact along certain blocks the walls of tenement houses are thin as movie sets, whose windows disclose the rubble of collapsed buildings. I used to have a dream that bombs had leveled the entire neighborhood and grass and trees and flocks of sheep been allowed to flourish there instead. But this will never be. The Lower East Side will go on just as it is, shimmering in waves of heat rising from the asphalt in summer, shrinking in winter in the pale light till it is nothing but a long gray wall hung with fire escapes on whose sidewalks every particle of dirt and trash stands out in the ashen air. Poor people live there. Artists and ghosts—Poles whose neighborhood it used to be and hippies who gathered there in the early sixties. But both of these have had their day, and St. Marks Place now belongs to hair stylists, pimps, and dealers in secondhand clothing. The building in which Malone took a room is a kind of history lesson of that part of town: It once housed the Electric Circus, a discotheque that began fashionable and white, and eventually became unfashionable and black, and then it was a center for the fifteen-year-old Maharajah Mutu who held prayer meetings there, when I used to see men in dark gray suits running down the sidewalk at five-thirty after work not to be late for meditation—and then a country-and-western discotheque, if that's not a contradiction in terms, that never got off the ground. Finally they closed the place down, and music no longer throbbed out the door on winter nights, and black boys no longer stood around the stairs combing their hair, and no one came in search of spiritual insight. And it just sat there, a huge hulk of a building painted shocking blue . . . a tax write-off for the Mafia. In the very highest part of the big black rounded roof a single window glowed late at night—and that was Malone, trying on T-shirts.

He found himself by now with a collection of clothes nearly as various as the contents of the closet Sutherland had showed him the night they met. He found himself with fatigues and painter's jeans, transparent plastic belts, and plaid shirts, work boots and baseball caps, and T-shirts in every hue manufactured and sold in stores, and then the shades he had created himself by bleaching and fading. He found himself on his empty, lazy afternoons, such as a hooker must spend, trying on clothes and looking at himself in the mirror. The mirror was a cracked shard and the clothes were heaped about the room in cardboard boxes and grocery bags, but he didn't care. He was like an actor in his dressing room, always preparing for a performance. He was free. Free to be vain, to be lazy, to dream. To stand in front of the mirror trying on one T-shirt after another, apple-green, soft yellow, olive drab, black, bright red, faded pink, beige, turquoise blue, and to discard T-shirts, pants, belts before he finally chose the clothes in which he went out into the street. For whom was he dressing? The love he inevitably met in the street. Malone regressed when he came to live alone on the Lower East Side: He went back to the dreams of adolescence, became the girl on her prom night, dreaming of clothes, of love, of the handsome stranger, of being desired. He'd wanted to live a life like this, of self-indulgence, long days, gossip and love affairs, and in his shabby room on the Lower East Side he was completely free to live this timeless existence.

For there is no sense of time passing when you live in that part of town. The Polish men stand in front of the stoop in dark suits and hats watching the crowd go by for hour after hour. The Puerto Rican women sit on the stoops down the street feeding their babies soda pop at dusk, and sometimes they dance with each other while a husband plays the guitar. The music on the jukebox in the bar the Polish men sit at every day, their hats pushed down over their noses, is ten years out of date. No one bothers to change the selections. They listen to Dean Martin sing, "I Want to Be Around to Pick Up the Pieces," over and over again, as a pall of incinerator smoke settles over the neighborhood.

There is no sense of time—the bums come and go; you learn to recognize a few, and then they disappear, on the train to Florida. The whores stand on the corner in their hot pants, shivering under the cold moon, and the sirens of half a dozen police cars rushing to a murder on First Avenue rise up into the sky like a chorus of heavenly voices and then die down. The palm reader dressed like a gypsy has been sitting in her window for years. The funeral home is next to the travel agency, and they look exactly alike. In the window of the travel agency is a poster of five young Polish girls running from a metallic house trailer toward a marshy pond; they have been running for years. It is difficult to say how long Malone had been there, but it was long enough for him (who had been horrified at the men begging for money, the boys folding up on the corner from drugs, the bag ladies asleep on their trash, the shrews screaming at the fruit-sellers on First Avenue over pennies of change, the decrepit, strange creatures on platform shoes with attenuated silhouettes) finally to feel he belonged there. He'd finally found a place whose streets he could roam, where time passed and one wasn't conscious of it, no one cared. He was a literal prisoner of love. Lying in his bed late at night, utterly exhausted, he would rise—completely against his will—to run up to the little park on Fifteenth Street because there might be a boy standing under a tree there looking for love. He loved everything while this erotic fever lasted: the empty streets in winter raked by the wind late at night, the bums sleeping in clouds of steam on the heating vents; in summer, the fragrant heat, the flies droning over the fruit stalls, the plash of water from the fire hydrants; the children screaming, the odor of cookies from the Polish bakery, days lived in a T-shirt and tennis sneakers, the acrid smoke of the incinerator smokestacks settling onto the street. He saw sunsets from his roof. In spring he loved the rains that left the subway stations damp and chilly, and he stopped in the men's rooms and made love there. Only the autumn, that crisp, hard, exhilarating season made him feel ashamed; made him feel trapped in the street, but it passed, and he resumed his life without consciousness of time. And so he lived there for years—and who can say if he stayed in that dismal tenement that so horrified and enthralled him simultaneously, pursuing love, or performing some strange penance for all the advantages he'd had? Love, and humiliation, at once. Malone became one of those boys you see walking home against the crowd at eight in the morning, his face wan, his eyes shadowed after a night with some man in Chelsea: a prisoner of love.

In fact the entire realm of daytime existence became meaningless to Malone, and he wondered how it was possible for men to do anything but pursue amorous interests; how it was possible for them to found businesses, build buildings, play squash. He found himself coming home on the subways in the morning, with crowds of people on their way to work—and while the man hanging onto the strap beside him was on his way to the headquarters of Citibank, he was coming home from a long night of love with one of its tellers. They swayed beside one another, hanging onto the straps, as the car hurtled through the tunnel: the one the servant of Vulcan, and he the servant of Priapus. When he saw, leaving his room at night, the hookers gathered on Third Avenue in their sequined hot pants and black halter tops, he only blessed them secretly in his heart. Rushing up Park Avenue one night on his way to a tryst, he saw an associate from his old firm leaving the offices of Union Carbide. He waited behind a pillar to avoid being seen.

He made love in deserted warehouses at three in the afternoon, and in piers along the river, with huge patches of sunlight falling through the ruined roof; he made love at night in curious apartments high above the city. He made love at rush hour in the men's rooms of subway stations; he made love at noon, at midnight, at eight in the morning; and still he found himself alone. He hurried back and forth across the city on the subway, on its sidewalks, rushing only on errands of love. And still he found himself on Sunday evenings rushing out to quell the inevitable sadness of that moment. He made love with Puerto Rican anesthetists at Bellevue, psychiatrists and Belgian chefs, poets and airline pilots, anarchists and bankers, corporate attorneys and copywriters, and he discovered that after the most passionate night of lovemaking, in someone's bed or at the Baths, he only wanted more. He went from going to bed with handsome people to going to bed with ordinary people, and finally ugly men; with Jews, Italians, Slavs and Brazilians, Dutchmen, Germans, Greeks and Arabs. He made a vow to sleep with everyone just once. He grew gaunt, even more handsome, his eyes shadowed and turgid with lust: He was a prisoner of love.

The building in which Malone and I lived, like a big blue mosque in the center of that neighborhood, was filled with prisoners of other things. The lower floors were full of elderly Jewish widows living on Social Security who were kept alive with the sandwich the Puerto Rican boy from the grocery downstairs brought them once a day. There were Polish couples left over from the days when this had been their neighborhood. There was a Japanese family who ran a tempura takeout restaurant on the street. There was a woman who coughed quietly throughout the night and whom no one ever saw. There was a sad young man in a wheelchair whose cousin came down from Queens each day to take him out. There was a courteous, old-fashioned German man who took his dogs out for a walk three times a day and said a courtly greeting to everyone, as if they were strolling on the Ringstrasse in Vienna. There was a hillbilly family who screamed at each other day and night and lived with twenty-nine cats and dogs. There was the bank teller at Chemical Bank who returned home, changed into an old black Chanel, put a lot of Cole Porter records on his record player, and lay on a chaise lounge all evening smoking dope as he leafed through old issues of *Vanity Fair*. And finally there was the woman who so affected Malone—just the sight of her, on the stairs, a tipsy blond woman with faded blue eyes who paused on each landing to get her breath before climbing to the next, and who smiled and said, "Go ahead," to whomever was behind her. She had once been pretty and she now lived with a husband who yelled at her, as she yelled at him, each evening. She once missed an entire landing coming downstairs, but she was so drunk she just picked herself up off the tiles and went wavering out the door. Her face, in the fluorescent light of that vomit-colored stairwell, had so much sadness and resignation stamped on its Dresden prettiness (long faded, wrinkled now) it sent a chill to Malone's heart and he could not look at her or smell her perfume without a feeling of panic.

Everybody was a flop there: failed artists, artists who'd never made it, disoriented people. Archer had nearly had his doctoral degree at Harvard when he decided that it didn't matter to him what Blake's opinion of applied science was, and he came to New York and lived as a call-boy. He spent two hours a day in a local gymnasium, and his tits were now bigger than his mother's. On the weekends he went to different cities along the East Coast just to stand in bars and show them off. The English girl downstairs came from a very good family and was forever being beaten up by her black lovers. She would call up at three in the morning when she was baking her organic bread, and her lover was breaking into apartments in the building, to see if you were home, and if you answered she would ask in her Oxford accent: "Oh, *do* you have any unbleached soy flour?"

Why was she, or any of us, still there in that place when anyone of modest sense would have moved out long ago? Rent was cheap. But that is too simple an explanation. The streets were made of quicksand, the air was an odorless gas, time passed and we couldn't rouse ourselves. It was simply easier to stay—and satisfy whatever appetites had brought us here in the first place; appetites that, once satisfied, left us exhausted. We became like the ashen air, the fire escapes, the warren of roofs and laundry lines glistening on a wet April morning. We were ghosts. And that's why I went to the discotheques last winter, and even worked in one: serving punch. It was the perfect form of life for a ghost such as I . . .

And ghostly I was—weak, without a will, or vision of another life—for years. I came to New York for love, too, like Malone, and I had been here so long by the time I first saw his incredible eyes, I could not remember. The first day of my life in that building I went to see an old woman who lived in an apartment on the first floor, two rooms in the back filled with the bottle-blue, milky light that gathered like glue at the base of the air shafts of these buildings. How horrified I was by that light! Exactly how long I had lived there I learned only when, going downstairs one day many years after this visit, I ran into the old woman at the mailbox, and she turned to me and said brightly as she turned the key: "Oh, hello! Are you still here?"

Yes, I was still here: trapped, like a fly in amber, in love with the sordid streets, the rooftops, the Puerto Rican boys, the little park at midnight where I could always find boys hungry as I was, their faces gloomy with lust, as they stood beneath the trees waiting to be picked up. I had come to town—when I no longer remembered—and stayed, and time ceased even to be measured, nothing was measured except the cyclical progress of love.

In the city nothing changes: It becomes cold part of the year, and hot another, but no trees lose their leaves, no crops ripen, there are only the streets, the fire escapes, the sky; the telephone, the echoing gymnasium, the angelic face of the Italian boy selling Christmas trees whom you see walking home from the Baths one cold winter night, glowing in the flames he has started in an old oil can to keep warm as he stands there on Second Avenue. Each winter you dance, and each summer you go to the beach. Each year you love someone new: Orientals in 1967, Italians in 1968; blacks in 1969, and bearded blonds in 1970; and always the Puerto Ricans, the angels, who take the form of messenger boys, waiting to cross the street across the pavement from you in their jeans and sneakers, their old leather jackets, on a cold winter day. You remember the eyes, as beautiful as bare trees against a sky: naked, cold, as they glance at you for a moment and then look away. Years pass loving such eyes. And the only way you know you're older is that you (once loved by older men) now find yourself loving boys younger than you . . .

How did time pass in this way? How was it possible for five years to seem like five weeks? I stalked people with the oblivious slowness of a man to whom time does not apply. If it took five or six years to finally speak to a man like Malone, no matter. Watching them so long made possession itself almost secondary. Love is a career with its own stages, rewards, and failures . . . a vocation as concrete as a calling in the Church, worth giving a lifetime to. So I do not know how long I had been on the circuit when I first saw Malone; but this sense of paralysis, of life without movement, had surely begun to affect him, too, by that time.

* * *

For that is the curious quality of the discotheque after you have gone there a long time: In the midst of all the lights, and music, the bodies, the dancing, the drugs, you are stiller than still within, and though you go through the motions of dancing you are thinking a thousand disparate things. You find yourself listening to the lyrics, and you wonder what these people around you are doing. They seemed crazed to you. You stand there on the floor moving your hips, wondering if there is such a thing as love, and conscious for the very first time that it is three-twenty-five and the night only half-over. You put the popper to your nostril, you put a hand out to lightly touch the sweaty, rigid stomach of the man dancing next to you, your own chest is streaming with sweat in that hot room, and you are thinking, as grave as a judge: What will I do with my life? What can any man do with his life? And you finally don't know where to rest your eyes. You don't know where to look, as you dance. You have been expelled from the communion of the saints.

And so we come to the night John Schaeffer, up from Princeton for the weekend, was taken to the Twelfth Floor and saw Malone come in the door and greet his friends. Friends who were nothing more than people he went to parties with, and who had long since lost their capacity to enchant. He stood talking to him and listening to the music with an oddly detached, critical ear. He was waiting for a song, the right song, a face, the magic face, to kindle in him again the old ecstasies—and when he found himself on the floor again, putting back his head when Patty Joe began to sing, "Make Me Believe in You," and touching Frank Post's voluptuous chest streaming with sweat, and wondering who the next boy would be, he was, like everyone else, just a prisoner of habit.

But he hadn't been there in a long time, living as he was with Rafael on the other side of town, and it was for some a thrill to see him again. For if Malone was, in the end, only a face I saw in a discotheque one winter, he was somehow the figure on which everything rested. The central beautiful symbol. As long as he was enmeshed, as long as that room could draw him back (as it now had), so was I. As long as it compelled that face it compelled me. You form relationships like that in a city, and especially in a society as romantic as homosexual society, with faces you never even come near but which stand for a great deal. Why did I never try to know these people whom I adored? I do not know. But though I'd never spoken to Malone, I loved him, and though I'd never tried to meet him, he was the only person in that huge city whose life, whose fate, I found absorbing; and the moment he appeared in that doorway once again, the moment he came back to the Twelfth Floor, I felt a great joy, as if the illusion of love were once more possible.

Nor have I even said what this man looked like, in a story that is really about physical beauty more than anything else—Malone was one of the few blonds I ever found handsome. In New York one is in love with Italians and Jews, and Puerto Ricans and Hungarians, with Sicilians and Venezuelans—the dark-eyed, dark-haired beauties in whom you wish to extinguish yourself, to drown, to disappear in, like a dark night—and blonds were as bland as the bankers and attorneys striding Park Avenue: the blank minions of a vast workhouse, who understood nothing of the secrets of the blood. Then there was Malone. He was the other kind of blond. He resembled those stylized warriors drawn with black lines on the umbrian hue of Greek amphorae, whose thighs were sheaths of muscle so clearly defined they might be plates of armor on the leg. He had the grace of a gazelle grazing on some golden plain in the heat of an African noon. His deep-set, extraordinary eyes were never superficial, empty, glazed over with that dead absence of feeling with which New Yorkers screen out the countless phenomena they must screen out each day in a city whose life assaults rather than comforts. They were filled with emotion; Malone's great strength was the fact that he could hide nothing. He had the perfect manners of a man of his upbringing; but even this restraint and formality could not extinguish the glow. On our deathbeds we will remember faces—not what we accomplished or failed to accomplish, what we worried over anxiously, but the face in the subway, the grace of two black boys who washed each other's shaven heads with shampoo one afternoon in an army camp in Georgia, the sight of Malone when his eyes met yours.

Nothing, however, could have been more startling than to notice Malone and Sutherland in our neighborhood. We had no idea one of them had moved there, but we now saw them every day, late in the afternoon, which is when they got up. Even on that street of crazies Sutherland stood out. There was something wild and breathless about his face, as if he had just seen the Blessed Virgin Mary appear above a subway entrance, or had just stepped out of one of those wind tunnels in which they test the wings of airplanes. Malone drew your attention for different reasons. He looked completely out of place. His eyes were so grave, and kind, and hopeful that meeting their gaze when you passed him on the street, you suddenly forgot where you were going and stopped to recollect.

Malone sensed some of this. By now those eyes had become a burden to him. He no longer believed in love himself, yet he saw people falling in love with him every day. Malone's eyes strayed—because he still was astonished by beauty—and he often found himself locked in an embrace with some nameless stranger on a street. He solved this dilemma by simply not looking at anyone anywhere he went; and if he had to meet them, he adopted from the first a breezy, impersonal form of friendliness that fairly declared itself a form of asexual courtesy and nothing more; which explains his peculiar ease and fluent charm when John Schaeffer saw him at the Twelfth Floor.

We saw this the afternoon they came into our store, and Sutherland went straight for the old, formal, floor-length dresses being sold secondhand. "They never have my size," he said breathlessly, "and I refuse to tell them it's for a friend."

Malone smiled and stuck his hands in his pockets and struck up a conversation with us while Sutherland inspected gowns: "By the way," he said in that breezy way, "I just moved to this neighborhood and maybe you can help me. Is there anyplace I can go at night to get a bit of air? A nearby park?"

We stared: The words made it sound as if we were living in a little village on the Rhine. Finally we told him of the three within walking distance: Washington Square, which was usually filled with people tossing Frisbees, selling dope, or playing bongo drums, and which wasn't very relaxing; Tompkins Square, which was dangerous; and our own watering hole, those two symmetrical parks on Second Avenue between Fifteenth and Seventeenth streets, where we went in the evening to sit and smoke a cigarette and watch men have sex under the trees, and which we warned him now was patronized by homosexuals.

At this point Sutherland arrived and draped a long, dark gray gown over the counter with marquisette appliqué and padded shoulders, and said in his breathless, vibrant voice, "Thank God I found this before Babe Paley did. Not to mention Marie-Hélène de Rothschild. Do you accept Master Charge, darling?" He suddenly yawned, and then said, "Excuse me," as he blinked back the moisture that had come into his eyes. "Frankie called at five in the morning," he said, turning to Malone as we began boxing the dress and writing the sales slip. "Quite gaga. Not only am I getting no sleep—and sleep is everything, darling— but I am beginning to be frightened, seriously frightened." And he yawned uncontrollably again.

"Why are *you* frightened?" said Malone.

"He reminds me of the Ruiz Correas," said Sutherland as he raised a cigarette to his lips.

"Who are they?" said Malone.

"The family who own the grocery store across the street," he said, "from my apartment. I reported them two winters ago to the Board of Health. I lived in com*plete* seclusion for weeks afterward. I did not set foot on Madison Avenue."

"But why?"

"I was afraid of reprisals," he said. "I was obsessed at the time by the death of the Duchesse de Cleves. She was executed during the Revolution, of course, poor baby, and afterward the soldier who had guarded her in prison went around wearing a little moustache composed of her pubic hair."

And with that they left the shop.

For a while after that we didn't see them at all. We began to see their pictures in *Interview,* and the *Post,* instead, that autumn: for Sutherland had begun to party on a grander scale, and Malone, having nothing else to do, went along on this latest excursion of his friend. Sutherland and Malone went to nearly every opening, premiere, gala, and charity ball given at which an element of gay society (fashion, the theater, the arts) made a momentary alliance with the society whose names monotonously sprinkle the columns (the Paleys, Guests, Guinnesses). In that interface they thrived: smiling in black tie beside Lee Radziwill or Françoise de la Renta as the photographer immured Malone, not in any pyramid, but a column of Eugenia Sheppard. He was simply identified in the caption as Anthony Malone. But he was only a partygoer *manqué.* Anything that was not a possible prelude to falling in love left Malone cold. He accompanied Sutherland because he did not know what other avenue he had not tried; he even, for a while, set out with him in the afternoons with their pockets filled with dried apricots, cashew nuts, and raisins, for a long night in the subway johns, meeting one another every three or four hours on the shuttle between Grand Central and Times Square to compare adventures. He forsook the subways after a month of that, but he was no longer chaste. That having isolated him more, he began to sleep with everyone. He went from the Venice Ball to the latest backroom bar and stumbled out of a truck on the waterfront at seven in the morning, his tuxedo stained with piss, his face gentle and bemused. One night they came down to the St. Marks Theater in black tie, with the Egyptian heiresses and a famous decorator, having left a dinner party to see a particularly atrocious double bill. The bill was *Once Is Not Enough* and *Mahogany,* and the theater was jammed with gay people, blacks, and Puerto Ricans talking back to the screen. Halfway through the first film a black man stepped on a Puerto Rican's foot as he was leaving his seat for a drink of water; he did not

137

apologize, and the Puerto Rican, a short man in a fake fur coat and peaked maroon hat, jumped up and ran after the black man, saying, "Man, I've got a gun, I'm going to blow your head off! You step on me, you say you're sorry!" The black man vanished, and the Puerto Rican continued stalking the aisles repeating his threat. At first no one paid any attention, and someone even yelled: "Go stick it up your ass and pull the trigger," and some queen yelled, "Now *that* would be a fuck!" But then the Puerto Rican yelled, "I count to five, I blow your head off!" and people started listening to him. "Everybody shut up! Or I blow this guy's head off!" he yelled, as he stood in the darkness down the aisle beside someone we could not see.

Then—while the ingenue sat on a rock in Central Park having a personal crisis beneath the windows of the Hotel Pierre—the almost clipped, confident voice of Malone said: "Go right ahead, I really don't care if you do."

And Sutherland chimed in breathlessly: "Shoot *me*, darling, I'm on so much speed that the only thing that could possibly bring me down now is to have you blow my head off. That *is* the source of all the trouble anyway, isn't it? We think too much! Blow my head off, darling, and leave me just a highly sensitized anus!"

And here Sutherland began telling Malone in his blithe and breathless voice about a course he had taken with a gay psychologist in San Francisco about getting in touch with one's anus as a source of sexual pleasure.

"Shut up!" the man yelled. "I blow your head off!"

"Go right ahead, darling!" Sutherland gasped. "Pull the trigger and let me come down." And he resumed his conversation with Malone, as the crowd hooted, "Thas right, thas right, you tell him!" and the Puerto Rican whirled around to point his gun at the people who had shouted that. Just then *Mahogany* came onscreen, and the man wandered down to the front row and sat down to watch Diana Ross sing her theme song.

They came out after the movie in black tie, with faces shining, and stood lighting cigarettes as Malone stepped into the street to hail a cab. Sutherland saw the Puerto Rican in the big fur coat and peaked hat standing on the sidewalk with a sullen, dazed expression on his face, as if he were only waiting for another pretext to threaten someone with his pistol. There was a certain ragged edge of human nerves in that part of town—a fine line between human life and violence. You were always missing a murder by ten minutes in that street. You came down to buy a paper and found the sidewalk roped off, as if they had just laid fresh cement, and a sign dangling from the rope: CRIME SEARCH AREA. "You see how dangerous bad art can be to the public," Sutherland said as he offered a cigarette to the Puerto Rican man, who stared at him with a wild, crazy look. "It spreads disorder, as Plato predicted. But *I* wasn't the one you should have shot," he said as the others called to him from their cab, "it was Jacqueline Susann. Darling."

And here he stepped into the cab and blew a kiss, as the man began screaming at him in Spanish.

And once more the city swallowed them up, and they led that strenuous life that existed for us in the newspapers, if there. More parties are given in New York City every night of the week than any other city in the world, surely. Malone and Sutherland went to three a night, and more, for weeks on end. Early in the morning, on our way home from the park, we ran into Malone standing in his tuxedo with a newspaper and carton of milk under his arm, talking to a bum in the clouds of steam that rose from the heating grates, a ghostly sight. "Any luck?" Malone would ask cheerfully when he saw us. He reached into his pocket for a cigarette and pulled out a studded leather cock ring instead. "Are those boys looking for love, too? And finding it?" For he was convinced, even as he went through the paces, that this was an arid way to spend a life. One evening when they had left a new discotheque that had just opened on East Nineteenth Street and strolled down Second Avenue to smoke cigarettes, they wandered into the park where we sat on a bench in the chilly darkness watching the silhouettes float around like sharks in that dark seacave of erotic love.

"He's that gorgeous boy who used to go with John Terry," Sutherland was saying as they sat down on a bench behind us, "the boy who's being kept by a businessman from Singapore, a tea tycoon, the one who masturbates with a lubricated boxing glove and who used to go with George de Rue, the man who is going to redo my apartment next month as a meat locker—"

"Stop!" said Malone all of a sudden. "I don't want to hear another word."

There was a moment of silence and then Sutherland breathed, "But, darling! Gossip is the food of the gods."

"I don't care anymore," said Malone, "whether fatigues are out, or Lacostes the kiss of death, and whether Eddie Chin has let his body go to pot, and will he be anally oriented again this winter, too! And who Terence Hutchinson's lovers used to be, and whether or not Jackie O is going to Halston's party Friday! I don't want to hear another word. I just don't care. I'd like to be serious," he said. "For a while." There was another moment of silence.

"I think I should change clothes if we're going to be serious," Sutherland said in a very low voice.

"You see?" said Malone. "You won't be serious. You can't!"

"These things are very serious," said Sutherland. "It is much more important to know who Terence Hutchinson's lover left him for than to know, to know—well, tell me, what do people consider serious these days?" said Sutherland. "I'm so out of touch."

"I'm tired of going to bed with people and being just the same afterward as I was before," Malone sighed. "How do all these men survive with all this perfectly meaningless sex?" There was a little click, and Malone said, "What's that?"

"The tape recorder, darling," said Sutherland, "I'm taping our entire conversation. Oh, wait, I want this." A button clicked, and we listened to the moans and hisses of a black man being blown in the bushes on our left. "They're talking dirty," hissed Sutherland. "And they're *not bad*." When it was over, he said: "I'm taping for the Duke of Alba, he wants three of my nights in New York to put in a time capsule he's burying on his ranch in Estremadura. Think of it, darling, they'll be listening to us a hundred years from now!" And he pressed another button, and the tape went on fast-forward. "The incredible Japanese," said Sutherland. "If only they had cocks. Now, we were asking the question, What is more serious than gossip?"

The question remained unanswered while the two men who had just engaged in fellatio in the flowerbed zipped up and went on their separate ways without a word, and the wind rustled the leaves of the trees. It must have been the contemplative atmosphere of the darkness and quiet, or the sight of so many bums on the benches, or the desire to escape the trivia he had just objected to, that made

Malone say next: "I want to get a job. In a little town with big front lawns and white frame houses and lots of trees."

"My dear," breathed Sutherland.

"I want to live in a big white house and sit on my porch and see fireflies blinking in the evening, and smell burning leaves in the fall, and see my children playing on the lawn."

"Children require a womb," said Sutherland, "and a womb is connected to a vagina, and the thought of cooze makes you vomit. Such a small detail. But I'll tell you what," he said. "A very rich Argentinian is coming to New York next month, and all he wants is a young man to keep. He doesn't particularly want to have sex with him, or even see him, but he wants to keep him from afar, as it were, like sending ten dollars each month to one of those orphans in Hong Kong. Well, he's coming next month and why don't we introduce him to you, and you might be able to settle down in your midwestern villa for the rest of your life, courtesy of Dr. Molina y Pran."

"But I don't want to be kept," said Malone. "I want to get a job."

"Get a job?" said Sutherland. "As what? A discaire? A janitor? What will you put on your résumé for the past ten years?"

"I . . ." said Malone.

"The only thing you could do at this point," said Sutherland, "would be to say you've been a prisoner of war in Red China. It would be far easier than what you were doing. What were you doing, darling?" said Sutherland.

"Looking for love," said Malone in a quiet voice.

"Looking for love," said Sutherland. He paused and then said, "No, I don't think that would get very far with Union Carbide. Or Ogilvy & Mather. Or the Ford Motor people. Looking for love is not one of the standard entries on the résumé. You see, *you* have been writing a journal for the past ten years, and everyone else has been composing a résumé. Don't think you will be forgiven that," he said. "After all, the Empire State Building is nothing but a mass of sublimated love." At this point we all looked at its silver spire, which rose above the trees of the park not fifteen blocks away, agleam with floodlights, an almost domesticated vision rising as it did from the banks of leaves.

At that moment a bedraggled bag lady came out of the darkness and stopped in front of their bench and said to them in a grating, raw voice as she bent over, a little hat on her head, a shopping bag in one hand: "Gimme a quarter, huh? I'm an alcoholic."

Malone reached into his pocket and gave her a quarter, and as she put it in her purse she said: "Thanks, pal." And then, still bent over, turning her head once to the bench across from her, where two men sat smoking cigarettes and waiting for each other to make the first move, she said: "Fucking queers, they should be arrested!" And she moved on to accost the people on a bench farther down the path.

"My dear," said Sutherland. And then: "That is what you are, you know. You can hardly go back to Winesburg, Ohio, or wherever it is you're from and live there. And lest we forget—does your family know? You're gay as a goose?"

"No," said Malone.

"Well, darling, don't you think you should send them a telegram? Or do you plan to stand at your father's grave and wonder why you never told him the most important truth of your otherwise opaque life? And think of the emotions at Mummy's grave! No, I think you owe it to them both to let them in on your dark, Hawthornian little secret. Let them know you're gay."

"I can't," said Malone quietly.

"Then I think you should drop this mythopoetic fantasy of the white house, the big lawn, the fornicating fireflies."

"I'll go live in the woods," said Malone.

"You'll be lonely," said Sutherland. "Even Thoreau went to town in the afternoon to gossip."

"You could come with me," said Malone.

"Not for a moment," said Sutherland. "I exist only in New York, take me off this island and I evaporate. I'm like a sea plant that is beautiful beneath the sea, but taken from the ocean turns another color altogether. You wouldn't like me in the country," he said, and paused to change cassettes. "There'd be no laughter, no gossip, we'd be deathly bored and begin to hate one another. Imagine having dinner each night, alone, the two of us. I'm amusing, I'm full of life, I'm a creature of the city. Transplant me and I'd die in your very hands."

"Well, I do love you," said Malone.

"Don't talk dirty," said Sutherland.

"But I do love you," said Malone.

"Would you carry my child?" said Sutherland.

"Are you taping this?" said Malone.

"Of course, darling, I am now taping everything. I'm doing a nonfiction novel."

"Well, I don't love anyone but you," Malone said.

"Only because I amuse you, that's not love," said Sutherland.

"Well, what is, then?" said Malone.

"Love is not caring whether he sees the bags beneath your eyes when you wake up, that first hour every day before they fade. That *must* be love! Or is it what Dr. Rose Franzblau says in the *Post*?" he said. "The mutual support of two mature people involved in separate quests for self-realization. It isn't love you need, anyway," he said. "It's money. All problems are essentially financial."

"Don't be absurd," said Malone.

"You have looks, intelligence, an excellent education—you're a National Merit Scholar—now get yourself a good price, Gigi," he said.

A black man suddenly raised his head and said, "Whas happening, baby?" And when no one answered him, he said: "Shit! Nothin' but faggots heah . . . shit! Nothin' but faggots! Shit!" He sat up and slapped one hand against his thigh, and then he said, "Got a cigarette, brother?" And Sutherland handed him a Gauloise. "Thanks, man. Boy, I was sup*posed* to be in . . . I was sup*posed* to be in Chicago yesterday. Whas today?" he said. "Saturday," said Sutherland. "The feast of St. Agnes, Virgin and Martyr."

"Thas right, thas right," he said. "Well, I was supposed to be in Chicago on *Wed*nesday, but I was too drunk . . . too damn drunk. And I'm still drunk!" he said, lying down and smoking his cigarette as he looked up at the trees. "Hmmmmmm," he said, lying there with one hand at his throat, clutching his collar. He turned over on his side with his back to everyone.

"You know, John Schaeffer," said Sutherland, "whose family, I learned last week, owns Union Carbide, has three thousand acres in the Tetons. Would you like to get your health back there?"

"No, but we do have to get out of New York."

"But don't you see?" said Sutherland. "We can't. We haven't got a *sou*. And even if we did, where would we go? They warn you about drugs, but this city is the worst drug of all. Where could we go, really? Oslo? Marrakech? The South Seas? Buenos Aires? Caracas, Santiago? Rome,

Munich? Ibiza, Athens? Kabul? Perhaps Kabul," he said. "We could wear blue eye shadow and live in a mud hut and listen to the wind, just listen to the wind . . . Of course there's that wonderful story of the English queen who threw herself ass-up across a pile of sheepskins outside Kabul and was raped by twenty-five members of a passing caravan. *That's* something to look forward to. Shall we go to Kabul?" he said.

"Actually I'd like to be an air traffic controller at a tiny airport in the Florida Keys," Malone said as if dreaming aloud. "I want to wear white pants and a white shirt. And a pair of silver airplane wings on my pocket. I want to sit in a tiled breezeway at dusk and have a beer while we're waiting for the mail flight from Miami. I am sitting in my starched white pants and my starched white shirt, I want to be an air traffic controller in a sleepy tropic town," he said. "That would be heaven."

"Is that what you really want?" said Sutherland. "You want to be a man?"

"How do I know," sighed Malone. "We are free to do anything, live anywhere, it doesn't matter. We're completely free and that's the horror."

"Perhaps you would like a Valium," said Sutherland. "I happen to have four or five hundred with me in my pocket."

But Malone was thinking now and as he watched the men lighting cigarettes for each other in the dark, having sex beneath the trees, he turned to his friend and said in a wondering voice: "Isn't it strange that when we fall in love, this great dream we have, this extraordinary disease, the only thing in which either one of us is interested, it's inevitably with some perfectly ordinary drip who for some reason we cannot define is the magic bearer, the magician, the one who brings all this to us. Why?"

146

Sutherland stood up and sighed. "I think we've both been taking the windows at Bendel's too seriously. We have brain fever. We've forgotten that elemental truth: that if the windows of Bendel's change from week to week, we, nevertheless, cannot."

"Are you leaving?" said Malone.

"I've run out of cassettes," said Sutherland. "Not to mention cigarettes. Good night, sweet prince! I'll be in East Hampton till Thursday."

"Good-bye," said Malone quietly.

We all sat there about another hour or so—the only sound was Malone sighing from time to time, heartfelt sighs. He got up finally and walked away, and we ourselves got up and left by the south gate and started down Second Avenue in the orange glare of those new safety lamps. The whores, the bums, the pimps, the boys folding up from too many downs, the pieces of garbage blowing in the wind, the metallic tops of garbage cans all stood out in the surreal, radioactive glare of an atom bomb. There wasn't a shadow in the place. Halfway down to St. Marks Place we saw Malone walking ahead of us; and when we caught up with him, he greeted us with that straightforward friendliness that was his manner, and made you think you were anywhere but Second Avenue at three-thirty A.M. ignoring the bum who was asking us for money to buy a beer. "How are you?" he said, putting an arm around our shoulders. "I've just been in your park. I love it! Did you see the fellow who came in with the Irish Setter? Those beautiful eyes? His, I mean, not the dog's," he smiled. "What a kind, beautiful, civilized face! I simply wanted to go up and say: 'Will you marry me?' " He was referring to a handsome mining engineer who lived in a townhouse on the northwestern block of the park, and who came in each night to let his Irish Setter run; he usually smoked a cigarette and sat down and introduced himself to someone and chatted—in the sweetest, calmest, most amiable way, poised, adult, and wise. You fell in love with him right away: with his fine blue eyes, his moustache, his red hooded sweat shirt and tennis sneakers, his slender form, his chestnut hair, the way he looked at you with that blend of humor, intelligence, and relaxed confidence. It was the confidence that was so rare in that park; for all women want to be swept off their feet. Why did so many men stand in that park immobile for hours, except in obedience to some profound law of psychology that causes a woman to insist the man come court her, seduce her, take her away? The mining engineer had just that poise and confidence. We all loved him, but he never went home with anyone; he sat beside you, smoked a cigarette, you fell in love with him, and he excused himself—saying he had to get up at six the next morning for work—and went off with his Irish Setter through the trees toward his townhouse. It left us breathless. And of course he had sat down beside Malone one evening—who made even the mining engineer nervous for a moment, till he found how amiable Malone was—and they had spoken with wonderful pleasure in each other and then, to Malone's amazement, he had stood up and said good-night. Malone was bereft. He still fell in and out of love like a baby. The next time he saw the man, nearly a year later, Malone had grown a beard, and when he came up to Malone and lighted his cigarette and glanced over, Malone remembered everything they had said a year ago. He thought of saying: "I know you, we met here a year ago last spring. Did I have a beard then? It doesn't matter. You've lived in New York seven years, you tried San Francisco for six months, but you'd rather be closer to Europe, you love Europe and New York, and you have to get up at six tomorrow morning to go to work. Now sit down. You wouldn't go to bed with me last time, but we're going to this time. What do you like to do? Do you like to get fucked a long time, deeply, slowly, searchingly? For such a nice person, I bet you're a bastard in bed—you probably love cruelty, you probably love pain. So come on, we're going to your place now and let's cut the small talk." It would have taken him by surprise; he would have gone; Malone knew very well that was all these people were waiting for, the mystical rape, as they stood immobile in the darkness, waiting like Spanish ladies of the fifteenth century to be courted. But he looked away from the man and simply thought to himself: Why bother? for by that time, he had already given up on this game and was doing something even more perverse himself: He was going home, not with the beauties from that park, but the ugly ones. He went home with huge, fat grocers from Avenue D, tiny boys with smashed-in noses who could barely speak comprehensible sentences, ugly boys, deformed boys, fat boys; everyone unattractive and repulsive Malone went off with and made love to. The neighborhood was now the perfect outer counterpart of his inner state: Its filth and ugliness corresponded to his lust. He wanted people the same way. The streets that had once enchanted him, that he had once set out on each night with exhilaration in his heart, now were ashen and sere—and he felt, not like an enchanted lover setting out for Baghdad, but like a roach scurrying down the sidewalk in the orange glare of the streetlights, the particles of mica glittering at him in mockery of all that was brilliant and bright. He gave up his trek westward to the purlieus of the West Village, in fact, and simply shuffled up Second Avenue to our little park along with all the bums.

But you would never have suspected any of this as he went on gossiping about the people he had come to recognize in our little park, thinking, no doubt, that was what we were interested in. And finally he stopped abruptly and said: "But how have you been? And what are you doing these days? Tell me everything!"

It was the old, original part of Malone, that terrific friendliness that was so instinctive a part of his character —even when he had concluded that it was something he would have to repress intentionally, like a twitch. Malone was simply too well-mannered. Too good-natured. How often Sutherland told him he must edit his friends; which meant, in Sutherland's eyes, getting rid of ninety percent of them. But Malone could not. He really was no snob. Dozens of people telephoned him daily with the fundamental rudeness of those who never think their own problems and desires are of little interest to anyone else; and Malone bore their rudeness and listened. And all because he was a friendly, affectionate, naïve fellow—who, when you came up to him on the street, even this street, put his arm around your shoulder and said: "Tell me what happened with that boy on Thursday night! Are you still in love?"

It snowed that winter and the snow gave to Manhattan those weeks before Christmas a surge of happiness of which Sutherland and Malone seemed to have more than their share. Throngs of people poured out of their offices at five, going to parties, visiting travel agents, hiring bartenders. On cold winter days when the ice lay crusted on the sidewalks of the Lower East Side, trumpets blared from the transistor radios the Puerto Ricans carried down the street with them, like tigers on a snowy glacier, and the naked branches of the trees gleamed in the sunlight against the sky. Forty blocks northward Malone and Sutherland swept through the department stores sampling perfume, trying on coats, giving people little presents of dope and handwritten poems, and attending the astonishing number of parties raised, to an exponential degree, by the time of year, including the slave auction the Fist Fuckers of America held a week before Christmas to benefit an orphanage in Hackensack. One afternoon I saw Sutherland surrounded by a group of drunken bums east of Astor Place—giving each one a dop kit from Mark Cross (he'd bought them all at a discount from the Mafia) and wishing them a good trip south. For, like his friends, the alcoholic ladies who lived in residential hotels, and the various millionaires he knew, they all went to sunnier regions at this time of year. Sutherland loved more than anything to shop at Christmastime: He liked to go to Gucci on Fifth Avenue and fart noisily at the counter, and if any of the help in his favorite stores—Cartier, Bendel's, Brooks, and Rizzoli—were rude, he would stop in a phone booth and have the store evacuated by phoning in a bomb scare. Malone followed him through the glittering rooms of merchandise thinking helplessly of Frankie and what he would buy for him. Sutherland presented Malone on Christmas Eve with a heap of gifts: a goose-down parka, hiking boots and backpack (for he saw this as the next fashion trend and wanted Malone to exemplify it), an amber scarab from the Fifth Dynasty, *The Duino Elegies*, a record of trained canaries singing to an organ recital (the product of a woman who had a shop beneath Rockefeller Center), a bottle of Joy, scented soaps from France, a first edition of Yeats, a recording of Pachelbel's canon (the music he played endlessly when alone in his apartment), and a cabochon emerald. All of these

151

things were stolen. He went into Bendel's dressed as Mrs. Charles Dickens and came out with trifles hidden in his skirts. Each evening he read the Gospel of Christ's birth to Malone and then jumped in a cab and went to the Everard Baths.

We all rushed to the Baths at that time of year: The halls were filled with circuit queens and out-of-towners who converged there before going back to Ohio or Maine or wherever it was they must return to participate in the family ceremonies. The rude old men whose attitude of contempt always chilled me as I slipped the money across the counter (framed now in a garland of Christmas cards from all around the world), the Puerto Rican attendant who walked me to my locker with an expression of hopeless melancholy, the fellow in his laundry cubicle on the third floor, glassy-eyed with boredom beneath the defiant centerfold of a big-breasted woman he had taped to the wall, slipping into slumber till a voice on the loudspeaker ordered him to change the sheets in Room Fourteen, the toilets filled to overflowing, the occasional turd that lay unaccountably in the middle of the hallway, the hot moans and hisses from the rooms you passed, the distant sound of someone being patiently spanked with the steady rhythms of a metronome, the leather queens standing in their red-lighted doorways in cowboy hats, dangling handcuffs—none of it mattered; only the rush of affection you felt when you rounded the corner and saw a friend you hadn't seen in five months, the two of you wishing each other "Merry Christmas!" before you went on your way, the soles of your feet turning black as you cruised the red, chill, fake-pine-paneled halls of the Everard Baths. It was Christmas in the Temple of Priapus.

Sutherland always brought several bottles of Campari

and a wicker basket of pâté, apricots and breast of chicken to the Baths and took a room in which to entertain. He poured Guerlain all over his crotch, and then popped around the corner, a cherub in a towel, his bright eyes and hilarious mouth making perfect strangers burst into laughter at the expression on his face. We always ended up outside his room at some point, watching his friends drop in for pâté and Negronis, and Sutherland himself dash out after a beautiful boy he'd just seen passing, trailing his towel like a child, revealing in his insouciance the cause of his problematical sex life. The Baths were humiliating to Sutherland: He entered rooms, closed the door, and emerged two minutes later. They had felt—like a house-wife examining eggs or squeezing cantaloupes—his cock, and found it wanting. He returned to his room and got drunk. Malone came out far less frequently than Suther-land, and when he did he nearly slid down the wall, in the shadows. But people saw him, and walking down the hall behind Malone used to amuse me, because I could watch the various expressions on the faces of people passing—even those who, catching sight of Malone suddenly, crashed into one another at a corner or simply walked into a wall. You had to bite your lip: Laughter was not *de rigueur* at the Baths. The Baths were serious. But to walk down the hallway behind Malone was to marvel at the various reactions people had to a fantasy-made-flesh: frowns, glares, studious attempts to avoid looking at him (so they would not be rejected; these were the proudest of all), in which the face assumed an almost prim, pained expression for an instant, like a maiden aunt who disapproved of all this; and then the wonderful expression of sheer joy, and awe, when the young boys gaped and turned to follow his prog-ress. The uninhibited hissed and talked to him from their doorways as he went past, like whores soliciting on a street-corner, or jumped up from the beds on which they'd been lying to call after him. The aggressive came up to Malone and offered him dope if he would come to their room, or simply grabbed his crotch; and soon, they had all left their doorways and were following Malone around like myself. Malone hardly went out of the room for this reason. He waited till very late at night, when most everyone was asleep, like little children who have just had a glass of milk, only it wasn't milk, it was another fluid. The halls were dark, and quiet, and chill, and only in the distance the sound of someone's moans, or the rheumatic wheeze of a stopped-up toilet, or the hum of the water fountain marked the otherwise unblemished silence. The Baths were almost peaceful then: The hot gloom of lust had lifted. The place for a moment just before dawn became an ordinary hall of closed doors, or open doors in which the occupant, lying invitingly on his bunk, had fallen asleep and was snoring ferociously. It was then Malone went out and took whomever he found, and made love. We all knew people who had their most magical experience very late one night at the Everard Baths with a man they never saw again, but of whose embraces they would think of periodically for the rest of their lives.

That year one of those predawn embraces gave Malone venereal warts, and we saw him shortly before Christmas in the lobby at Bellevue, leaning against a pillar as he listened to a Bach cantata being sung by a group of doctors and nurses for their patients gathered in wheelchairs around them. The snow fell outside the huge windows as they sang. Malone was a sentimental man and he grew sad as he watched this scene. His Christmases had always been re-ligious, charitable, and familial; this year he was staying in New York alone. "I've got venereal warts," he said with a wry smile when the concert had ended and we asked him what he was doing at Bellevue. We were still just people who saw each other when we went out dancing, but Malone was nothing if not friendly. "I'm staying in town to have them painted. But how about you?" And he stood there listening to our plans with his customary consideration. "Well, Merry Christmas," he said with a smile. "And let's get together, please? Sutherland's in Venezuela, and I'll be all alone," he said, "and God knows one hates to be alone at this time of year." He went out the door, turning once to wave to us in the crowd of poor people who came to the free clinic as he did now, for he was poorer than any of them.

Christmas came and went: a dull, gray day on which the snow blew across the empty streets and the bums lighted fires in trash cans on the Bowery. Malone came home one night from a party and was unable to sleep. In the darkness the frivolous evening he had just spent evaporated and he was left with the certainty that he had neglected the very people he truly loved. He had ignored them for the company of people who meant nothing to him but with whom he danced, had fun, and spent the weekends. He sat up, his heart racing in the darkness, flooded with the memory of those members of his family who had been kind to him, and loved him as no one else did with a fundamental, unquestioning love—and he resolved, an hour before dawn, to write them all tomorrow, to return home even, and cling to these souls for the rest of his life. It was then—alone, panic-stricken, flooded with a strange love as he sat there in bed, hearing only the hiss of the pipes—Malone convinced himself that Frankie was only waiting for a sign from him. He would get him a Christmas present for that

Latin day of celebration, the Feast of the Epiphany. And the next day he went out—all thoughts of his family forgotten in the brilliant sunshine—to raise money for his gift by seeing a few clients. And that was how he spent those gray and snowy afternoons after Christmas, rushing across the city amid the crowds that flowed out of the huge department stores exchanging gifts, a merchant among merchants.

We ran into him on the street a few hours before midnight on New Year's Eve. He was in black tie and black coat (like most of Halston's entourage, like most of us who had been living in New York awhile, we had all arrived at the color black; it was in the end a preference that I never could decide was our sophistication or the fact that we were in mourning for our lives), and carried a bottle of champagne in his free hand. He had just left a dinner party uptown because New Year's Eve (like Christmas, Thanksgiving, and Easter) was a sentimental occasion he had always celebrated with his family; he did not want to kiss strangers at the stroke of midnight who meant nothing to him. He was on his way to the Plaza Hotel to visit an executive from Minneapolis staying there whom he had taken to the discos the previous night—the easiest work was as an escort—and who wanted to photograph Malone. He seemed glad to see us, and asked us up to his room for a drink and dancing afterward. In fact, we had spent the entire day on the telephone trying to ascertain from the jungle drums where everyone was going that night; there were so many discotheques now that life was no longer a simple matter of going to the Twelfth Floor its first year and finding in that tiny room everyone you wished to love. No, even that precious fraternity was splintered now, and half were in the Caribbean, or Paris, or various clubs that had opened around town now that discotheques were an industry. Not only did we not know where to go that night, but we had no heat in our apartment, and when Malone learned this he gave us his keys and said to wait in his place till he got back. "I've got a portable heater," he said in his brisk, cheerful way. "The couple next door have violent fights and you can listen to them till I get back. I'll just be gone an hour!"

We went inside the building and began going up the stairs under the thin tubes of fluorescent lighting fluttering spasmodically on the vomit-colored walls. At the very top we found Number Thirty-Six and unlocked the door. It was an old apartment and it was simply a cell—except for the telltale signs of one-night affairs who had left cigarettes stubbed out on saucers, and notes scrawled on the wall ("Call me! 555-3721. John"), a bottle of wine and glasses, and a wicker basket filled with scraps of paper on which more phone numbers and more names were written, no one might have been living there. A squash racket and the Bible and the first issue of *Playgirl* lay on a desk. We sat down and looked around at the filthy walls, and sure enough the couple next door began to fight in angry, drunken voices. Time passed. We grew depressed at their brutal dialogue and turned on the radio to drown them out. Outside snow began to fall past the filthy windows, into the chasm of fire escapes behind Malone's apartment, while uptown it drifted past the tall windows of the suite rented to an executive of a Minneapolis encyclopedia firm who had decided not to pay Malone for the pictures he'd just taken of him nude since the price was too high.

"I'll leave your camera at the desk downstairs," Malone said as he picked it up from the coffee table, "but the film I'm going to remove, of course." Before he got to the desk in the lobby two security guards met Malone and took him to a room on the second floor, and broke his arm. They called a doctor several hours later. It was shortly before three when the telephone rang; we had just begun to think of going on without him. "Hate to bother you," his voice, strangely hollow underneath the familiar briskness, said, "but something unpleasant has occurred, which I thought only happened in East Germany. I'm kind of in jail, and need to see a doctor, kind of thing? Perhaps *this* is the place to spend New Year's Eve. There's a girl here wearing a coat Sutherland and I have been looking all over Manhattan for." And that is what he did, with the muggers, thieves, rapists, and lunatics: saw 1977's first dawn bleach the towers of Wall Street south of his window, eating a wooden peanut butter sandwich with a black girl who had slit a woman's throat while trying to rob her purse on Riverside Drive. But the choicest irony awaited Malone when we took him up to Bellevue after they had released him to have his arm set. The doctor attending him turned out to be a man he had slept with several times. "Oh, God," Malone said weakly just before surrendering to the drug they had given him, afloat on the white pillows of the hospital bed, "is it really time to move to San Francisco?"

6

MALONE only laughed when Sutherland declared that no one past the age of thirty should have more than three good friends; but he knew an awful lot of people. We had not been in his apartment five minutes the evening we left Bellevue to get the Social Security card the hospital requested, when there was a knock on the door. Two boys came in to go out dancing with Malone; two faces we had seen for years and never spoken to. They were shocked by our news that he had been beaten up, could have no visitors, and was spending the night at Bellevue. "But who did it?" said the short one. "Frankie?" We said no, and when we asked who Frankie was, the tall boy replied: "You can't have known Malone very long. Frankie is a drop-dead Italian who was madly in love with Malone and who, when Malone told him it was all over— "

"An inevitable moment," said the tall one, as he sat down on the edge of an upended milk crate, "an inevitable moment in the lives of all lovers, of every persuasion, a moment we must all learn to accept with grace and dignity."

"However, at that inevitable moment," said the short one, picking up the story, "Frankie did *not* behave with grace and dignity, no, he threw Malone down on the grass in Central Park and began breaking each rib and was about to knife him when Sutherland and the police arrived and saved Malone." It was all inaccurate, but Sutherland with the freedom of an artist had arranged the plot to make the tale more vivid, and so the afternoon when Frankie had sat sobbing beside Malone was now, in the vast library of gossip, a scene of violence. "And ever since," the visitor said, "Frankie has tried to learn the location of Malone's cold-water flat"—he turned to us—"we call this place a cold-water flat, it is *not* an apartment—but with no success."

"Is Sutherland at the hospital?" said the other.

"He's in South America," we explained.

"Oh," said the first, turning to the second, "he's with Kenny Lamar, they went over with that count, you know, the one who has every record the Shirelles ever made, the one Sutherland told you was the direct descendant of Diane de Poitiers, *that's* where he is," he said, with the breathless tone of someone fitting two pieces of rumor together. "Oh, God, they're having a fabulous time."

"Well," said the second, standing up, "so will we. Malone would *not* want us to miss the party." It was five o'clock in the morning, and the laundry lines that sagged between our building and the one behind, the fire escape, the flat tar paper roofs were emerging in the gray light. A pigeon fluttered in a gutter, a cat stared at it from the window opposite, its tail flicking back and forth, its teeth chattering, its eyes wild with the expression one saw sometimes on the faces of people at the Twelfth Floor. "Especially since all the beauties will be there," the short boy said, "twisted out of their minds. Oh, God! Was Malone tripping when he was assassinated?"

We said we didn't know.

"Probably not," said his friend. "Malone *never* does drugs." They turned to us at the door after saying they would visit Malone tomorrow, finding us suddenly attractive, and introduced themselves before leaving. The vast majority of Malone's friends had slept with one another. "By the way," the tall one said, "you are now a part of a strange brotherhood, you know?" And the other took up the theme: "Yes, you have to come over some evening. We're all very different, but we do have one thing in common." "We adore Malone," his friend said.

And they went out the door, and it was morning.

Sutherland returned from Caracas the following Monday and came down to Malone's in the uniform of a nurse in the Crimean War to sit beside him and read Rudyard Kipling. He appeared each afternoon in his starched white dress, bearing a poppy and a volume of *The Jungle Book*. He put the book down in the middle of a tale, one day, to tell Malone of a project that had come to him, full-blown, while sitting in the courtyard of Nony Dillon's house in Caracas one evening waiting for her to finish playing a hand of bridge. He had decided to sell Malone. Sutherland was a citizen of the Upper, not the Lower, East Side, after all: He had lived so long among people who sold things— Egyptian scarabs, Turkish rugs, party concepts—to alcoholic ladies in residential hotels, rich folk passing through, the affluent in search of objets d'art, that it occurred to him to convert Malone to cash. For you cannot live in New York City very long and not be conscious of the niceties of being rich—the city is, after all, an ecstatic exercise in merchandising—and one evening of his visit to Venezuela Sutherland sat straight up when he read a line of Santayana's: "Money is the petrol of life." He who had been raised to consider money slightly vulgar suddenly wanted, now that the illusion of love gripped him infrequently, material things: He wanted a house in Cartagena, he wanted to go to Rio if he cared to. He wanted to be able to leave New York from time to time, and not to have to be nice to people in exchange for it. He set himself up, then, in the only business his past years in New York had prepared him for: He became a pimp.

Malone—who considered Sutherland essentially insane —said nothing as he heard this plan described, but being rather lost himself, let Sutherland carry on anyway. The little truce he had achieved with the world that peculiar week of Christmas, when everyone had thought him out of town, the mood of that spontaneous retreat, fled more quickly than the crowd when it decides a bar is passé. When we went over to see Malone that week, the place was jammed, for it took some accident such as Malone's to bring New Yorkers together who were otherwise constrained by the rules of public life to be strangers. When did people talk to each other but at a fire, a robbery, a man dropping dead of a heart attack on the street? Yet people took care of their kind. The bums helped each other: You would see them late at night in winter bending over a friend, saying, "Come on, man, get up, get up!" and finally dragging their friend into the entrance of some tenement where they would all sleep on top of each other, out of the cold, and coming home yourself at dawn from the Twelfth Floor, you would step carefully over their bodies on the landing and even stop to look at their faces and wonder what they were dreaming of. Well, our little society (so tiny, in fact) gathered around the wounded, too. But such was our disposition to turn everything into a party, that when we got

there we found the detritus of expensive fetes uptown—
flowers, caviar, champagne—brightening Malone's room,
the gift of boys who had tended bar at openings the previous night. A tape made for Malone by a popular discaire
was hardly audible beneath the roar of conversation. How
they talked: The quantities of gossip spilled into the air
every hour, which convinced you in the end that none of
us had the slightest secret trait (we were fools to think so
if we did), the analyses of love affairs, apartments, careers,
faces, bodies, gymnasiums, parties. Passing through the
mob I heard a remark, delivered with a condescending
shrug over a glass of carrot juice, which stood for all of
it: "But he shaves his *back*!" Poof, another beauty had bit
the dust. "He's the reason I saw a shrink," someone else
was saying. "Everything was wrong. He lived on the Upper
East Side, he bleached his floors, he thought the Twelfth
Floor was for lonely people." As Sutherland went around
in a crisp black maid's uniform, emptying ashtrays into a
brown paper bag, the most successful model in New York
was asking people's advice on how to attract a boy he'd
recently fallen in love with who was reputed to be indif-
ferent to clean-shaven men. "I could grow a beard," he
said. "But then you know what they say about facial hair."

"What?" said a bearded poet, who had been unable,
after all, to leave this round of discos, bars, and baths he
had denounced on many occasions.

"That it is the same color as one's pubic hair," said the
model. He removed the cigarette holder from his lips and
hollowed his cheeks in a comical expression of hauteur.
"How many times I've gone to bed with dreamy people,
only to discover their pubic hair was a dull, uninteresting
gray. Of course my beard would be blond."

"And what if he doesn't look at you then?" said the poet.

"Then I'll try a moustache," the model shrugged. "There must be some look he's crazy for. It's all just a matter of packaging. Perhaps," he frowned, "he doesn't like blonds!"

"Oh, come see," said a boy sitting by the window. "The sunset is very beautiful."

"Then pull the shade," said Sutherland, wiping out an ashtray with his apron. "I never look at the sunset across these rooftops. It is too depressing. The more beautiful the sky, the more hopeless the neighborhood."

"You must track him down, learn his habits," said the poet, once again intrigued by the problem of seduction at hand.

"The way you moved to Montauk to be with the surfers," said the model.

"Yes," he said. "If you are in love with giraffes, you should live on the Serengeti, if you are in love with surfer boy, you must go to Montauk. And that is what I did."

"But, Rafael!" said Sutherland. "You never slept with any of them!"

"So what?" he shrugged. "One smile from them was ten times more thrilling than the most expert blow-job by some queen at the Baths. I did not have sex with them, but I surfed with them, drank with them, baked clams together, fell asleep side by side in motel rooms—who wants a blow-job?"

"Millions of American boys, thank heaven," said Sutherland in his breathless, throaty murmur. "Oh, God," he said, staring at himself in the mirror, "I been bitten by the love bug!"

Several people shrieked and stood up and said they were on their way to dinner; they filed by Malone's bed and all spoke to him—and what was striking, for those people, they sounded sincere. As they left, however, the open door admitted a new flood of visitors. We watched in astonishment as those mysterious faces we had been so in love with came into the room. Janos Zatursky came, a Hungarian physicist who rarely smiled or said a word (and everyone was in love with him), and Andrew Litton, a beautiful boy who had once been his lover, and Stanley Escher, a struggling architect, and Robert Truscott, the heir to a California forest, and then a host of nameless cocoa-colored boys one sees all around Manhattan, delivering messages, playing handball in empty lots—those Hispanic angels, a blend of Cuba, Africa, and Puerto Rico, whose dark eyes and bone structures no plastic surgeon could create: All of them stopped by to kiss Malone or share their dope with the other people in the room. Raoul Lecluse came, of the Lecluse Gallery years ago, and Felipe Donovan, the owner of the Twelfth Floor, and a man who had pierced his nipples years before it was a fad and shaved his head before that, and John Eckstein, a dancer with the American Ballet Theatre, and Prentiss Nohant, the boy famous for appearing in public in costumes made entirely of gas masks.

The circuit queens came: Luis Sanchez (who played the music at the Twelfth Floor on Saturday) and John di Bellas (a gymnast we had loved till learning he was arrogant); Ed Cort and his lover, Bill Walker (an anal masochist who went to work with a seven-pound ball bearing up his ass); Edwin Giglio (who was so disliked that at his birthday party on Fire Island the guests brought in a candlelit cake and then threw it in his face—while he was tripping); George Riley (a melancholy architect who had never recovered from his affair at Stanford with a professor of mathematics); two airline stewards whose names we didn't know; Eddie Rien, Paul Orozco, and Bob Everett (all hustlers who were no more than five feet four, or twenty years of age); Bill Morgan (who looked like a portrait by Titian, always had gonorrhea, and worked at the airport fueling jets); Huntley Fish (the famous tits), Edwin Farrah from Australia; and Bob Chalmers, a millionaire who went to the Baths every night and lived at the Hotel Pierre watching old Tarzan movies till night fell.

Lynn Feight, a handsome man from Philadelphia being kept by an Episcopalian bishop; and Bob Giorgione (the photographer), who had attempted suicide too many times to recall; and Tom Villaverde (who had a penis so large no one would go to bed with him); and Randy Renfrew (whose penis was so small no one would go to bed with him); and Alonzo Moore, who roller-skated through town in a chiffon ball gown waving a wand to passersby, all came by to see Malone.

And, at the very end, Bruno Welling, a famous drug dealer from the Upper East Side, and Leonard Hauter, a short, dark, enigmatic boy who never said a word but went everywhere with Bruno Welling and served, people said, as a human guinea pig for the newest drugs, which Bruno could not sell till he learned their effect on people. They came by and left Sutherland with a lid of Angel Dust and his favorite drug of all: speed. Everyone in New York was waiting for Sutherland to disintegrate before their very eyes—he shot up incessantly—but by some perverse fate, he went on blooming like a cherub, the very seraph of good health.

They were talking to Archer Prentiss, the chinless, ugly boy who was such a good dancer and who lived in our neighborhood, when we arrived. He lived in a fifth-floor walk-up above a Polish funeral home and spent all his time reading newspapers in his room; he went out only to buy cottage cheese, and newspapers, and to dance.

"But I have never seen you, in the *faubourg!*" said Sutherland in a voice whose passionate excitement gave you the impression he had just been someplace marvelous and was going to be someplace marvelous again.

"I'm a recluse," said Archer in his warped monotone.

"Ah," said Sutherland, tilting the cigarette holder by his lips. "Ah," he breathed.

"A real recluse," said Archer.

"Tell me," said Sutherland. There was a pause, and Archer leaned forward. "What does one wear?"

Archer stared at him until Sutherland said, with a wave of his hand, "No, no, surely there are more intelligent questions than that, it is not your fault I am concerned," he said, "with surfaces."

"With surfaces?"

"Yes, with hats, with gloves, you understand," he said. "I was a recluse myself once, due to a . . . grocery store," he said, waving his hand. He spoke with the most fluid languor, and never above a breathless rush, and as you looked at him, reclining on some pillows that had been thrown onto an old sofa in the corner beside Malone's bed, he produced an impression of almost soporific languidness until your eyes traveled down the figure and saw his one foot, tapping the air with the regularity of a metronome.

"But the whole affair blew away," he murmured throatily, "and I shop at D'Agostino now. Why did *you* become a recluse?" he asked Archer.

"Because I was burned out," droned Archer, "because I was a doomed queen, because I got tired of the same faces, and the same places, because I had been standing in the Eagle's Nest for ten *years.*"

"My dear," breathed Sutherland as he expelled a stream

167

of smoke. "At least you weren't in the men's room at Grand Central."

"I know just how you feel," said Malone all of a sudden. "I want to become a recluse, too."

"The Schaeffers have a place in the Berkshires," said Sutherland, turning to Malone. "Will that do? Is a thousand acres enough for you to be alone with the wildflower and the loon? Will a thousand acres suffice, darling?" he said.

"I think so," said Malone, looking at him with a smile.

"Don't you think he looks just like a wounded airman of the First World War recuperating at Sandringham?" said Sutherland, getting up to hover around Malone like Betty Furness displaying a refrigerator. "If you walked in and saw him, could you resist? Could you?" he said. "I wonder," he said, standing back like a designer appraising a gown, "if we should hang dog tags around his neck. Or sprinkle talcum powder all over everything? Talcum powder and cheap after-shave cologne?" he said, asking us all to survey Malone.

"You see," he said, turning to us, "this is what our client will see when he walks through the door tomorrow. We mustn't make a mistake!" He put a hand to his lips. "We could always ask Harry Kaplan to come down. He's done brilliant things with the windows at Bendel's."

But evidently this was not required, for the next afternoon when we came up with his groceries and his mail, Malone looked as we had left him. And the handsome young man with horn-rimmed glasses whom I had last seen sitting beside Sutherland on the sofa at the Twelfth Floor was now sitting on a pillow in the corner. "You really can't think of five things in life you've always wanted to do," Sutherland said to him when we walked in.

"Well," he said, "I've always wanted to spend a year on the Serengeti, and go up the Amazon, and visit the Galápagos, but do you mean things like that? I imagine everyone wants to do those."

"Well, not *everyone*," breathed Sutherland. "Some of us prefer, like Thoreau, to journey in the *mind*. I was thinking, nevertheless, of fantasies deep within you. Secret wishes of the heart, so to speak."

"Well," said the boy, whose calm had given Sutherland no entrée till now, "I suppose what we all want is to—not be lonely," he said, his voice growing small. "What I really want is someone to love."

"Ah," said Sutherland.

"But you see," he said, "I don't think two men *can* love each other . . . in that way. It will always be a sterile union, it will always be associated with guilt. Sometimes I think that God was sitting up above the world one day, after He had created it," the boy sighed, "and someone said, 'Now what could we throw in to spoil it? You've created such a perfect existence, how could it go amuck?' And someone said, 'Confuse the sexes. Have the men desire men instead of women, and the women desire women. That would do it!' And that's what they did," he said. "You see, life *would* be marvelous if we weren't homosexual. To grow up, to fall in love, to have children, grow old and die. It's rather nice. But then God threw in that monkey wrench. As if out of sheer mischief!" he said.

"Does your family know you're gay?" said Malone, from his bed.

"Oh, no," said the fertilizer heir. "Oh never. I can't imagine. I simply can't imagine it." He stared at the floor and he said, "They were talking about it one night in Maine, and my uncle said, 'If I were queer, I'd put a

169

rifle in my mouth and pull the trigger.' " He looked up. "*That's* what they think of it."

"They wouldn't cut you out of the will, would they?" said Sutherland in a breathless voice.

"I don't think so," he said.

Sutherland quickly fanned himself before the boy looked up at him.

"But then they'll never know," he said.

"It's just as well," said Sutherland. "But I must disagree with you totally about the impossibility of love! There are hundreds of beautiful young men who want just what you do," he said, "but they are afraid! Cynical! Pessimistic! Self-loathing! Love bids them follow, and they say, 'No! I'd rather spend my evenings in the men's room at Grand Central!' But you, you are too intelligent, too sensitive, for that. You need, in the words of the Jefferson Airplane, someone to love. And before the summer is through, you'll have him."

"I will?" said the boy with a smile that dissolved in the irony of his little shrug. "Ah, then show me, please, I am anxious for this person."

"Wonderful," said Sutherland. "I have someone in mind at this very moment."

"Who?" he said.

"Ah, that is not the issue just yet," said Sutherland. "As Ortega y Gasset says, 'Love is an experience few people are capable of,' and I must first find out if you yourself are one of those happy few. Let's go. I'm taking you to a cocktail party on Bank Street."

"Oh," said the boy as he got to his feet. There was an expression of disappointment on his face. He had been happy sitting there in the shaft of sunlight by the fire escape telling Sutherland the answers to his questions while Malone lay there listening.

170

"*All* the boys you saw at the Twelfth Floor last night will be there," said Sutherland.

"Oh," said the boy.

"At least you love beauty," said Sutherland.

The boy walked over to the bed and shyly shook Malone's free hand, and then, after bidding us good-bye, went out the door. "He is deeply in love with you," said Sutherland to Malone the moment the door had closed.

"What do you mean?" Malone said. "He hates being gay and said that he doesn't believe in love between men."

"My dear, that was all for your benefit!" said Sutherland. "He wasn't talking to me, he was talking to you! He was pouring out his innermost doubts, and fears and despair! He was putting forward all the reasons he couldn't believe in love, while he was already dreaming of your damp kisses! He wasn't talking to me, he was talking to *you!*" he said, gathering up his cigarettes and dark glasses and beret. "He was saying, 'Love is difficult, love is impossible, help me make it through the night!' You'll be in the will by Labor Day. Good-bye, darlings, I'm taking him to the over-decorated home of a burned-out queen whose beautiful and alcoholic guests will only make him long for you, Malone, recuperating in this slum! I'll call you tonight!"

He gave Malone a cocktail kiss and turned at the door. "He is young, he is innocent, he still thrills to Patty Joe when she sings 'Make me believe in you, show me that love can be true,' and not only that, he believes the lyrics! Have you never been sitting beneath a tree beside a lake, when a young girl comes on her bicycle, and thinking she is alone, walks down to the water and wades out to swim? Have you never seen a nine-year-old boy on a Georgia road playing by himself in the noonday sun? Have you never seen innocence? Well, this afternoon, you have!" And he was out the door.

"He believes the lyrics?" said Archer with a grin.

Malone waved his hand, and smiled. "So do I," he said, as he leaned forward to breathe the scent of a single rose that John Schaeffer had brought that afternoon.

"But the one who just left—is nuts!"

"Oh, he believes the lyrics, too," said Malone. "At the same time, I have no idea what he wants from life, or where he thinks he is heading, or what really matters to him. But then"—he shrugged, smiling at the absurdity of a statement so unlike everything in which he had been taught to believe—"he says no man can know anything for certain in this life, except how to be well-dressed."

7

SUTHERLAND loathed money—partly because he belonged to an old Virginia family that considered it vulgar, and partly because Sutherland, while not serious, was a man to whom wit and beauty were the true source of happiness. He loved to tell the story of his paternal grandfather, who spent hours in the bathroom reading novels, and who was doing so the afternoon a remote cousin came by from Atlanta with a block of stock in a new company that he wished Sutherland's grandfather to buy; but his grandfather refused to come down, engrossed as he was in a novel of Jane Austen. "Tell him I'm taking a very long shit," the old man said to his sister at the bathroom door; and the young man went away, and with him, a fortune in Coca-Cola stock. The family remained poor.

And so we sat on the stoop those spring evenings and watched the bidders for Malone come and go. Sutherland was hardly interested in the sympathy of circuit queens who could do nothing but shake a tambourine and look pretty. He was suddenly all business. The fact that he was joining rich men and a beautiful friend did not bother him at all—he loved to do it, rather—but the fact that he was doing something for money bothered him a great deal. The right hand knew not what the left was doing. As he waited on the sidewalk beneath us for a client to arrive, a beggar approached Sutherland and held out his hand and said: "I'm hungry." And Sutherland said to him, with that suppressed hysteria that lurked behind his breathless voice: "I'm hungry, too, for love, self-esteem, religious certainty. You are merely hungry for food." And he gave the man a Valium. And standing there in the twilight waiting for some enormously wealthy art dealer to arrive—an art dealer who had seen Malone at dinner parties with Sutherland and always ached to know him—he nervously tapped his foot against the pavement, hating, even now, the fact that he was doing one thing for gold. "But I have all the things money can't buy," he wailed to the waiting moon, the whores clustering at the soda counter, "charm, taste, a curious mind. Why run after *gelt*? Because," he reminded himself as he stood there, "plane tickets cost money. God! Not to mention houses in Greece."

Since coming to New York Malone had received numerous offers from wealthy men amounting to very little effort on his part. People wanted Malone the way they wanted vases from China, *étagères*, Coromandel screens. And so, while spring arrived on the Lower East Side, and we sat out on our stoop in the evenings, we watched them come and go: the fertilizer heir, the Argentinian architect, rich screenwriters, decorators, owners of textile firms— Sutherland had them all filing through that apartment, like the people uptown at Parke-Bernet viewing the works of art before they go up on the block.

Meanwhile the Poles in their dark suits and hats watched it all go by, their hats pushed back on their heads, as if a funeral were about to begin in the church down the street. The street had come down to that, the Poles and Puerto Ricans, the two races of man, northern and southern, inundated in the garish chaos of hustling for a buck.

One evening we came downstairs and saw an ambulance pulled up in front of the building—and five minutes later a body covered up on a stretcher came out. It was one of the tenants, the Coughing Lady, who had lived alone on the fourth floor for thirty-five years in the same apartment and who had died nearly a week ago without anyone knowing.

"Oh, God, that's how we're all going to end up," droned Archer in his flattest monotone.

"Not if we use *lots* of Estee Lauder," said Sutherland breathlessly as he went inside to bring Malone some ice cream and cigarettes.

Sometimes Malone sat with us on the stoop at dusk and watched the rectangle of sky at the western end of our street glow a burnished orange as the sun set, and then red, and then a pale blue that deepened and deepened at the cornices of buildings till it turned a rich and intriguing indigo that one saw only in the city. Malone was perplexed by men like our clump of Poles who stood for hours talking and watching the crowds go by. "You know, when I first came to the city," he said one evening, "I could not understand how these people could just sit out in front of their building all day and in the evening, too, just watching people go by. It drove me mad! I thought, how can anyone be so stationary, how can anyone reduce his life to that, and just waste his life standing in front of a tenement watching the crowd go past! I used to think it was their Eastern European souls," he said, "some dark sloth and pessimism, you know, that allowed them to do this. But now," he said with a sigh as he himself turned his attention back to the passing throngs, "I understand perfectly why they do it." And there he sat, his chin on his hand, an American no longer chary of time.

He sat there with his shirt open, bathing himself in the breeze blowing across town, up those ascending streets, which curved away to a blue horizon and then dropped down to the Hudson. The fire hydrants gushed water with a soothing plash. Two Puerto Rican mothers sat on the adjacent stoop feeding their babies bottles of orange Nehi, and halfway down the block a man played the guitar while two women in shorts and curlers danced the merengue together. How the city baked! The geysers of water, the gushing gutters, the cool breeze at sunset that touched his sweaty stomach with a chill, the deep blue of night that thickened in that square of sky at the end of Eighth Street to the west, and then became a deep, heartbreaking indigo, while a dozen radios blared advertisements for Clorox and Goya flour through a dozen windows, all bathed him in beauty; and as the city began to cool at last, sitting in the camaraderie of queens, he sat thinking that at least he had stripped his life down to that one single thing—love—and this was where love had led him, this was where he was, as his father had been led to Ceylon in search of oil.

Furthermore he saw as he sat there that what he truly was in love with—or any of us, for that matter—was not Rafael, or Jesus, or the man we had been watching on the dance floor for four years now, but our own senses, the animal bliss of being alive. He had come to adore, true climber on the ladder of love, not only Rafael but all the Rafaels in this street—and that what he loved, finally, was only the city. And that if we had no human lover at the moment, we had instead the color of that indigo that precipitates like an extraordinary dye on late-summer evenings at the end of city streets; the breeze bathing his face and shoulders; the sweet comfort of the sweat, drying on his chest; the merengue coming through a window, the fragrant heat, the warm, redolent, perfumed evening; the little moon hanging in the band of light blue sky high above the indigo, floating in a silvery blaze high above the island, the rooftops. He sat there long after everyone else had gone inside, finally brought to rest, a witness of the summer moon.

His only concession to self-improvement began when his arm healed—around eight o'clock each evening he would leave us and go to a gymnasium uptown to lift weights and use the rings and parallel bars for an hour. He who had given up on a human lover nevertheless maintained the temple, as if some day, years from now, the god might return. For if anything is prized more in the homosexual subculture than a handsome face, or a large cock, it is a well-defined, athletic body. Having all three is devastating; add to them the peculiar charisma of Malone, his capacity for love, for giving himself, and the parade of prosperous men who came up those steps is understandable.

Sutherland had to schedule them, in fact—he had divided up Malone's week very neatly. On Wednesday evenings he would pull up in a taxicab with the fertilizer heir, in a Hawaiian shirt and dark glasses. The fertilizer heir had just come from a game of squash at the Racquet Club, and his black hair was slicked down from his shower; in his chinos and white polo shirt and sneakers, he might have been on the deck of his family's boat, which had been sailed up from Florida for the summer at Mt. Desert, only the week before. Sutherland (still picking up the tab when they went out together) had never carried a wallet in his life and simply pulled out a fistful of bills from the pockets of his painter's jeans, half of which flew away in the wind, so that we had to chase them down on the side-walk. Sutherland said breathlessly when we returned them: "Thank you so much, I have so little rapport with *phys*ical money, you see. Like keys and locks. You know Scriabin put on white gloves to pay his rent!" And with that he thrust the bills through the window and said something in Italian to the driver, who smiled and drove off.

"These cab drivers are so young, and so beautiful," he breathed as he stood there. "Am I terribly late? Has Malone come home yet? We were involved with Mrs. Farouk-Hasiid at Bendel's, she had lost her charge plate and couldn't decide on a picture hat, anyway, which, I assured her, is never out of style."

"He hasn't come back," we said.

"Ah!" said Sutherland, looking askance for a moment at the filthy stoop on which he finally sat down, smudging his white pants. "Then we shall wait. We shall drown for a moment in the life of the street. And what a street! Not since Juvenal have such harlots and fags been parading through a major capital!"

And he began to explain to the fertilizer heir the various meanings of the outfits going by: the red handkerchief in the left pocket (fist-fucker), or right pocket (fist-fuckee), the yellow handkerchief (piss), the shaved heads, chains and leather, the bare chest with tiny gold rings inserted in the nipples. "Oh, I know her!" said Sutherland when one such went by, to the wonderment of the fertilizer heir. "We used to work at Bloomingdale's together. When the store closed, we'd put on their very best suits and go to drinks in the Oak Room—and then put them back in the morning."

"How is the Oak Room?" someone said. "Has it changed?"

"Yes, dear," said Sutherland. "It's all black." He blew out a stream of cigarette smoke. "Poor baby," he said, still looking at his old acquaintance who had paused to buy a newspaper at the corner. "She looks *very* tired, of course she has been in New York since the fall of Constantinople. She achieves orgasm only after hot wax is dropped on her pierced nipples, they say. When *I* knew her she was all cashmere sweaters and penny loafers. I, however, had just invented velvet nipple clamps."

"You what?" said the fertilizer heir as he looked up at Sutherland.

"Velvet nipple clamps," Sutherland repeated in that low, breathless voice, his face a mask of innocence and raised eyebrows.

"Velvet nipple clamps," repeated our visitor.

"I invented them," said Sutherland. "Please, darling. In those days I never had to use the toilet, I—"

"Enough!" said Archer.

"I was the household god, the mascot of sadomasochistic New York. *I* was in the taxi when John Jerome bit his lover's nose off outside Sanctuary. One of the legends of SM New York. *I* used to shit on John's lips and then *he* would turn to his lover and kiss him with my shit. Heavy," he said with a long sigh. "I was into heavy SM. Now all I want is a hug and a kiss." He stubbed his cigarette out on the stoop, and said in an aside to the garbage can, as he tossed it there: "And an emerald parure." He looked up to see a gaunt, handsome young man go by with half-moon shadows beneath his eyes, and the grim expression of someone living for lust. "Now there's a boy who spent the night tied to a bed, in a room in Chelsea!" said Sutherland happily.

"I—I don't understand sadomasochism," said the fertilizer heir in a tentative voice, with the frown of a scholar, as he sat on the bottom step holding his squash racket and paperback volumes of Hawthorne and Henry Adams, which he was reading for his Master's exam in July. "Why would you want to feel pain?"

"My dear," sighed Sutherland. "You would have to read all of *The Fall of the House of Savoy* to understand that," he said, referring to an obscure six-volume work of German history, which was his favorite reading. "Not to mention the *Autobiography of St. Theresa,* and the life of Mahatma Gandhi. Darling, it would take at least a year on Fire Island to make you understand. Don't worry, you shall have it," he said, for Sutherland had taken a house in the Pines and already moved a large part of Malone's wardrobe out there, where he might be seen in a setting more appealing than St. Marks Place by prospective clients who would not have been caught dead on the Lower East Side.

"Fire Island?" said the fertilizer heir.

"Fire Island Pines," sighed Sutherland. "A strange seaside community where people are considered creative because they design windows at Saks. But don't worry—it has other things. Wild deer, in the fall, and even wilder beautiful boys at almost any time of the year. You'll see. I'll show you the Dangerous Island," he added.

"Why dangerous?" said his tutee.

"Dangerous because you may lose your heart," he said, standing up. "Or mind. Or reputation. Or contact lenses," he said. "Horst!" he called, waving at a boy across the street who had recently told Sutherland he had four thousand Quaaludes to sell at seventy-one cents apiece—a very low price, and a chance Sutherland could not pass up now that he was escorting John around. "Excuse me," he said to us, "I have to see a man about a shipload of bananas.

I'll be *right* back!" And he dashed off around the corner to follow Horst up Second Avenue.

As we were watching him rush off after Horst, another cab pulled up at the curb, and out stepped Malone, looking still like the German sailor recuperating in Malta. His arm was in a sling (which he still wore to certain clients), and he wore white pants and a pale, blue-striped polo shirt. "Hello everyone," he said with a smile when he turned around after paying the driver. He had just come from an hour with an elderly retired psychiatrist who had paid him a hundred dollars to stand on his Aubusson in a pair of blue Speedo bathing trunks while he, the psychiatrist, masturbated at his feet. John stood up and said he was waiting for Sutherland to return from some errand he had just dashed off on. "Something about a shipload of bananas," John said slowly.

"Oh," Malone laughed, recognizing a line of Sutherland's. "Well, let's wait for him upstairs. We'll have a beer if you like."

John stood up and said, "Oh, I'd like that." And then he went pale at the thought. Like all shy lovers, the last thing he wanted was to be alone with his love—he wanted to adore him secretly for a while longer. But he could not say no; the moment of truth was here. He nodded at us, and the two of them went inside. A moment later Sutherland returned to the stoop. "And where is my chickadee?" he said. "He went up with Malone," we explained.

"Ah!" said Sutherland. "Perfect! I shall leave them alone for just a little bit. But not too long!" he said, sitting down on the stoop with us. "Falling in love is such a delicate matter," he said, lighting up a Gauloise. "Really like timing a roast."

"Timing a roast," said Hobbs.

Sutherland stood up. "But even that is small potatoes," he said. "Wait till we marry him off!"

"Marry him," we said. "To whom?"

"Why Malone, of course," said Sutherland, as he went up the steps. "The contract is already drawn up. Malone gets several buildings in midtown, and I . . . well, I shall button my lips. But you'll come to the party, won't you?" he said breathlessly. "I promise it will make the marriage of Venice to the Adriatic look like a policemen's ball. And Lally's do at the Plaza," he added, sticking his head out the door of our tenement, "look like a Tupperware Party!"

And he vanished inside.

John Schaeffer had dropped an envelope, however, in getting up to accompany Malone upstairs, an envelope that had fallen out of one of his books, and someone reached down now and picked it up off the steps. Queens inured to gossip, we listened rapt as he read it out loud. The letter was not what one would have expected from this recent graduate of Princeton, whose own shyness had led us to regard him as a snob, and whose life—Sutherland assured everyone—had been spent in that longitude that circles the globe but appears on no maps and is inhabited solely by the very rich. He had spent nearly all his life away at schools in France and England, Sutherland said, learning Latin with the van der Heydens and the Goelets, or on his grandparents' ranch in Montana, or simply his father's schooner; and life had always been for him—and would always be—an almost rural, certainly seasonal, nomadic existence. He had never had to deal with reality, Sutherland declared with a passionate sense of triumph. People had appeared and disappeared in his life like the islands he sailed through with his family each summer, a different one each day, as permanent as the cantaloupes they ate beneath an awning on the stern. "John Schaeffer," Sutherland said, "has, in a curious way, been brought up with the stillness, the manners, the loneliness of a shepherd!"

But the letter disclosed a soul more complicated than that. "Dear Andy," it read.

First let me say how much I miss everyone. I lay for three days in my room after commencement and could not even come down for food. My parents understood. I think you, and a few others, and myself, were very, very happy. Hopefully we shall be once again in life. At any rate, I'm in New York right now, since the trip down the Danube fell through, and while I hate cities, I have met someone absolutely wonderful whom I want you to meet, too, if you manage to come home this fall. He runs around with a dreadful crowd, lots of drugs and insincerity, and lives in a roach-infested slum (on the Lower East Side), but it's because he's in hiding from a former friend who wants to kill him. Yes, I'm afraid that not only have I fallen in love for the first time, but fallen in the wrong, the inconvenient *sort of way, if you understand. He is perfectly calm and humane about it all; I think he's suffered, too, though his manner is very— straightforward and high-spirited. He's someone you'd love to play squash with. He reminds me a bit of Tom Esterhazy —and, in a way, of Bunny Molyneux—and yet he's not like anyone else. You know, life is so dreadful now—for all of us, I mean—so dull, that all that matters to me, more and more, are individual people. The few people I care about. He seems so strangely lost, so sweet-natured, and kind, and bewildered. But he strikes everyone that way, I think. That's why so many people are after him—God, the vulgarity of some of them! I am so happy when he just looks at me.*

His eyes are so extraordinary that when he does, I feel that same deep peace we felt at Mont-Saint-Michel, remember, that October evening in the chapel. The same calm *is in his eyes. They are grayish blue. He is almost a painting by Burne-Jones. In fact, he affects me so much that when I'm with him—when we meet on the street, say—my legs actually shake. I can hardly stand up. This has never happened to me before! I of course never even dreamed that he had noticed me, but this friend of mine who's been taking me everywhere (an unusual person in his own right), told me last evening that he is interested in* me. *I couldn't believe it! But he insists it's true. As you can imagine, I'm living in a kind of dream.*

I am keeping my journal, of course, and will show it to you someday. I'll be in Maine next week for the family reunion and then will probably return here; all I care about at the moment is Malone.

John.

P.S. Eliot said an artist must know when to be self-conscious and when to be unconscious. *Well, that's always been my problem, too! And this is the one chance I have to simply go with the stream of life. My one chance for love. You see, I have to take the risk. Or I'll be like that man Thoreau speaks of, who, when it came time to die, realized he hadn't lived. I must leap, as Kierkegaard said, not into the arms of God, but into the arms of Malone. (Please excuse all this.)*

"Poor *baby*," someone said as the letter was put back in its envelope, and we all got up to trek to the Morton Street pier to mingle with the crowd.

* * *

Thursday evenings belonged to Dr. Valeriani-Winston, the Argentinian neurosurgeon Sutherland had met in Paris on New Year's Eve. He was a very handsome man in the prime of life who was the scion of a famous family, and a surgeon, a sharpshooter, and an erstwhile sailor for his country in the Olympics. He had once seen Malone walking down a beach in the Hamptons several years before and he had fallen in love. In Argentina any suggestion of homosexual desire is tantamount to suicide; and so this handsome, olive-skinned man, with his high brow, thin moustache, and muscular body, came to North America as often as he could. After all, it was the American boy he was in love with: the American boy who was the best friend of his youth in Argentina, the son of an American oil executive with whom he had learned to sail, and shoot, and play tennis. This boy had since left Argentina, married, and was now a lawyer living in a suburb of Seattle. Dr. Valeriani-Winston was left with his memory, like a pressed flower from a wedding that had occurred years ago, and now wandered the earth searching for that blond youth with whom he had spent those hot, happy summers in Rio de la Plata. Such is the life of any homosexual like Malone: He isn't even aware of all the things he's stirring up inside another man's soul. How was Malone to know, walking down the beach at dusk that day in East Hampton, that an Argentinian doctor had been devastated at the sight of this reincarnation of a figure in his youth?

And so as we sat on the stoop Thursday evening watching the local branch of Hell's Angels pull up at a barbershop to have their hair cut, a cab pulled up and out stepped Sutherland with the Argentinian neurosurgeon, in his suede jacket, polo shirt, and boots, fresh from an afternoon of hunting at a friend's estate on Long Island. They stepped out of the cab into the last oblique, ruddy rays of the sun setting on the Hudson, far down the length of Eighth Street. The homosexual young men walking down the sidewalk at that moment and looking at him with intense, glowering glances, meant nothing to him. He was a homosexual where only one figure was concerned—the friend he had loved in his youth—the blond American youth: Malone.

"He's so lonely," Sutherland would say to Malone when they sat on the stoop discussing him, "and such a gentleman. The old-fashioned kind, who would gladly fight a duel over you. He'll buy you a townhouse here, darling, and just fly up every month or so for some medical conference, take you to the best parties, and then fuck you to oblivion in the den afterward. Every girl's dream . . ."

"Hah," Malone shrugged. "But he's a block of ice. So exact, so competent, so macho. Why is he interested in me?"

"You resemble a boy he was once in love with, the great love of his life, when he was young—oh, when he was young," Sutherland sighed, "you should see the photograph I saw, he looked like a Greek god."

"He is very well-built."

"Well-built? You could do your nylons on his stomach."

"My nylons?"

"He has a washboard belly," said Sutherland. "You know, all those bumps and ridges."

Malone said nothing.

"Girls have committed suicide over the man," said Sutherland breathlessly. "And he *is* from a major B.A. family."

But Malone just smoked his cigarette, and looked at the beautiful Puerto Rican boy passing, and said nothing; he was still in love himself with those dark eyes, those slender angels, who were on the street day and night in our neighborhood. Malone still had a wistful memory of that romantic dream, of a kind and beautiful Latin youth, lying in his arms in some room somewhere, a dream in which the things the world cared about were irrelevant . . . he was even now still hoping to see a boy he had seen one night that winter, while walking up Second Avenue from the Baths, a night so cold the people selling Christmas trees on the sidewalk had filled empty oil barrels with trash and set it on fire to keep warm. He had looked up at a little family group, and on the edge of it, a young man looking at Malone behind the flames of the trash barrel, his eyes dark and glowing . . . eyes he would never forget, or the flames at three A.M. on a cold winter night on the Lower East Side. He could not forget that face even now and went down to the fruit stands of that block from time to time, hoping to see him again.

He did not find him, but one evening he met another boy, as dark-eyed and grave and beautiful: a bank teller who lived in an apartment on Third Street beside St. Jude's Cemetery. It was a quiet street, and the boy led a quiet life. He was studying to be a Rolfer. When Malone went to see him one evening he found him seated in his bathtub, reading a book on anatomy in the light of a dozen candles set about the tiles on little saucers. He came home each day from the bank and got into the tub and memorized the names of muscles in order to pass the state licensing examination for a masseur. He spoke very little. Malone knelt beside his bathtub and kissed him above the faintly fragrant greenish water in the tub, as a tiny trickle from the tap plashed in the silence. His white penis floated on the surface of the water like a lily pad. Malone felt as if he were in church, at those banks of candles in red glass cups his mother had taken him to as a child to pray for some aunt or cousin in America. He felt a curious peace flood his limbs: the warmth of the candles, their flames all around him, the slightly humid air, the moist high space, the trickling water, and the beauty of this young man submerged in the tub reading a book filled with the precise drawings of human musculature. Through the half-opaque window the silhouettes of trees made a pattern. They made love much later on a mattress in the living room, as the cries of children playing in the street echoed around them, and when Malone left he had fallen in love; not with the young man, but the thought of him in the bathtub with his candles reading books of anatomy; and when Malone went to see him the next time, he simply sat with him in the bathroom and did not even ask to make love. The next time he merely paused on Third Street one evening while walking past the cemetery and looked through the trees and gravestones at his milk-white window and watched the blurred form moving about the room, setting candles on the tiles. It was six o'clock. He had come home from work, Malone surmised, and was sitting down in the tub to read his book. The breeze rustled the trees. The street was still, the cemetery dark. There in the darkness of the silhouetted trees and empty summer street Malone felt a great peace descending on him. This was all he needed now: the blurred grace of the bank teller bending down to light a candle—in the unconscious beauty of a figure on a temple frieze. He wondered if he should ring the bell; but what would be the point? He loved him as he stood there in the street, remembering his penis floating on the water like a lily pad. He loved these boys, as did I, to be among them was enough; he was in thrall to them, he was in the thrall of Puerto Ricans.

He watched them now even as Sutherland continued talking about the advantages of an alliance with a rich and prominent family in Buenos Aires, walking down the street in their sneakers and jeans and cheap leather jackets, until a cab pulled up and a screenwriter who had once been very successful in Hollywood got out. And while Malone talked to him on the sidewalk, he saw, walking behind him, an adolescent Puerto Rican who had nothing at all to do with wealth, success, or glamour: a boy named Juan Rafael, who worked as an orderly on the night shift at Beth Israel, and who came to our little park afterward in a denim jacket and sneakers, and allowed himself to be blown in the flowerbed by some man while he stood there looking at his watch and saying, "Hurry up, man, huh? I gotta go."

His dark, cloudy eyes, eyes that cloud in cold weather, were what still made Malone glance wistfully over the screenwriter's cashmere shoulder. He preferred Juan Rafael. He loved the bank teller who came home from his day and got in the tub after setting lighted candles over the tiles in little saucers. He liked his homely and modest life. If Malone danced with the decorators, designers, and discotheque owners who bought Maseratis one year and Mercedes the next, and then traded that in for a Rolls, he considered them realistic in a way he didn't want to be. But I'm so tired, he thought as he stood there on the crowded sidewalk, I must get out of New York. And so the three of them, Malone, Sutherland, and the screenwriter, went off for dinner at the townhouse of a wealthy textile manufacturer on Beekman Place.

Of all these candidates for Malone's hand, however, the richest by far was the youngest and least sophisticated, and the one most painfully in love: John Schaeffer. At the age of eighteen, he had inherited twenty-six million dollars, and at the age of thirty, he was to inherit twenty-six more. His family had raised him in so subtly normal a way—had essentially quarantined him from contamination by the unnatural fact of this great fortune—that he was indistinguishable from any well-brought-up, idealistic, unassuming young man. He seemed in fact unworldly—his pale face, the watchfulness in his eyes as he sat listening to whoever was speaking. Even so, six men were assigned to his trust at Morgan Guaranty, despite the democratic intentions of his parents. Sutherland started to check the stock market in the morning now, to see how Union Carbide was doing, and loved to refer to its enormous tower on Park Avenue as John's little townhouse. A moral man is essentially dumbfounded when confronted by a man who is amoral—everything the latter does is met with a certain disbelief. And since no one could decide whether Sutherland was actually amoral, or so moral that he had given up on any relationship with other men, in the first place, we all wondered if he actually planned to sell Malone. We had heard of boys who had been given property, of course; kept boys, lovers, who were ultimately given a legal share in some huge estate, or an apartment building on Third Avenue, or a house at Fire Island; but it seemed improbable to us that anyone, especially an American, could be so coldblooded about the fleecing of an amiable young man. But then we were average people, and Sutherland was not. He began to tattoo, for instance, the closing price of Union Carbide stock on the inside of his wrist each morning, where he could glance at it throughout the day as he continued to solidify his position with John wherever they went.

No one knew better than Sutherland the pathology of

love; and he was not hesitant to strengthen Malone's hold on John with a little suffering. And not such a little. John Schaeffer was in a weak condition, anyway; a month ago, he had graduated from college, and with this event, said good-bye to a long, long phase of youth, along with the friends, the green courtyards, long evenings of talk of poetry and life, carefree adolescence which ends officially at twenty-one in this country. A homosexual will never have such a close relationship with his heterosexual peers again, unless he enters the army, a relationship that sublimated sexuality makes even more moving. John Schaeffer was an affectionate, idealistic fellow, and these friendships' end had left him as with a limb cut off. He was twenty-one, shot through with Shakespeare's sonnets and the novels of Henry James; he was young, and to many people the very image of the handsome American, the gilded youth; yet all he wanted himself was affection, a true friend, a companion to assuage the loss of what he sentimentally saw as his last youth (he hardly could know how we extend our youths at the end of each succeeding decade, like a man postponing payment on a loan), and in this state—of melancholy despair, poignant sensitivity to the sensual, romantic aspects of life: green courtyards, bluffs above the sea, faces, friendships, long lunches, iced tea in summer, in short, all that Princeton and his happy summers had meant to him— complicated by the fact that he was now expected to do certain things (marry, begin a career, repay the world what it had given him), he met that figure whose kindness, whose beauty seemed a magic bridge between his youth and the next phase of his existence. He fell in love with Malone while the two of them left the stoop and went down the street that first afternoon to buy peaches on First Avenue; that was all it took. The sunlight glowing on the golden hair of Malone's forearm, the veins in his hand, the peach it held, the dusty trees, transfixed him. He found the city hideous, but in it was Malone. He wished to take him out of it, to stand with him some summer morning on a mountaintop at dawn and watch the fog roll back from the farms spread out below. He wanted to go with Malone to Greece. He had just begun to interpret the world in terms of love, and as is the case with converts, now nothing else mattered. The universe had shrunk to one manifestation of nature: Malone. He watched Malone standing there in the sunlight surveying the cartons of fruit to see what they would take with them, and he felt as if the cherries, peaches, raspberries, and tangerines had not existed until Malone caressed them in his hand. He wanted to buy Malone every peach on Second Avenue. He did not know if the whores were laughing at him, with his arms loaded with peaches when he walked back with Malone, but it did not matter: He felt safe beside Malone.

And when John Schaeffer was not with Malone (which, by Sutherland's machinations, was most of the time), he thought about Malone. His heart was heavy, his throat thick, with the thought of him. He played over and over again in his mind what they had said to one another, how Malone had looked, the moment at which he had walked into the room, Malone's relationship with whoever else was there, Malone's parting words. Malone was so confident, so at ease. He sometimes did not answer his own telephone for days—an indifference to the invitations of life that not only astonished but struck John as extremely erotic: the thought of Malone sitting in his chair, bathed in sweat, while the phone went on ringing and ringing through the hot afternoon with importunate lovers unable to break through the thorns of his perfect indifference.

Malone's parting words to him were subject to the most painful, exhaustive interpretation: What had Malone meant when he said, "Keep in touch"? Or, worse, "Good-bye"? Or, still worse, not even noticed his departure? Malone did not return his calls. John stayed in his uncle's apartment on East End Avenue all day on the chance that he might call. Malone was always out with other people, but when Malone was with him, their moments were so mysteriously moving to John he lay for hours in the study feasting on the memory of them. The phone did not ring. Sutherland ignored him. He seemed to either shower John with invitations or leave him utterly alone. Finally he started going down to the Lower East Side, on the pretext of buying secondhand books or seeing a movie, in the hope that he might run into Malone on the street returning to his apartment from the newsstand. This is the most humiliating and painful stage of love. One warm spring night when Malone had left town for a dinner party in Bucks County, John came wandering down to St. Marks Place after getting drunk himself for the first time in his life at a dinner party at his uncle's and, still in black tie, showed up at the little park on Fifteenth Street.

He paused like a little boy entering a cathedral at the gate of the dark park, as if wondering whether or not to dip his hand in the font of holy water, and then began walking slowly up and down with a pale, frightened face. He knew Malone sometimes came here to smoke a cigarette. He did not wish to appear as if he were looking for Malone—he did not want Malone to realize how he was suffering—but at the same time he hoped desperately his Malone would be here. But the dark figures he peered at as he walked down the benches, half of whom assumed he was cruising and asked him to sit down, were not Malone.

Then he came to us, and he sat down and blurted, "I'm looking for Malone!" We said he was out of town. "Out of town! For how long? When will he be back? Where did he go?" he gasped. And we told him he would be back that night. He was drunk, and excited, and the tension of his search, the warm darkness, made him confess with the gentlest of questions how he felt about our mutual friend.

"He's all the boys I've ever loved in all my life," he said as the black man in the trench coat snored on the bench beside us, and the glowing butts of cigarettes floated about in the darkness like votive candles beneath a shrine, "the boy I fell in love with at Le Rosey, the boy who was mowing the lawn of Hampshire House the day we drove by to my grandfather's funeral, my cousin Paul, the Irish medical student I met in Africa that night in the hut above Ngorongoro, all of them I'll never forget! On my deathbed I will remember their faces! But Malone, Malone is all of them, all of those boys, those summers, the smell of grass when it's cut in August, the heat of a summer day, talcum powder, empty rooms, tiles gleaming, the Swiss lakes, the fir forests around Heidelberg, Malone is all of them!" he said. And with that, he lurched to his feet and rushed out of the park and hailed a cab.

That was the last we saw of them for a while—John went off to Maine, to sail up and down its coast with his family, all in white, and Dr. Valeriani-Winston returned to Argentina. Sutherland remained uptown. Malone went out on calls. It got very hot very soon that summer—tremendous heat that made the East Village almost sensual for a spell: shadows, and breezes, and the sun beating down till dusk, when it broke up and rose in shimmering waves from the pavements toward the clear blue sky. The fire hydrants were open, gushing day and night. Peaches were ripe in the fruit stalls on Second Avenue, the streets south of Astor Place were empty at dusk, and every figure you came upon walking south shimmered for a moment in the distance, then materialized into a group of boys playing ball in a lot littered with broken glass. Even Sutherland, when you ran into him on Fifth Avenue after the office workers had rushed home for a game of tennis in the country before the light had failed, was ecstatic as he stopped to talk, after an afternoon in the men's room at Grand Central, picking pubic hair out of his teeth: "Oh, my dear, there is no other time, no other time at all, but now, when the city is over-ripe, like a fruit about to drop in your lap, and all the young stockbrokers' underwear is damp! My dear!"

In the worst of the heat, we sat in our park till four in the morning because the apartment was an oven.

The park was the only place to go to get cool in that neighborhood, and as the nights got hotter, it got very crowded. The park was used by two classes of people, who came there at different hours. The first group came early to walk their dogs before going to sleep in the air-conditioned bedrooms of their townhouses, which lined the northern side of the park; they were usually gone by midnight, and then, like ghosts, like gremlins, the derelicts, faggots, drunks, and freaks moved in. It was where the slimiest creatures of the Lower East Side swam to the surface for a moment, in the dark, when the middle class had left the beach, only to go back to the bottom before dawn. At dawn, they vanished. Dawn, that most insulting moment for the homosexual, when the sky goes white above him, and the birds begin to chatter, and still on his knees he looks up from the cock he's been sucking to see the light, like a man making love in a dark bedroom when the door has been flung open. Until that moment, however, it was the perfect place to rub the itchy sore of lust —the perfect cave in which to lick your wounds—for half the lamps did not work, and in the shadows of those trees, it was very, very dark.

We were sitting on our usual bench one hot August night watching the characters come and go. We hadn't seen Malone or Sutherland for weeks and assumed they had gone to Fire Island for good. There wasn't any wind at all, and the dregs of life were busy in the bushes. Around one o'clock a man came in and sat on a bench nearby and began to croon, with the careful modulation of the would-be nightclub singer, songs by Cole Porter and Rodgers and Hart. "I've got you . . . under my skin," he sang, loud, as if trying to project to the balconies, the farthest tables at El Morocco, "I've got you . . . deep in the heart of me." And after a few songs, the black men trying to play craps farther down the benches yelled, "Shut up!" and he went right on with his extensive repertoire. He sang of a New York City many blocks and many years away from where we sat now—making our own kind of music when he finally left, the beautiful music of regret, rising to a roar like cicadas in high grass in summer:

"But what is life *for*?" a man who ran a bookstore on St. Marks Place said unhappily. "You must admit there is no real reason for us to *do* anything. We have as much *pur*pose in existing as these trees."

"But you'll never find an intellectual reason for living," said the next. "It has to come from the heart. There is no reason per se to live. People do things from the heart, not from reason. There *is* no reason to live."

"Exactly," said another. "But isn't the idea of using our reason the most irrational thing of all?"

"It was so simple," someone else sighed, "when you just had to get an A on your exam. I was very good at that, but now that it's no longer a case of making the Honor Roll . . ." and his voice trailed off.

"Did you see Frank Gilbert last night at Flamingo? He shaved his body," someone said, bringing philosophy down to earth and banishing our malaise with the concrete magnetism of gossip. "And waxed his stomach. He looked incredible!"

"Someone said he never wipes his ass, he goes out dirty on purpose. Now *that's* confidence! And he can get away with it!"

And they went on like cicadas, like crickets, in the summer night, sawing their legs together, a quartet playing the music of regret—regret over places they hadn't lived, decisions they hadn't made, men they wanted to sleep with —till Malone appeared at the western gate and sat down with a cigarette. "Oh, God, I'm exhausted," he said. "I've just come from two enemas and a fist-fucking!"

"Oh, what was it like?" said someone who had been writing fiction for ten years now with no success. "Who were your customers?"

And Malone, knowing this fellow wanted to write a novel about a homosexual callboy, would patiently recount the fantasies he had pandered to that night. He himself always looked so cool as we sat there in the stagnant heat, the thick air laden with the fumes of passing cars lying on our skin like the soiled, damp towels in a cheap bathhouse. He always wore white pants and a pale blue polo shirt, and he always asked how our day had been: our day! Our stagnant little day! Filled with the most awful trivialities! He was like the officer visiting the amputees in the hospital after a battle, and everyone poured out his thoughts to Malone, his complaints, hopes, opinions, and vanities—never dreaming they were of no consequence to the fellow listening. They would have gone on forever. No one listened like Malone. No one asked the intelligent, perceptive questions he did, questions that opened up a further flow of revelation, which would not have stopped if the others had not grown impatient with their woes. Malone would have listened indefinitely. "But tell me about the people you see!" said the fellow anxious to gather material for his novel.

The bright red nylon of a striped bathing suit was sticking out of his coat pocket, and as Malone took this out and held it up, he told us about the man who paid him to stand in his bedroom in these Speedo trunks impersonating the captain of the swimming team. Another client pretended to be a fifteen-year-old German Jew at Buchenwald, and Malone was the camp guard he begged for mercy. Another pretended that Malone and he were in bed at his college fraternity, and that his fraternity brothers would be returning at any moment from a mixer at a nearby sorority. He gave enemas to some, tied up others in their bathtub and pissed on them, or simply sat on the sofa and listened to them talk about their mother. He saw Moroccan millionaires, and Mafia men in Brooklyn, men from Detroit on business trips, bankers and marine biologists, film producers, newscasters, ballet dancers. He impersonated sailors, Viet Nam veterans, British lords, dead cousins. "But the most peculiar," he added, "*and* the most charming, I think, of them all, is the man who comes to town from Cedar Rapids, Iowa, once every two months and who just wants to smell my hair when it's wet." He turned to his interrogators. "But this must bore you all."

"Oh, no!" came a chorus.

"What did you do this evening, for example," someone said. "Did anything crazy happen to you tonight?"

"Well, one extraordinary thing," Malone said, blowing out a stream of smoke. He was tired, and this incident had been more unsettling than he had allowed it to be at the time. "I answered a call on East Sixty-fourth Street," he said after a pause, in a voice hollow with fatigue, "and when the door opened—there was a boy I'd gone to school with, in Vermont! A boy I'd had a crush on, in fact. We were both astonished."

"Did you have sex?" said the novelist, who saw a two-act play trembling on the horizon.

"No," Malone laughed. "I couldn't. I played soccer with him in school. He was my proctor sophomore year, I worshiped him! So we took out his yearbook and talked about everyone. It was fun." There was a pause, and then someone asked, "Hey, when is the marriage?" for they knew about John Schaeffer.

"Soon, I guess," said Malone. "We're building up to it, gradually. It's like training for the Olympics," he laughed.

He fell silent then, too tired to go on, and caught by the memory of that yearbook photograph with its list of his activities and awards underneath. He sat there thinking that he had, over the past ten or fifteen years, erased that photograph, bit by bit, until that person had vanished utterly. The people he knew now he had not known last year. As homosexuals tend to do, he had simply ceased to communicate with his former world; like a brother who, once he enters the monastery, renounces all his former life. And so he wrote in his journal that night: "I hate to see John Schaeffer falling for all this. I should just say to him, 'Don't bother, it's a mirage.' Or must everyone discover for himself?"

He felt himself growing more and more tired, deep inside, as he sat there, so tired he was unable literally to move. He blessed the darkness, the fact that gradually the people on the bench began slipping away with a deprecating joke to pursue some boy who had just slipped in through the gate. The sudden arrival of a trio we'd never seen before caused everyone but myself to slip off the bench and go after the new boys. Malone and I fell silent for a long time, watching the activity around us, listening to the occasional wail of a siren down Second Avenue. There was something almost peaceful in the park that faced us: the bell tower of the church bathed in floodlights, the banks of leaves etched in brass by the amber-colored streetlights, the flower-bordered fountain, all might have been in a little park in Baltimore or Boston. In fact, as we watched from our dark grotto, a young couple strolled past, arm in arm, as their Irish Setter ran around the cleared space of dust beneath two trees. They stopped and watched the dog run off, and then the man started to call it back. "Sugar! Sugar!" he called. His voice carried in the dark summer night, gentle, calm, domestic: "Su-u-u-u-gar . . ." and finally the Irish Setter burst out of the darkness and stopped, panting, at his feet. The man put the leash on its collar, and together they drifted out of the park, passing for a moment beneath the streetlight. "Oh," Malone said, passing a hand over his face, "how easy it must be, how easy . . . to come out in the evening, to call your dog, to walk home with your wife's arm in yours. Have you ever noticed," he said, stirred now by this vision of domestic bliss that was beyond his reach, and shocked earlier that evening to find himself crying in the subway on his way home from a client, "that gay people secrete everything in each other's presence but tears?

200

They come on each other, they piss on each other, or shit, but never tears! The only sign of tenderness they never secrete in each other's presence. They come, piss and shit together, but they cry alone! God!" he said, with a short, hard laugh. And then beside me I felt a shudder pass through his body and he fell silent. A man stopped at the bench and held out his hand. Malone removed a roll of bills from his pocket and gave it to him. The bum walked on, too drunk to know how much had been given him. It was the money Malone had earned by impersonating so many dreams, on his trips to these apartments all over town. He liked to get rid of that money as fast as he earned it, spending it on things that left no trace. I looked at his face in the half-light of one of the streetlights. He looked like a man who has been crossing a desert, a place without shadows, for some time now. He resembled those people at the beach in summer who fell asleep in the sun and awakened with parched, dry lips, and skin drawn so tight it gave their eyes the hollow look of a prophet who has long been in the wilderness. There was no shelter for him anywhere and so he continued to sit there in the darkness, watching the others look for what had once enraptured him and which now left him sick with loneliness. We were still sitting there, in fact, with some people who were arguing over who had the biggest cock in New York, when Sutherland walked into the park after dropping John Schaeffer off after an evening on the town together. "Oh, you must know!" one of them said to Sutherland. "Doesn't Allan Miller have the biggest dick in New York?"

"He would like to think so," said Sutherland in his most velvet and sinuous voice as he sat down on the bench, fresh as the gardenia in his buttonhole, which he had plucked from the finger bowl served at the dinner he had just left.

"However, the issue is in some dispute. Does Allan Miller have the biggest cock? Or Martin Fox, or Jorge Forbes? Or Mitch Graves, for that matter, who used to astonish the janitor in the men's room at Grand Central when he would pull his rubber hose out at the urinal, and who is now in Saudi Arabia working for TWA. Or some unknown apprentice electrician working for Con Ed? Unfortunately, there is no entry in the *Guinness Book of Records* on this subject, though I am willing to turn over to them the results of my research if they should inquire."

A man with one leg up on a bench across the path reached down now to insert his pack of cigarettes into his sock. "Oh, I like that," Sutherland cooed. "I find that *very* Merchant Marine, very sexy. He keeps his cigarettes in his sock! I bet *he* doesn't read *GQ*! I am looking for a man who has never heard of *GQ, Women's Wear*, or the Twelfth Floor," he explained. "One gets so tired after a while . . . should I marry him?" he said, looking at the man from whose white sock a pack of cigarettes protruded.

"That one has no cock at all," someone said. "We went home together last summer. What a mistake!"

"Please," sighed Sutherland. "I am sure his cock is no smaller than mine," he went on with smooth, drunken confidence, the only homosexual Malone knew who was not afraid to admit this. "Do not be harsh on us untouchables. We lepers of homosexual society. In fact, I have only encountered three cocks smaller than mine, now that we're on the subject of that perplexing organ. The first was a medical phenomenon, an ex-monk I met at the Baths who loved Greeks. The second was a Puerto Rican I sucked off in this very park four summers ago. And the third, oh who was the third? I think a boy in Pittsburgh," he said in a musing voice. "But no matter," he said, sitting up. "A homosexual with a small cock makes no sense, that's all, like a man who rushes to the tennis court without a racquet. An opera singer with no voice. Oh, there are hundreds of analogies," he said, but by this time he was talking to Malone, for the others, depressed by this dreary subject, had all gone off to find someone unafflicted in this way. He immediately turned to Malone, holding the gardenia taken from the dinner he had begun the evening with in a building Malone himself had visited on a call, and said: "Well? Don't you want to know what happened? He asked only for you," he said, not waiting for Malone to inquire. "I did not tell him you were downstairs in Thirty-four B slapping your penis against the face of Louis Rothstein and yelling 'You dirty kike, you!' He was crushed. When we went to the Eagle's Nest afterward, where he nearly fainted—"

"Fainted?" said Malone.

"The boy was struck dumb," said Sutherland, "he was petrified at finding himself in the thick of so many fantasies-made-flesh. When I took him out finally he was shaking like a leaf—but still he asked for you. 'Does Malone go there?' he wanted to know. 'Does Malone like that bar? Who were Malone's lovers?' Whenever I propose anything, he asks if you will be there. I have told him you are too busy to run around with ne'er-do-wells like me, and then he asked if I couldn't get you to come to a party, a really big party, if we gave one on Fire Island. He would not be dissuaded. I had to give in. And so," he sighed, "two weeks from tonight, we are giving at the house in the Pines the fete of the season, we are giving," he said, blowing out a stream of smoke, "the Pink and Green Party. And all, *mon cher*, for you."

"The Pink and Green Party?" said Malone, weakly.

"Yes, darling," said Sutherland. "I could think of nothing else at this time. Fellini has been done, Carmen Miranda has been done, Egypt too," he said, ticking off the great and famous parties on Fire Island of the past five years, "Leo has been done, the Big Heat, the Black Party, the White Party, the Fantasy, Magic, and Dreams, the Quo Vadis, the Bombay in July, they have *all* been taken, darling, and we cannot, like any artist burdened by the tradition of those who have gone before, like the novelist who must write after Proust, Joyce, and Mann, we are faced with a constricted area of choice, not to mention a deadline of two weeks. Ah," he said, as a boy staggered out of the bushes zipping up his leather pants, "it is so good to get back to the original source, the Ur-text, of it all," he said, looking around at the dark figures bobbing at crotches, "to refresh ourselves with the original mysteries and rites around which, really, our whole lives revolve. It is just this," he said sitting back to regard the life of our lagoon.

"I'm not going to the beach," Malone said. "I don't ever want to go there again."

"Just for one night, darling!" said Sutherland breathlessly. "Just make an appearance, my sweet, and then leave with John. In fact, the whole party is being given so that you two may leave it," he said. "This enormous mass of people is being gathered so that you and he may feel more satisfactorily alone. Do you understand? This party is being given so that you may leave it?"

"God," Malone sighed, throwing his cigarette away and standing up. He turned on Sutherland. "Don't you think the moral thing to do is just tell John Schaeffer to go back to Princeton, his family's house in Maine, his suite of rooms, and forget this charade? There isn't what he thinks there is out there, and he might as well be told. Look where it got me!"

"Oh, dear," sighed Sutherland, "would you at this moment prefer to cease upon the midnight with no pain?"

"Kind of," said Malone.

"But don't you see that this is all there is?" said Sutherland. "Don't you know what it means to be a woman? My grandmother on her eighty-ninth birthday only wished she could walk down the street and be looked at!"

"Oh, God," Malone said.

"There will be two salsa bands," said Sutherland, walking away with him, "and we will draw up the guest list tomorrow, in deepest secrecy, of course. I am confining it to two thousand intimate friends. Guards, and numbered invitations . . ." he said as they wandered out of the park, Malone's head down as he went, staring at the ground. In a moment the first birds began to make their noise, and by the time Malone and Sutherland had disappeared down the depressing waste of Second Avenue, the sky was turning light, leaving the pale, human, wasted faces no longer mysterious or beckoning. It was as if a sink had been emptied by someone pulling the plug: the green water gone, odd things clinging to the porcelain. Within five minutes the park was empty and then a local character came in with a ladder and pail and went around to each tree, on the innocent mission, his own spontaneous deed, of feeding the squirrels.

8

IT was very hot that summer by the end of June and even queens who cared nothing about dancing had taken their tambourines to Fire Island. The city was deserted, and Sutherland found a house in the Pines taken by an Italian princess whose husband had once been his lover. Even when he was on welfare his first summer in New York, he managed—like so many others in the same straits—to make the annual migration to Fire Island; it hardly mattered how you got there, who you were, or where you came from. He was handsome; he was witty; he was taken in, even though he moved soon afterward to the more domestic pastures of East Hampton. But there was a part of his character that always brought him back to Fire Island. It was there he could wander down to meet the arriving boats in a nun's habit, it was there he could have two hundred intimate friends over for drinks and to see him burn his Lacostes. It was there he would appear at dawn on the deck of a strange house, daiquiri in hand, claiming to have just seen a man get fucked by another man's wooden leg in the dunes, where he had gone simply to chant his mantra to the rising sun. Fire Island was for madness, for hot nights, kisses, and herds of stunning men: a national game preserve annually replenished by men who each summer arrived from every state in the Union via an Underground Railway of a most peculiar sort. Dressed as Harriet Beecher Stowe, Sutherland went down to the dock each time a boatload of new protégés was to arrive.

The fact that there was little in their heads was what finally shifted his loyalties to the Hamptons, however, where, if the homosexuals tended to be fatter, older, and attired in pastel-colored slacks, they could at least discuss, over cocktails on a clipped lawn, Samuel Beckett or the latest novel of Iris Murdoch.

As for Malone—though now the most gorgeous stretch of beach was inferior in his mind to the most dingy street of the Lower East Side where Ramon and Angel were playing handball against a tenement wall—he felt he had found Paradise his first visit to Fire Island; and it took him three or four summers to even admit it was anything else. Both Sutherland and Malone, in fact, had been coming out to the resort more summers than they cared to admit; for it was always there, all summer long, and irresistible, at the very least, to people who loved to dance. And so Sutherland—who found it vulgar—and Malone—who found it cruel—still came, because nowhere else on earth was natural and human beauty fused; and because nowhere else on earth could you dance in quite the same atmosphere.

Each summer saw a hundred parties, but Sutherland's was greeted with great anticipation: because of the house it was to be given in, because of Sutherland's reputation, because it was the perfect time to end the season with a blowout. The guest list was already a matter of sensation, and the usual rumors that Liza Minnelli and Truman Capote were coming circulated the community. They were rumored to be coming several times each summer, and rumored to have been there, but were never seen. This year Florinda Balkan and Bianca Jagger were mentioned besides. Sutherland laughed his low, throaty laugh. It had entered his mind to give a really tasteless party, to do something against the mode, since he considered the Pines a community of window dressers incapable of intelligible conversation. At the same time his inherent playfulness spurred him to do something astonishing and memorable, and outdo the past; he regretted halfway through the preparations that he hadn't made it an SM affair, since several boys he knew had already offered to hang from a cross and perform unnatural acts onstage during the gala.

He flew out from time to time to see how our work was coming along—he had come down one afternoon and hired us to get the beach house ready. We washed windows, polished banisters, swept decks, and began installing the pink and green panels, the sculptures made of teaspoons, the mannequins, the sacks destined to release carnations, glitter, and pills on the guests. A crew of men from Sayville came over to install the lighting, and the premier discaire of New York came out to hang the speakers and set up the playing booth. Sutherland arrived each time with a different entourage: a man who had been writing novels in Rome for ten years, with no success, a tall, gaunt, bearded fellow who lived in the woods of upstate New York, prophets, intellectuals, artists, models. We walked down to the harbor one day to meet them. "You must write a story, *the* Fire Island story," Sutherland said excitedly under his breath to the novelist as we walked past the big white boats moored in the harbor, "about a very rich Jewess on one of these boats, and a young man, her social secretary, playing canasta on board her boat in autumn.

Oh!" he gasped, as a woman in a cerise caftan came out of the cabin of her Chris Craft and lighted a cigarette as she surveyed the harbor with the grim, puffy face of someone who has just arisen from sleep, "there she is now! Her *entire* fortune is based on vacuum cleaners! Yes!" he said breathlessly. "If you press a single button, her boat vacuums itself! What *will* the children think of next?" He smiled nervously at the world in general, and then hissed suddenly between clenched teeth as we passed two beautiful young men coming from the grocery store like barefoot angels with sacks of yogurt. And he continued muttering, hissing, gasping, and urging us to look at some extraordinary example of philistine display, or physical beauty, as we walked back to the house. "Do you think the reason Americans are boring," he said breathlessly, turning once at the edge of the harbor to look back on the white boats, the boutiques, the awnings, the hotel, "is that they believe in happiness on earth?"

There was a man Sutherland saw nowhere else but here, once a year—a Swiss pediatrician who spent his annual vacation in the Pines the last two weeks of August. Each year they saw each other, the doctor's face grim with longing as he stared at Sutherland on the beach, at parties, in the bar, and each year they failed to speak. For the past month Sutherland had been going daily to a gymnasium to resuscitate the body he brought back to life each year at this time. "My breasts," he said in a husky voice as he leaned forward with arms crossed on his chest and a finger massaging each nipple, "are now bigger than my mother's. It is these breasts they want to suck, and rip, and tear," he sighed, as we walked down the beach. "Do you understand? As Auden says, we want not only to be loved, but to be loved alone," he said as he saw the man on the beach in front of the house he rented each summer, watching him, his annual dream-made-flesh.

"He is sick with lust," Sutherland smiled softly as he paused in the shallow water and pretended to be looking for shells, "he glowers at me, like a dog dying of poison. He has a sensation in the pit of his stomach," he smiled, "which, I am glad to say, is beyond the reach of commercial antacids, beyond the reach even of drugs, beyond the reach of anything but these tits," he said, his hand straying to a nipple and gently touching it, in the pose of Botticelli's Venus arriving on the foam. "Yet he will make no move, and neither will I. Come children," he sighed, beginning to walk down the beach again, "enough meanness for one day."

"What a novel!" said the man from Rome. "Two people come to a beach resort each fall, once a year, they never speak to one another—"

"Never speak," said Sutherland in his low, throaty voice, looking straight ahead as we marched past the people viewing us like guests selecting food from a vast buffet, "and then at the end of their lives, when they are both old, but still coming to this beach resort, they finally speak. And!"

"And?" said the man from Rome.

"You are the novelist," sighed Sutherland.

"But I have no imagination," he said, gnawing his lip as he stared down at the water splashing his ankles. "I can't make anything up."

"What would they say?" someone asked.

"They would say," sighed Sutherland, "one of three things. 'Are you Jewish?' 'Do you come here often?' 'Do you live with your parents?' Love is, after all, my darlings, all anticipation and imagination, and when they finally met they would say something perfectly mundane! Too, too mundane. It is merely the story of Fire Island you have just recounted." He stopped and said, "The story of the Dangerous Island. Well," he sighed, "there is nothing in that direction but what the copywriters refer to as sun, sea, and sky. Let's go back."

He turned in the direction of the Swiss doctor and the people watching the parade of flesh, and said to himself with a shudder, "Oh, God, the years I've wasted here! The dear friends gone!" And then in a louder voice: "We're going home now. Has everyone seen my tits?"

Malone came over Tuesday afternoon to see a client and when he was through, he lay with us on the beach for a while. But he was too keyed-up to lie there like a corpse turning brown. Just when he seemed to have finally surrendered to the stillness, and the others were nearly asleep, he sat up suddenly and lighted a cigarette and stared at the people passing by along the water's edge. "You must admit," he whispered to me as he lay back down with a sigh, "that sunbathing is far more arduous than chopping down trees. I'd rather be clearing a forest," he said, blowing out a stream of smoke, and then smiling at me. And finally, when the others had gone back to their houses to shower and dress for Tea Dance, and he and I remained behind to enjoy the dusk, he said: "You know, I spent the whole afternoon sunbathing on the beach between a discaire and one of Gotham's biggest dealers. A drug dealer, a callboy, and a discaire. This has been," he smiled gently, looking out at the wheeling gulls, the foam turning gold and rose in the setting sun, the clear blue sky, "the nadir of my life." He laughed and lay back down again and fell silent. The moon appeared, very clean and very silver, and the skein of clouds strung across the sky, no larger than the fantail of a passing jet, turned gold, and apricot, and lavender. Later, when everything was turning blue again, he was lying on his stomach watching two people struggle with a kite, when he said in an idle, musing voice, "Isn't it peculiar, where you end up through what seem like such minor decisions? Really, in life, if you just let yourself float," he said in the voice of a child wondering over some extraordinary fact, "you can end up anywhere! There are tides flowing anywhere!" he said, looking over at me with his chin still resting on his hands.

"Why," I said, "do you think you've wasted your life?"

"Does it matter?" he smiled. "And do I have enough strength to save it? If I do want to?" he said.

He shuddered, got to his knees, and turned to look out to sea, where two shrimp boats were marooned on the horizon. Down the beach, in both directions, people faced the sea in the Lotus position, meditating. The sky behind us was a tumult of gold- and salmon-colored clouds in the west, and before us the day had already died, unwitnessed, to give birth to the primal dream of this particular place, the musical, glittering, erotic night. Everyone—everyone except us, and the people meditating on the ridge of sand facing the sea—was preparing now for that magical night, showering, dressing, locating the pills they would take at nine o'clock after a light supper so that by midnight the night would be even more illusive.

Already people in white pants, their faces blooming with a day spent by the sea, in the sun, were walking up the beach to cocktail parties in Water Island; a very popular model came down with her Afghan and her agent, to stand at the water's edge on tiptoe, in the pose of a nymph by Maxfield Parrish, as she held up a transparent blue scarf that fluttered from her fingertips in the breeze; and two lovers lingered to play with one another in the surf, their bathing suits cast on the sand, their buttocks white as the chaste moon floating above the green waves in which they stood waiting for the next breaker.

"Why am I such a puritan?" Malone said all of a sudden. He stood up, gathered his towel and cigarettes, and looked down at me, as if I could answer him. "A puritan is like an inveterate criminal," he smiled. "He can never be reformed." Then he excused himself to get ready for the seven o'clock boat back to the mainland, and walked off, leaving the world to twilight and to me.

It became very hot in the city—so hot we lay in bed at night, immobile and streaming with sweat. Cats lay about the sidewalk in the sprawl of animals who've been struck by automobiles. Everyone moved into the street and sat there as long as he could till it was time to go to bed. Sutherland and Malone went back and forth to the beach, which bored Malone to distraction at this point, since he was in love with the very heat of the city. He loved to go downstairs in the morning and find the Puerto Ricans walking down the streets with their shirts dangling from their pockets. He would set off these summer days to wander the city. He wandered the streets and parks with the deep pleasure of someone who is saying good-bye to a place, which, once it has been relegated to the past, now seems especially touching. He lay on the grass in Central Park watching the faces that had so held him in thrall pass by, or flash about in games of soccer on a dusty field.

Malone realized at this point in his life that he had ceased to be a homosexual, so much as he had become a pederast. The fellow who caused him to stop one afternoon and sit down on a grassy rise to watch the soccer game was no more than twenty, in the first flush of beauty; and yet, as he ran with the ball through clouds of dust stirred by the game, Malone watched him with a certain detachment, earned by years of desperation. Five years before, this person would have stabbed him in the heart, engendered such despair that he would have obsessed Malone the rest of that day and night; and he would have gone out to the bars or baths hoping to find someone of his type. And the next afternoon he would have returned to the Sheep Meadow on the chance that he might be playing. Now it was something else. He wore old white gym shorts and a faded red polo shirt. He had black, black hair and large dark eyes and he had not spent the summer in the sun for his skin was ivory-white. Years before, Malone would have gone home and called someone up and said, "You should have *seen* the kid I saw in the Park today!" as if something, someone had to memorialize such wonders. Now he simply accepted it. Now he knew very well that this young man's beauty was just that—a fact: his beauty—and that he, Malone, could not worship it, or worse (the fault of so many people he knew still), possess it, consume it, digest it. The boy's beauty became for Malone as he lay there on the grass watching him run around in those clouds of white dust, handsome as a myth on the plain of Troy, an impersonal fact, as impersonal as the beauty of a tree, or a sky, or a seacoast, a fact that did not compel him to embrace it any more than it seemed necessary for him to embrace a particularly lovely copper beech. He lay there watching the boy play his heated game of soccer, but he looked at the clouds passing over the sun, too, and when the team finally broke up and walked across the grass toward Central Park West, Malone rose and walked away, a calm spirit.

And so Malone came that afternoon to a kind of truce with the city: He was leaving it, now he had found a way, and its faces no longer kept him there against his will. He was free. Free to go. Free even to please Sutherland one last time and show up at the party on Fire Island, which till now had seemed reprehensible. He was very cheerful when we all got on the train, for a reason we could not imagine, and sat down with Sutherland, who promptly fell asleep. Halfway to Sayville a young man with moustache and glasses, looking as if he were on his way home from a piano lesson in Kew Gardens, sat down across from our little band of gypsies, and after half an hour of staring at Malone with the bright intensity of an anarchist about to blow up the train, began to masturbate. "How many people I fell in love with on this train," Malone said as he raised his head from his book, his eyes sparkling. He nudged Sutherland and explained in a low voice why we would have to move; but Sutherland only yawned and said, "It depends, darling, on how big it is." He leaned forward and then remarked: "My dear, I don't think that's any reason to call the porter. If there is a porter on this ancient caboose," he murmured, closing his eyes again; and then the train came to a stop and the conducter shouted, "Sayville!" and we all said good-bye to Sutherland and got off.

Sutherland remained on the train to go to East Hampton to pick up a wig a woman had borrowed from him months ago, "and with the usual tact of the obscenely rich," he said with that breathless high dudgeon, "allowed her Irish wolf-hound to pee on it and then forgot to return it to me." The wig, he learned on arriving in East Hampton, had gone back to the city the previous week with the woman's maid, and so, Sutherland, on the eve of his party, found himself riding back and forth across Long Island in stuffy trains pursuing his favorite false hair. "The story of a generation!" he gasped when he finally arrived by seaplane the next afternoon in the Pines. His arrival was a sight I shall not forget, in fact: Sutherland on the pontoon of the seaplane as it drifted into shore shortly after three, spike heels in one hand, a daiquiri in the other, and a bright red wig on his head, and tiny pearl earrings. He had fourteen pieces of luggage for us to take to the house, and was nonplussed when he learned Malone was somewhere far down the beach in another town reading the collected works of Saint Augustine.

"Mummy's very nervous," he said breathlessly as we came up to him, wading into the water, "about too many other things. Have the flowers come?"

We assured him they had, and then hoisted the Vuitton onto our heads.

"I'm so sorry about the luggage," he said, "I know it's pretentious." He gnawed at his lip. "But it wasn't when my grandmother bought it, in 1926."

We followed him ashore, like slaves in the Cameroons following their master, past the crowded deck of the Botel where four hundred glossy homosexuals drank cocktails beside the white Chris Crafts on which Jewish families played canasta, oblivious to the mob ten feet away; a talent for ignoring people bred in the elevators of New York.

"Do you think this house," said Sutherland, as he wiped his brow in the resplendent, mirrored living room, "is ostentatious enough? They offered me the one next door at four thousand the month, but I told them it wasn't enough. No," he said as he strolled about, "I wanted something really meretricious. So this is the room in which we are to give our daughter away. Reading Saint Augustine," he snorted, "in Point o' Woods. Malone has, I'm afraid to say, a streak of melancholy that is quite unfortunate—though half the secret of his success. We're all in love with the sadness of life—that wistful, grave, forlorn rue that suffuses his eyes like a perfume of Guerlain whose name I can't recall. I've tried to keep him blithe," he said, standing at the glass door and staring out at the sea, "but he wants more than Estee Lauder can give, poor baby. Reading Saint Augustine indeed! He's a perfect match for John Schaeffer, who, if he reads one more book, is going to ruin his complexion. Well," he said, turning back to arrange the gladiolas and white nasturtiums in a spray more to his liking. "Darling, is there any Perrier in the fridge?" he said, removing a pill from his little box. "Mummy thinks she'd like to take a nap."

He went to the glass wall and stared out at the bodies baking on the beach in the crisp, ferocious heat, just over a sand dune. "You don't think they'll get so burned they will be in a bad mood and come to our do with tempers as hot as their skin. Well," he sighed, turning away to ascend the polished staircase, his fragile form reflected in half a dozen mirrored walls, "one can't, at their age, insist they come in out of the sun and take a nap . . . which is what sensible girls from Richmond have done since they were tiny tots . . ." His voice trailed off, and he turned on the balcony to regard the room below, as a hand strayed up to remove the pearl clip earrings. "Do you quite know," he said, "what it means to be a mother? To bring out of the womb a child, and rear this child, worrying about her teeth, piano lessons, first period? To get her the best French teacher, the best playmates, the best schools. To hope against hope that she will be beautiful and witty and wise? And then to have her reject the millionaire you've chosen? If you *knew* how John Schaeffer is suffering!" he gasped.

"Malone said the only reason he would go through with this affair tonight is the chance that John will meet someone else and fall in love. The reason, of course, everyone comes to this island. Lord, what fools these mortals be!" he sighed. "Awaken me only for the most vile of emergencies! Otherwise, I wish to sleep, and receive the full benefit of my moisture-pack!" And with that, he turned and vanished in a billow of white curtains, murmuring about the ghosts of parties past.

As Sutherland surrendered to the white pill he had extracted from the little silver case, sacks of ice arrived in wheelbarrows trundled over from the grocery store, and the caterers set up the bars around the rooms. Outside, the beach emptied as people went back to get their costumes ready and the beautiful, unnoticed twilight fell on the deserted sea. To the seaplanes descending from the violet sky the Island glowed one last instant in the rays of the sun sinking into the Great South Bay. Its golden dune grass caught the light and burned an intenser gold as the rest of the Island was bathed in blue light and rumors of suicide. It lasted, this peerless dusk, for just an instant as Malone sat gossiping on the harbor dock, and he came nearer to the people in the seaplanes, with the faces, trees, and boats, and they could almost hear the soft roar of gossip rising from the holly trees. Everyone at Tea Dance was talking about the boy who had jumped to his death that afternoon from a rooftop in the city, and when that topic was exhausted, their love affairs of the previous week, the new faces, the music last night, the party to come, and—at least in the circle who sat with Malone when I arrived at the dock and joined him there—how they planned to fly back to the city after the party to go to the Everard Baths. Before leaving to return to their house for cocktails, they had persuaded Malone that he would fly back with them.

But once they left Malone looked at me with a smile and only shrugged: happy to watch in silence the air turn milky blue, the white steeples and sails across the bay, without the demands and needs of other people. A great peace descended on us. We hardly had a thing to say to one another because we had seen this so many summers. I glanced at the fellow beside me. He was one of us now—and I began to wonder why Malone had fascinated us so. He wasn't, in the end, any of the things we had thought all these years: a doctor, a designer, a victim of bone disease, an Episcopalian protégé. Of all the faces we had been in love with, some in fact had been these things; but most of them, whoever they were, had disappeared to farms upstate, California, or the Hamptons. Only we were still on the circuit. In a country where one is no more than what one does (a country of workers) or the money one possessed, Malone had ceased, like us, to have any identity at all. He was simply a smile now, a set of perfect manners, a wistful promise, as insubstantial as the breeze blowing the hair across his forehead. And he had been, all those years, just as lost as we were, living on faces, music, the hope of love, and getting farther and farther away from any chance of it. In a year he would be cleaning houses and living alone in some obscure room in the East Village and seeing none of his former friends; and when he went out to the old places to dance, he wouldn't dance—but stand on the edge of the floor, dancing alone, perhaps, or shaking a tambourine when an especially good song came on. It happened to us all. It was either that, or travel somewhere else, like Montana, Oregon, where he could begin the illusion again, with new faces, bodies, eyes to fall in love with: the occasional stranger passing through. A beautiful dark-eyed boy in a red bathing suit was floating past on a sailboat at that moment. He looked at Malone. Their glances held, and the dark-eyed youth continued moving, out into the channel, turning his head in the sunset breeze to keep his eyes on Malone as long as he could, until his boat was but a blue and rosy blur in the viscous dusk settling on the bay. "That's where I want all my relationships," Malone smiled. "Disappearing into the sunset in the West." For there were Latin youths in San Francisco, surely, and in Chicago, too; in Los Angeles, and in the public parks of Bogotá and Rio de Janeiro. This thought—of all the boys he might sleep with still (the comfort of every romantic heart)—vanished in the memory of the one boy he had not slept with, when another boat went by. It bore four water-skiers going out for a final run, and one of them, a handsome Puerto Rican doctor, called to Malone: "Did you hear about Bob? It broke my heart!" And Malone only nodded, and then shook his head.

It was the most beautiful illusion of homosexuals and romantics alike: if only I'd loved that one . . .

What had that twenty-three-year-old young man, whose blond beauty had caused even Malone to believe in the springs of his wasted youth again the day he saw him at the gym, done by dying? His face took on a sad cast as he spoke of the news that had put the whole island into shock, as shocked as it could be, and which, as he spoke of it now, made Malone's limbs begin to tremble under his cotton shirt. That twenty-three-year-old beauty who had his whole life before him; that boy from Idaho—who had slashed his wrists, and then his throat, and then hurled himself nine floors from the top of his apartment building to the steaming pavement below on this hottest of all hot afternoons just four hours ago in the city? What had he accomplished by that? Malone knew the dead boy's lover, he had been Malone's own ideal once, and their love had been for him one of the reassuring things of this neurotic life; and now the boy, with his fine bones, his gazellelike grace, his long thighs, and high buttocks, had slashed his veins, hurled himself down to that soiled, grimy sidewalk Malone himself had walked nearly every day, lined with a dozen cheap grocerias and bodegas in front of which men sat drinking whiskey and making bets. This blond youth from Idaho had smashed himself against the hot, hard sidewalk before the eyes of those drunken cardplayers, hating his youth, his beauty, his lover. Of all the people Malone had listened to, had tried to help, he now felt responsible somehow for this one's suicide; for he had spent many afternoons at the YMCA with him doing gymnastics. "Why didn't I sleep with him?" he said. "When we're all so terribly alone. The least we can do in this life is love one another . . . just a hug and a kiss . . ."

He was right, of course; but how could you love everyone? If only enough of us loved enough—perhaps by some arithmetical progression, everyone would be given this gift. But that was useless speculation for those of us left behind, who were not going to hurl ourselves off a building in the pressure of a summer heat wave, a lover's quarrel, a drug, I thought as we sat there now. There was no such end for the rest of us, or glorious legacy of love: Fate in America was quite different, as Malone knew staring at the waters at his feet—one went back to work, bought a house, accepted. As a child Malone had consecrated his life to Christ; as an adult, to some adventurous ideal of homosexual love —well, both had left him flat. We sat there in silence for a while as the throngs who had come down to the bay with drinks to see the sunset went back to their boats, and parties, and restaurants. "Well, darling," Malone said, standing up with that necessary ability, acquired over the years, to eschew the serious and return to the blithe, to move, literally, from funeral to party, "I'm off to set my hair and choose the right nail polish." He looked down at me and smiled. "This is my engagement party, after all." And we walked off the dock, even as a seaplane at our backs touched down with John Schaeffer, two elderly designers holding Lhasa Apsos in their laps, and the discaire who would play at Sutherland's party, a seventeen-year-old Moroccan from Brooklyn they had discovered on one of their forays to the boroughs.

By the time the pontoons touched the water, darkness had descended, and John Schaeffer came ashore into a crowd of people streaming home from Tea Dance, brushing their bare chests, bronze arms, listening to their warm voices spilling laughter and gossip on the evening air. The lights in the harbor came on, their reflections trembled in the water, a breeze fluttered the awnings, and the millionaire and the discaire—who had never been here before—searched up and down the boardwalks till they found Sutherland standing in a nightgown and wig atop a house blazing in floodlights and a mist of sea salt. Sutherland had awakened to eat supper. The three of them shared fried chicken, as Sutherland, still groggy with sleep, tried to dispose of John Schaeffer's excited questions. "These men I flew out with," John Schaeffer said, "one was taking a German friend here for the first time, and I overheard him tell the German, 'You must remember that the boys who come out here are all in love with themselves.'" He put down the fried chicken. "Do you think that's all it is?" said John Schaeffer. "They're in love with themselves?"

Sutherland dangled a wing and looked at him, speechless, for a moment. "Well, surely you know we homosexuals are just a form of ingrown toenails . . ."

222

"But—" said John Schaeffer. "But I'm in love with Malone, not with myself."

"Of course," said Sutherland. "Oh, don't worry," he sighed, nibbling at the wing, "you have a cock thick as a sausage, love will most certainly come your way in one form or another. By the way," he said to the discaire, "what are you doing tonight? I think it very important for the hostess and the discaire to be on the same drug. Do you think I should have put it on the invitation? I suspect that most girls will be doing THC, don't you?" And they began to discuss, Sutherland and the discaire, the various drugs that had risen and fallen in popularity that summer, and if any Angel Dust had arrived recently from the Coast. John Schaeffer took this opportunity to move to the sink and begin washing dishes as he listened to this outlandish conversation.

"Oh," Sutherland yawned, "I'm too *old* for this. Centuries ago these affairs used to leave me a quivering lump of jelly, but now, I want them all to go home, and they haven't even come. Oh good evening, darling," he smiled as the first huge headdress swayed through the door.

There are parties and there are parties on Fire Island, and Sutherland, who had devoted himself to nothing very purposefully the past fifteen years of his life, had learned along the way to give a party: He had been to so many, he knew exactly why the great ones were great. It was a public event. People had come by train and boat for this one, from the Hamptons, and Montauk; from Paris and San Francisco by plane. People from the past he had not seen in five years reappeared and were lined up on the boardwalk outside, feathers rustling in the breeze. People had spent a week's salary on their costumes, had made sure *Women's Wear* would be there, and *Interview*; someone from cable TV was interviewing the guests on the boardwalk for Anton Parrish; but so strange were most of the faces to Sutherland, that he was grateful to be suddenly embraced by the Swamp Lady —an ancient queen who had been coming to the Pines since it was a collection of shacks occupied by poets, and who had seen it become a Malibu mobbed each summer by hordes of youths. She came. Theatrical agents and actresses, models and a new designer's entourage; the Warhol stars of ages past; men who flew in from Topeka and Dallas, eye surgeons from Omaha and Phoenix; boys who had been living in Rome for ten years: All of them came. To Sutherland's dismay. "My dear," he breathed as another crowd of strange queens went by, "who are these people?" And they began lamenting their old age.

By three the discaire was playing sambas for this crowd of unknown creatures, and the platform built over the pool had begun to bounce visibly to the beat of the dancers, when a stockbroker from Kuhn, Loeb cleared the floor to whirl around in a passionate dance in swirls of pale green organdy. Sutherland tried to place a scene vaguely similar in his mind: Had he cleared the floor at the Leo Party in 1969 too? In the same dress? But the memory failed him, and he sighed and said to Malone: "Each tab of acid, they tell me, destroys a hundred neurons."

So Sutherland and Malone gawked at a quintet of handsome Latin youths who were dancing with their arms on each other's shoulders under the holly tree. "Young girls who come into the canyon," Malone decided.

At four there was a commotion in the room and they were delighted to recognize Lavalava and Spanish Lily at the door arguing with a guard. "She threw garbage in my face!" the guard said. "She doesn't have an invitation and I told her to go home!" Lavalava flicked a pink boa at the guard and began expelling a rapid stream of Spanish. "Oh, she may stay!" Sutherland said, loyal to his nights at the Twelfth Floor and remembering that Lavalava had murdered a friend of his years ago by voodoo. "We don't want her going home and making little dolls of *us*," he murmured to Malone. The furious guard left. Lavalava beckoned to a companion to come forward, a tall, dark, handsome man in pink tights and green suspenders over his bare chest. There was something prepossessing about him as he stood for a moment surveying the crowd, something still, motionless, and sinister even before Sutherland gasped: "Frankie!"

Was it Frankie? Or someone who looked like Frankie, for there are a dozen Frankies every season on the circuit in New York: dark, saturnine boys with grave eyes and faces that one instantly imagines on a pillow in a shadowy room. There were several Frankies at this party alone, and when Malone arrived from his dinner party in Water Island and Sutherland told him his fears, Malone said, "Oh, I know, he was on the boat coming over. Don't worry. It's over at last. He's staying with this rich old Cuban feather queen, he loves the Island, he has as much interest in me as a used popper." They watched the real Frankie from the balcony, standing on the floor beneath them in a circle of people who were putting poppers to his nose, and dancing around him, and when Frankie stripped off his shirt, Malone smiled. For it had come full circle. It was the final proof, the final piece of data that confirmed Malone's view of the whole world: watching Frankie dance without his shirt, adored by all the people near him, conscious of his beauty. And he wasn't the only one. Malone stood with Sutherland on the balcony marveling over the number of them. So many of the people at this party they did not even know— especially the young ones, come into the canyon for the first

time, quiet as deer, some of them, coming to your hand for
salt: their dark eyes wide and gleaming with the wonder
and fear we had all felt at seeing for the first time life as
our dreams had always imagined it . . . at seeing so many
others like themselves, at seeing so many people with whom
they could fall in love. The old enchantment composed of
lights, music, people was transfixing them for the first time,
and it made their faces even more touching.

Friends came up to embrace Malone, people he had
known for years—how many years, they did not want to
think. They were all looking at the new faces with an odd
sensation of death, for they had all been new faces once.
Each summer on Fire Island has a star: the boy who moves
through the little society with the youth and beauty he has
just begun to squander (and what else can be done with
them?). The old friends embracing Malone and Sutherland
had each had his summer, had once caused hearts to lurch
when they walked into a party like this, quiet and nervous
as fawns. And now they were wondering—as men had
wondered about them—if they could get any of these stars
into their beds, or were they older than they thought they
were? Were they as old as X, that man who had stared at
them their first summer with that terrible despair in his face,
and whom they had refused even to meet? None of this
bothered Malone. In his mind he was seeing this for the last
time. He could enjoy it as he hadn't since he first arrived on
the Island how many summers ago.

"*Look* at that one!" Malone would cry as he grabbed the
person he was standing with, in a voice charged with that
delight which everyone loved in him, and which they flocked
to after their own capacity for wonder had vanished. "To
die! To die over! And what about the green T-shirt! Oh
my Christ! Get me a transfusion! I am dead on arrival! He's

flawless!" And he would turn and say to John Schaeffer, who stood beside him wanting to ask Malone to dance but having no idea how to, "You must admit this place is incredible—we, who've grown used to it—" "Just a bit," breathed Sutherland, flicking an ash onto the crowd below. "Forget the sheer style, and beauty," resumed Malone, "in this room. It's all *we'll* ever see of the Beatific Vision!" "I'm glad you like it," said John Schaeffer with a smile. "Oh, I loathe it," said Malone. "Loathe it? Why?" gasped John, staring at Malone. "Because . . . because . . . oh, I guess because I'm thirty-eight," said Malone, "I'm afraid that's all it comes down to. You have all this before you, and I have all this behind me," he said to John Schaeffer. "I'm in mid-passage, darling," he said, beginning to talk like a queen so as to demystify himself, so as to destroy the very qualities John Schaeffer had fallen in love with, "I'm menopausal, change of life, hot flashes, you know. Wondering how much longer I can go without hair transplants and whether Germaine Monteil really works on the crow's feet. I've had it, I've been through the mill, I'm a *jaded queen.* But you, dear, you have that gift whose loss the rest of life is just a funeral for—why else do you suppose those gray-haired gentlemen," he said, nodding at his friends on the floor, "make money, buy houses, take trips around the world? Why else do they dwindle into a little circle of close friends, a farm upstate, and become in the end mere businessmen, shop-owners, decorators who like their homes filled with flowers and their friends flying in on Air France and someone pretty like you at the dinner table? It is all, my dear, because they are no longer young. Because they no longer live in that magic world that is yours for ten more years. Adolescence in America ends at thirty." And John Schaeffer stood there, dumbfounded, not wanting to hear any of this, because he loved Malone. "You have ten years of adolescence stretching before you," said Malone in an acid tone, stubbing out a cigarette in a plate of aspic, "and *I* am a professional faggot. What is gay life," he said, looking down at the dancers, "but those bumper cars at an amusement park, that crash and bounce off each other? Like some Demolition Derby." He put his hand on John Schaeffer's shoulder and said in a kind voice: "You must remember one thing, if I can leave you with anything, if my years out here can benefit you at all, then let it be with this. Never forget that all these people are primarily a visual people. They are designers, window dressers, models, photographers, graphic artists. They design the windows at Saks. Do you understand? They are a visual people, and they value the eye, and their sins, as Saint Augustine said, are the sins of the eye. And being people who live on the surface of the eye, they cannot be expected to have minds or hearts. It sounds absurd but it's that simple. Everything is beautiful here, and that is all it is: beautiful. Do not expect anything else, do not expect nourishment for anything but your eye—and you will handle it all beautifully. You will know exactly what you are dealing with," said Malone, his arm around John Schaeffer as they faced the crowd of beautiful dancers.

"But I don't want to deal with it," said John Schaeffer now, turning to Malone. "I want to go around the world with you. Go anyplace you like. I love you," he said now.

"Oh, God!" Malone said with a laugh and simultaneous shudder that passed through his upper torso. "Those words. Expunge them from your vocabulary, it will save you a lot of trouble. You don't love me. I am a professional faggot. Now what other lessons can I pass on to you?" he said, moving on to put that moment behind them. "Indifference is the greatest aphrodisiac," he began carefully, trying to sum up in three minutes the experience of ten years on the circuit, and distill it properly for this fellow to whom he was passing the torch, "never underestimate the value of indifference, it is, finally, the great freedom. *Try* not to be self-conscious," he said, "or so critical. Don't mope around looking for someone else to make you happy, and remember that the vast majority of homosexuals are looking for a superman to love and find it *very* difficult to love anyone merely human, which we unfortunately happen to be. Oh, God, let's dance!" he said, for they had started to play Zulema.

The discaire was mixing old songs with the new, unlike the mediocre ones in town (who must play new music, music the crowd loves; or worse, music the crowd has never heard), and the old songs brought back the magic of whole summers to the people there. He danced with John Schaeffer in a corner, allowing him finally to be overcome by the music, and showing him without a word a step he could be comfortable with. They danced together as if they were falling in love, but John Schaeffer's love only produced in Malone a gloomy helpless guilt. They faced each other at opposite ends of an illusion. And then those first unmistakable beats of the bass guitar, those first few notes of that song that had made everyone at the Twelfth Floor holler in a communal shout of ecstasy began, those first, repetitive, low notes that had caused Sutherland to say with great hilarity one night: "Each E-flat is like the thrust of a penis," that curious song that had the power—even though it was just a song played at discotheques one year, was never the most popular there, or surfaced in public—to change the whole tenor of the place. Malone drew John Schaeffer nearer to him, closed his eyes, and began shaping the words that Patty Joe sang: "Make me believe in you, show me that love can be true," his eyes wild when he finally opened them.

He came back to the balcony drenched with sweat, his polo shirt sticking to his chest. On his face was an expression of radiant exhilaration; that expression that led people to think Malone took speed, when he didn't. It was his joy that there were men who loved other men. "How is the party, darling?" he said to Sutherland, catching his gloved arm as he swept by in a swirl of taffeta. Sutherland held his cigarette holder in the air and said: "On a scale of one to zero? Beyond credence, dearest," he said, embracing Malone. "Absolutely everyone showed up. Except Pam Tow, thank God . . . Don't mess my hair," he said, drawing back. "Mummy's so pleased. The pigs-in-the-blanket were delicious, the music is to die, and everyone seems to be on the same drug, which is so important. The bathrooms, of course, are filled with people sucking cock, I can't even get to the drawer with my world-famous collection of rare and antique Valiums. Are you happy, dear?" "Yes," Malone said, embracing him again. "Even John is having a good time, and Frankie is the star of the summer." "I never said you hadn't taste," said Sutherland in a sinuous voice. "He's bought a house in Freehold, New Jersey," said Malone, as they sat down for a moment and Sutherland slipped off his satin pumps. "Do tell," said Sutherland, massaging his foot. "Yes, he's making twenty thousand a year now, and he'll have a pension, too. Never say America isn't a worker's paradise!" "Grandfather always said that," sighed Sutherland. "And we haven't got the price of a bus ticket to Denver. Oh, well, we lived for other things," he smiled. Malone put his arms around him and held him close. "At least," he murmured in his ear, "we learned to dance. You have to grant us that. We are good dancers," he said. "And what," said Sutherland, "is more important in this life than that? Nothing!" They grew melancholy in each other's arms as they sat quietly there, suddenly tired for a moment, or was it years, and the party seemed to drift away; and Malone, who had become an insomniac, so anxious was he over his life, began to feel sleepy—the index of happiness—until Sutherland, looking over Malone's shoulder in a daze, noticed a tall, gaunt, bearded man standing in the hallway looking glumly at them. "But who is that?" said Sutherland. And Malone, looking around, replied in his ear: "Roger Denton. The size queen who moved to San Francisco because he had had everyone in New York. She's back, dear, and looking for new meat."

"Oh la," sighed Sutherland, his arms still around Malone's neck, "send her to that village in the Philippines filled with young men who are all that way. Don't worry," he smiled back at Malone as he slipped out of his arms and stood up to greet this guest. "I have our tickets already. Darling! How are you? Was San Francisco what they say, a weekend city?" And he embraced a giant praying mantis who had just arrived behind Roger Denton.

The crowd suddenly roared as the lights went out, and the room was bathed in a low red feverish glow, and John Schaeffer appeared at the same instant at the top of the stairs, white-faced, terrified. "I waited for you," he said to Malone, his eyes anguished. Malone took his hand and led him to the balcony and put his arm around him as the violins of "Love's Theme" began their ascent, and they leaned on the balustrade to look down at the scene.

An hour later Malone pushed John Schaeffer down the stairs in front of him, for at that moment "Law of the Land" had begun. It was one of those parties that people were not going to leave: Everything was as they wanted it. The people, the music, the drugs, the place. Around five Malone and John Schaeffer, exhausted, sweating, came out onto the terrace where I was cleaning up glasses. John Schaeffer walked back inside to get wine, and Malone walked down the deck to the bay. His face was calm, and innocent, and fresh in the way some faces are after a night of dancing. "Well," he said, as he stripped off his soaked green polo shirt and shoes and waded into the bay, "at least I learned to dance." He saw me there and called: "Tell Sutherland it was a wonderful, wonderful party, tell him I'm going out west, tell him I'll write." He waded deeper as I stood there. "I'll only be happy working in some little town in Idaho, and living a decent life. First I'll build a cabin and then I'm going to dental school," he said, waist-deep now in the still, dark bay, turning one time to wave good-bye, his slim white figure and grave eyes visible in the lights from the throbbing house, and then, with a single splash, suddenly vanished in the darkness. I stood at the water's edge and wondered if I should go after him: especially after listening to his reflections on the young man who had killed himself in Manhattan that afternoon. Someone was always dying at one of these parties, trying to sniff a popper at the bottom of a swimming pool, or jumping off a balcony on Angel Dust, but as I listened I could hear no cries for help. And the warm, dark night descended on me as I stood there with an armful of glasses, napkins, and discarded scarves and ribbons. "Malone!" I yelled. But there was no answer.

Even as Malone was swimming across the bay, Sutherland searched for tranquillity in his own way. He was still at the party when word got back that twelve men had died in the fire at the Everard Baths, and the rumor went around (via one of the boys on the dock that evening who had heard Malone agree to fly back after the party) that Malone had gone up in smoke, too. Did Sutherland think Malone had gone back to the Baths? And assuming the worst, did he go upstairs and take a pill? Or did he go to his room even before Malone had waded out of his life, simply because the party had exhausted him? Whichever is true, shortly before dawn he awoke (as who would not in that deafening house) and reached for another Quaalude. He had taken so many drugs that evening, mixing them in his bloodstream with the equanimity of a chemist in a research lab, and not even remembering what he had taken, half-asleep, he reached reflexively for another pill. He pulled the pillow closer and shortly afterward, while the distant strains of "Love's Theme" crept up the staircase and down the hall, his heart stopped beating. The host of the Pink and Green Party was not discovered, much less thanked, till Tuesday afternoon when a writer who had taken a mid-week share to finish a book on gay consciousness and who planned in fact to interview Sutherland entered the room. The writer found a note on the table beside Sutherland, which he had left to deter any guests who might stray up to his bedroom, and which made no mention of suicide— for Sutherland had little use for suicide and less for suicide notes: "Don't awaken me. It was kind of you to come. I'll call you in the city. Kisses to you." A forest of X's followed, which looked like crosses, but were really kisses.

In a letter Sutherland had once composed on the funeral of his dreams, he was to be laid out on the high altar of the cathedral of Cologne, while an orchestra played "Pavane for a Dead Princess"; but instead he was sent off at Frank

E. Campbell's on Madison Avenue. The wake was exactly the sort Sutherland would have loved, attended by everyone he considered beyond the pale of simple good manners, but who could have danced him into the other world: the crowd Sutherland called "the hard-core tit-shakers," with whom he had danced for nearly twenty years. The dealers and the astrologers and the psychics came. Even in a week that saw many gay funerals, half of Seventh Avenue was there, and people whose names appear monotonously in the columns: a man from Halston's read the eulogy, and one of the two Egyptian heiresses read a few lines from Schopenhauer, and Sutherland was cremated. The coffin was closed, which prompted a hairdresser at Cinandre to ask: "But how do you really know he's dead?" Others came up to an old friend of Sutherland (a retired queen who had been to Sutherland what Sutherland was to Malone) and claimed the dead man owed them money. Others—the old guard of New York psychics who still practiced such things, and felt it a favor to offer their services like this—inquired if they might put us in touch with Sutherland now that he had passed over. A professor from Rutgers pointed out that John Quincy Adams and Thomas Jefferson had died on the same day, not four hours apart, on the Fourth of July; and the departure of Malone and Sutherland on the same night was just as curious, and even more symmetrical, to some queens. The whole ragtag crowd who came, all the people Sutherland had supplied with drugs all those years, were buzzing with it: the models, illustrators, pimps and hustlers, the boys like Lavalava and Spanish Lily who lived only to dance, the yoga gurus and brahmacharyis, the antique dealers and screenwriters, the jewelry designers and doctors, the psychiatrists and weight lifters, the waiters and the copywriters. Nearly everyone assumed Sutherland had killed himself. They talked of karma, and dying the way one had lived, and getting back what you had given out. After all there had been Angel Dust at the party and no one was himself in the hands of that particular drug. And so they went on gossiping that evening, and others that followed. No one bothered to correct anyone's interpretation of the event; it made no difference now, certainly not to the deceased, whose ghostly laughter we could hear whenever we looked at the people in the room: these émigrés of the South Bronx who had become far richer and more successful than Sutherland in careers inconceivable to someone of Sutherland's upbringing; for Sutherland, while he would have been a pimp, would never have been a copywriter.

The tape played at the wake was a tape Sutherland and Malone had once declared the greatest work of art since the Sistine Chapel, made five summers ago, when they had been happiest dancing on Fire Island, by the discaire who was now in Paris recording for a homosexual count. Afterward the mourners went out to the opening of a new discotheque in Soho. There were too many discotheques now, and the songs one heard in them had become what we considered music to roller-skate by. But these people would never stop dancing. The only member of Sutherland's family who came north was a bald, well-mannered brother we didn't know he had; but then one couldn't imagine Sutherland as having a family at all, composed of the usual figures in the usual house on the usual corner, with a driveway in which the children played with the hose on hot summer Saturdays. His mother was ill in Richmond and could not stand the journey. It was just as well, somehow; for most of us forgot that anyone had a family, living among queens in New York City. Families belonged to that inscrutable past west of the Hudson, and when a queen walked out a window, and you heard the family had come east to claim the body, it was like hearing that some shroud had come out of the darkness to pick up the dead and return whence the Three Fates sequestered, in the hills of Ohio or Virginia. There was no family to mourn Sutherland. John Schaeffer was at that moment off the coast of Nova Scotia, reading Proust in a skein of silver sunlight that stretched inviolate for miles around him. The only figure who was missed, and missed by everyone who had seen the two of them together for years, thinking they were lovers, was Malone. It was Malone whose absence was the chief topic of conversation; because by then the rumor had become generally accepted that he had died himself, in the flames of the Everard Baths, and the fact that he was not at the wake was considered proof positive. Malone had gone up in flames with the sleazy mattresses, the queens waking up in drugged confusion in a stranger's arms to find the walls in flame around them, the hundred and thirty beds on which he had adored so many dark-eyed angels like a man drinking at a holy spring.

Whether or not he did, it was that image which I recalled now: of a night in winter, when the Everard had been the place we all went to, especially after a night of blissful dancing at the Twelfth Floor, when the only thing that could cap the music was a lover's embraces. I came upon Malone in the dark hallway of the third floor, beside the little window from which people jumped the morning of the fire, broke their bones and died, like roaches falling from a hot oven. It was cold and snowing that night, and the hallway filled with bodies was even more voluptuous because of it. Malone stood at the window, looking out at the falling snow through the web of ice crystals that had formed on the windowpane, watching the snow fall on Twenty-eighth Street, on the tops of garbage cans, the silver throats of the streetlights; while against him brushed the bodies of the muscular men who wished to catch his eye, thinking that once Malone saw them, they would have him. But Malone continued standing there, within the house of flesh, the Temple of Priapus, staring out at that sparkling snowfall. That was it. That was Malone—standing in the crush of voluptuous limbs, enthralled by the cold, lonely, deserted street.

It was autumn now, however, in the street outside the funeral home, where I stood watching the mourners stream out to go dancing at the opening of Flamingo, and the night was crisp and thrilling. Autumn always gave our lives an inexpressible undercurrent of hope, for winter meant, if not the promise of new love affairs, at the very least a change of clothes. How strange, how perfect, that one did in the end grow tired of summer, and long to leave the beach and see faces in the drama of early darkness once again. I stood there for a moment, the sound of taxi doors closing crisp, the trees fluttering in the frigid wind that had floated down from Canada, along with the geese that even now were flying south down the deserted beach that this crowd had lately quit. Everything—the doors closing, the faces disappearing, to dinner parties, assignations, love affairs, bodies, smiles—was, like Malone, elusive and thrilling. Out of the darkness a voice that resembled Sutherland's addressed us, that low, breathless voice that always gave the impression the speaker had been somewhere marvelous and was going somewhere even more exotic in a moment (the promise, in the end, of New York City). "My dear," said the queen of an earlier generation who had taught

Sutherland much of his style, "do you think the girls are right when they tell us only our lovers are our friends? Or even worse, that each of us has only one friend in Gotham? If he had only awakened from that sleep, Sutherland could be dancing with us tonight. Let us pray, darlings, that he has found an angel like himself and that for those of us still left on earth, the music at this dump will not be too dreadful." And with a wave, he disappeared into the darkness that had fallen early, it seemed, for the first time that evening.

Midnight
The Lower East Side

Darling,

By the way—Spanish Lily OD'd on some strange new drug that even the Angel Dust aficionados won't touch, so we won't be seeing her on the dance floor anymore. John Schaeffer went off to Europe to either hike the German Alps or attend the London School of Economics, or both; with twenty-six million it hardly matters—we'll never see her again. Frankie has become a perfect circuit queen—he left that Cuban crowd, and is now being kept by some guy whose family owns Sydney, Australia. Half those people who used to go to Sutherland's to shoot up have moved to San Francisco, and I heard Rafael opened up a plant store in Queens. For the truth is, darling, what happens to most of these people anyway? They have their fling and then they vanish. They have to take jobs eventually *as telephone operators, bartenders, partners in a lamp shop in some little town in the San Fernando mountains . . . and others take their places . . . but mostly they just vanish, and you forget about them unless you hear, one day, a certain song.*

Well, no one will forget about Malone; I saw a man one evening this winter coming out of 399 Park Avenue in a Chesterfield, his hair very blond, one of those young associates with Shearman & Sterling, I suppose, and my heart stood still. In the depths of all that grayness, in the late-winter afternoon light, that big man as handsome as a prince, as a Nordic warrior: which is what it's all about. All societies, Oliver Wendell Holmes, Jr., said, are founded on the blood of young men; and if they don't get it through a war, they get it some other way just as definite . . .

Everyone is the same here—suicide notes on Monday, found a lover on Tuesday, divorced on Thursday—the only things that change up here, darling, are apartments, haircuts, and winter coats; and good faggots still go to San Francisco when they die. (All the more reason to, now that the Everard is gone; there is just no place to go and everyone's in a funk over it. Do you know they have fifteen major baths in San Francisco?) Write soon. I await your reaction to the novel.

Rima the Bird Girl

The Deep South
Stinking Hot

Raison d'Être,

The novel is more vivid than I had expected, and frankly brought back things that are a little too close to me still. I had to leave New York, you know, not for any practical reason but for a purely emotional one: I simply couldn't stand to have it cease to be enchanted to me. How could it? Our hearts can't change, and yet those riots of the soul that carried us on, sequined swimmers in that aquacade of

240

sex, simply failed us one day and we looked up, as if the refrigerator had stopped humming and the current in our apartments had failed. Those streets, those corners, every one of which I loved, were just streets, just corners. Malone was possibly more committed to it than any of us—whatever "it" was—for to be perfectly honest, I cannot name the disease, the delirium of the last ten years; even now, having thought and thought about it, I have no idea why I was living that way unless, if you'll excuse me (now that our hair is down, earrings off and shoes too), it was for the same reason a man as reasonable as Malone goes out into the street at night: because he is handsome, infertile, and lonely.

As to where he went—if he ever finished that swim across the bay—I've heard a half-dozen different things. Lots of people in New York are convinced he died at the Everard Baths, where he was headed the night he came back from Fire Island. But I don't think so: The fire broke out at seven in the morning, and Malone seldom stayed long at the Baths. When he first came to New York he used to stay for days, and wanted to live there; the Baths were a kind of paradise. But as the years went on, he would go and stay no more than forty-five minutes, since he either knew everyone there, had gone to bed with them, or worse, could no longer deal with people in that way— the way that used to thrill him (the beauty of the body, the communion of flesh) and which now, as he was growing older, repelled him slightly and could not warm his heart. No, if he went to the Everard that night, I think he stayed an hour at most and then went on his way, a last farewell to places of his youth. He also was seen at the Eagle's Nest that night, you know. (Remember the first night we saw him there. I shall never forget that!) I admit that, to you, the novelist, it would have been perfectly appropriate to have him burn up in that fire—because when those baths went up in flames that morning, so did those ten years Malone presided over like an angel, our youth, our dreams, our crazy hearts. But life so seldom imitates art; if only it did, I wouldn't have retired to a farm and be sitting now in the shade of this dreary live oak.

To go on with the rumors—a friend traveling around the world on sabbatical wrote me last February that he'd seen Malone in Singapore, and gathered that he was teaching at a girls' school in the suburbs. But when he took a car to the school the next day, no one had heard of Malone. Malone might have changed his name; age may have changed his looks, for that matter (though it hurts to think this; it means we are aging too), and it's possible the nuns simply didn't understand whom my friend was asking for. Five of their teachers had gone on holiday to Bali that day, and perhaps Malone was one of them—but Hank couldn't stay, he left the next day and never found out. It's odd how it was important to several people to learn how Malone ended up; he was the emblem of so many demented hearts.

So you may take your pick, really—did he burn to ash with the others in the flames of the Everard Baths? Did he slink off to the Far East and is he teaching English there now to a roomful of pale Oriental girls with voices like little birds, who all sing to him verbs and adverbs in the suburban stillness of the morning? And does he have a lover, a slim Eurasian boy, who lives with him in a little bungalow under the oleander trees? Or is he a steward on a passenger ship belonging to a shipping line based in Mombasa, as Jody Myers claims—and does he look now like one of those Dutch sailors he loved as a child, the ones who used to come out on the veranda of the sailors' home next to the church he attended in Ceylon, the sailors in their freshly ironed white shirts who would sit in the shadows of the porch, smoke cigarettes, drink gin and beer and watch the women (and men perhaps) go walking by, those sailors who with their combed hair and cheap cologne symbolized to Malone the radiant world of masculinity? Is he one of those freshly showered, bronze Dutch sailors now, on the porch in some suburb of Djakarta? The one thing I can't imagine is Malone growing old, Malone dying. When I see these old men at the gas station here, sitting in their rocking chairs and waving at the cars that occasionally go by, looking for the expressway to Savannah, I stare at the bones of their sharp or flabby faces and think: These were handsome men once. Very handsome men. The city hall is filled with their photographs, of baseball teams of 1910 and July Fourth fish fries and the installation of the county's first telephone pole. Not to mention the fact that I'm in love with half their grandsons!

For what were those summer days we shared, in truth, when I could not sleep, so anxious was I for the next hot morning, afternoon, and night? When I lived like a neurasthenic, when on getting up each morning in that revolting tenement, I was happy because the air baking over those asphalt roofs, which still bore the puddles of the thunderstorm the night before, was incandescent with heat, and the street below adorned with Puerto Ricans walking down the sidewalk with their shirts dangling from their pockets. Those weeks in midsummer when I got on the subway at night to ride back and forth beneath the city meeting drunken soldiers trying to get back to Fort Dix, and queens as haughty as Cleopatra coming back from a night in the bars where they had refused everyone; nights so warm, so beautiful, I could not close my eyes. What was that ragged, jagged craziness, when we could live a whole summer on a cheap song played on WNJR, but the pride of life? It was all in our demented minds, it had to be. The greatest drug of all, my dear, was not one of those pills in so many colors that you took over the years, was not the opium, the hash you smoked in houses at the beach, or the speed or smack you shot up in Sutherland's apartment, no, it wasn't any of these. It was the city, darling, it was the city, unreal city, the city itself. And do you see why I had to leave? As Santayana said, dear, artists are unhappy because they are not interested in happiness; they live for beauty. God, was that steaming, loathsome city beautiful!!! And why finally no human lover was possible, because I was in love with all men, with the city itself. And Malone was crazier than I. You could tell from his face how deep the disease had eaten into his system. The life of his flesh dwindled, but his spirit ascended like the angels into a perfect love—and yet he was still stuck with his mortal body and his mortal lusts and mortal loveliness: You can't live on the promise of a casual smile which passes while you sit on the stoop waiting for the breeze from the river—demented queen! You can't love eyes, my dear, you can't love youth, you can't love summer dusks that washed us out of our tenements into the streets like water falling over rocks—no, dear, madness that way lies. You must stick to earth, always, you must love another man or woman, a human lover whose farts occasionally punctuate the silence of your bedroom in the morning and who now and then has bad moods that must be catered to.

What lover could possibly have matched what Malone

had stored up in his imagination? Or any of us, for that matter. We were lunatics, I'm sorry to say. Our lovers weren't real. Wasn't that finally the strangest thing of all? The way we loved them? We were just queens in the end. We would not even speak to most of them—were we cowards? Shy girls waiting to be serenaded? Or did we all suspect that half the beauty and the shimmer of that life was in our own hypnotic hearts and not out there? If that was the case, then we were fools: for being romantics. You know, we queens loathed rain at the beach, small cocks, and reality, I think. In that order. Anyway, that's why I left—the madness of it all offended me, finally, I wanted a real porch, a real front yard with real live oaks and real flowers in real pots—and that is what I have now, dear, retired faggot that I am, content with the quiet pleasures of life. Even as I put down this pen (my hand is numb) *I can hear the mockingbirds in the gardenia bush outside my window, and there is,* croyez-moi, *no sweeter sound on earth.*

Diane Von Furstenberg

Full Moon
The Lower East Side

Vision,

I have submitted your letter to the Columbia Graduate School Faculty, for I can understand about half of it. As to your friend who thought he saw Malone in Singapore, I heard that story, too. I also heard from a Pan Am steward who swears he saw him in Australia, on a street in Sydney. Could you give me Hank's address? I think I'll write that parochial school in Singapore and inquire after our friend.

*I have tried to contact his family in Ohio already. Because
I, too, want to know where he ended up; it's important,
because he was somehow the one who seemed above it all,
and what he is doing now that it's over (and it is, I'm afraid,
though I hate to admit it) fascinates me. I doubt that he
died at the Everard, for the same reasons you do; though
it's possible, of course, since the majority of those bodies
were just cinders and ash and could not be identified. It
would explain why no one has heard a word from Malone
—which surprises me, because Malone was the best friend
of so many people, even though he probably considered
none of them his best friend. Do you think that all that time
Malone cared for no one? THAT'S an interesting possibility.
It's often the case with people who have that profound
ability to charm, who charm without even trying, or know
too well how to charm. It's possible Malone went off to
Singapore or Sydney and has absolutely no interest in any
of us back here. Yet I believe he was too genuinely affectionate (his whole tragedy, really). Is the silence due to pride
then? Like that countess in Paris who, the day she discovered her first crow's foot, drew the drapes of her mansion
and never went out into society again? My dear!*

*There is another possible explanation for the complete
silence, other than pride, indifference, or the extinguishing
flames of the Everard Baths—and that brings us to my last
theory. Do you remember how fascinated Malone was—
stunned, really—by that Italian circuit queen, Mario Pross,
who joined the Franciscans? We all knew queens who joked
about taking the veil, but when Mario actually did it,
Malone was breathless. Mario Pross was, after all, one of
the most doomed of doomed queens. One week he was
working on his tits at the Sheridan Square Gym (he was
really handsome, you recall, and had a terrific body), going*

to Fire Island, doing poppers and drugs, dancing till dawn, fucking in the Meat Rack, and doing windows for Macy's, and living with a very hard-core crowd, and the next week, poof! he was in bare feet, praying the Stations of the Cross. Without a word to anyone! He just did it. Do you think Malone is pruning grapes somewhere in a monastery above the Hudson?

You see, I think what really explains Malone is that he was religious: *He had grown up with those nuns in the tiled colonnades in Ceylon, under the thorn trees at noon, and if he loved the sailors sitting on the veranda drinking beer, he loved Christ and Mary and the Saints in the darkness of that church, too. I think the sunlight, the palm trees, the transparent sea, the bronzed sailors, the happiness of his childhood, and the death of Christ all got mixed up and he never knew where the aesthetic stopped and the religious began, and vice versa. You know, when people who were once religious no longer believe in God, they never really change; they just go on, hunting for the ecstatic food, trying to satisfy that hunger. You must admit this search took Malone places he never would have gone otherwise; and who knows where it has taken him now?*

Because he dreamed with the best of us, my dear, dreamed even more outlandish dreams—and then when they failed him, he left. In silence, for what could one say? You remember what Sutherland said to me coming back on the train one day when I asked him why Malone was so restless, and talking about moving to Denver, San Francisco, Charleston. "Dreams decompose, darling," he said, "like anything else. And they give off gases, some of which are poisonous and all of which are unpleasant, and so one goes away from the place in which the dreams were dreamed, and are now decomposing before your very eyes. Otherwise,

247

you might die, dear, of monoxide poisoning. Tant pis," *he*
said. Well, maybe that is why Malone split. You think?
Decomposed dreams?

Betsy Bloomingdale

Sleepytime
The Deep South

Ecstasy,

I would love to talk about this forever, but don't you see
what we've become: old hags chewing the fat, like the men
down here who want nothing more than to sit all day at the
post office or gas station, chawing and gabbing away. About
the fish they caught and whose daughter divorced and went
off to Atlanta. Very rural, dear, very golden years. What is
so incredible about homosexuals is that, if they live as
homosexuals (that is to say, as women: beings whose life
consists chiefly of Being Attractive to others), they die much
sooner than heterosexual men. Here we are talking as if life
were over. Malone has disappeared, true, and we have no
idea where he is or what he is doing (as if that would tell us
what to do and where to go, when in fact we must find the
answers in ourselves), and with his departure from the city,
the city ceased to be enchanting. (That is what your novel
is about in the end, you know: the city. Hot summer nights
in that city. So you did what I said a novel should do, for it
can't be anything more.) And now that you've done that,
you have to go on. We can't just fold our wings and sleep,
like two blackbirds in a magnolia tree; and what does one
do next? Living for beauty is all very fine, but it's a hard
regimen and burns up the heart very quickly. I hope we
don't become quiet old farts sitting on a bench in some small

town watching the fellas play baseball. *Remember Shake-speare's sonnets to the beautiful young man, telling him he must marry or his beauty will die with him? The point is that we are not doomed because we are homosexual, my dear, we are doomed only if we live in despair because of it, as we did on the beaches and the streets of Suck City.*

Let us not, after all, dignify Malone too much: He was in the end a circuit queen. He was handsome, true, and good-mannered and kind—and it's sad to think that such a romantic soul will have to wander (if he is alive) like the gypsies, the Jews, expelled from some walled city in the Middle Ages—but then love, in the best of circumstances, is hard to find. Malone was determined. He wouldn't give up. He hung around as long as he could and—who knows? He may come back. We may come back. You remember all the men who tried to escape—who had their firms transfer them to Saudi Arabia, to Cleveland, who went to the country to manage stores, or just retire with their aging parents—and who all reappeared. Once that life is in your blood, my dear, it's hard to live elsewhere.

And even so, do you realize what a tiny fraction of the mass of homosexuals we were? That day we marched to Central Park and found ourselves in a sea of humanity, how stunned I was to recognize no more than four or five faces? (Of course our friends were all at the beach, darling; they couldn't be bothered to come in and make a political statement.) I used to say there were only seventeen homosexuals in New York, and we knew every one of them; but there were tons of men in that city who weren't on the circuit, who didn't dance, didn't cruise, didn't fall in love with Malone, who stayed home and went to the country in the summer. We never saw them. We were addicted to something else: something I lived with so long it had become a tech-

nique, a routine. That was the real sin. I was too smart, I built a wall around myself. I might as well have been living in the desert, where the air is, after all, cleaner.

Well, dear, the sun is burning overhead, incinerating every leaf in the garden; the lake is smooth as a sheet of polished lead; the birds are napping; the pine trees look as if they were plugged into an electric socket, their needles glowing with current; the clouds overhead are incandescent, and edged with silver, and in about three hours they will gather to a point in huge, towering cumulus mountains and disgorge a violent thunderstorm that will leave the air exquisitely soft. What I said earlier was wrong: We don't have to do anything with our lives. As long as you are alive, there's an end to it. I feel like a child who's been awakened from his sleep and taken downstairs in someone's arms to see the party and the guests. Who knows how long it will last, who knows when that considerate adult will send you back to bed and life will once more be that poignant band of light beneath the door, beyond which all the voices, laughter, and happiness lie? No, darling, mourn no longer for Malone. He knew very well how gorgeous life is—that was the light in him that you, and I, and all the queens fell in love with. Go out dancing tonight, my dear, and go home with someone, and if the love doesn't last beyond the morning, then know I love you.

Paul